"MCGAVIN, YOU'RE GOING INTO THE *BARRIO* . . . INTO THE GHETTO . . . INTO HELL . . ."

The captain shared his self-amused grin with a sergeant who was manning a clipboard for him. "Give this kid to Hodges. Go ahead and read off the assignments."

"McGavin and Hodges . . . Central *and* South bureaus on rotation. Allen and Stephenson . . . West Bureau. Young and Diaz . . . South Bureau . . ."

Danny McGavin craned around for his new partner—and located him by the disgruntled way he rolled his heavy-lidded eyes. Bob Hodges was leaning against the wall, one of the salts, a vintage Patrolman Three with two stripes *plus* a rocker on the sleeve of his dust-faded monkey suit. He'd segregated himself from the youthful company in the chairs. He looked like a balding Kansas farmer. And he appeared to be so drowsy it'd take a .357 to fully rouse him; even then he'd probably only blink and mumble, "Is it retirement yet?"

"Great," Danny said to himself, "just great. I'm teamed up with a mummy."

A ROBERT H. SOLO PRODUCTION
A DENNIS
SE
ROBE
C
MARIA CO
Co-Produc
Music by HE
Director of Photography
Story by MICHAEL SCHIFFER and
RICHARD DILELLO
Screenplay by MICHAEL SCHIFFER
Produced by ROBERT H. SOLO
Directed by DENNIS HOPPER

An **ORION** ® PICTURES *Release*

COLORS

**A NOVEL BY JOEL NORST
BASED ON THE SCREENPLAY
BY MICHAEL SCHIFFER**

**FROM A STORY BY
MICHAEL SCHIFFER
AND RICHARD DILELLO**

GRAFTON BOOKS

A Division of the Collins Publishing Group

LONDON GLASGOW
TORONTO SYDNEY AUCKLAND

Grafton Books
A Division of the Collins Publishing Group
8 Grafton Street, London W1X 3LA

A Grafton UK Paperback Original 1988

ISBN 0-586-20509-8

Printed and bound in Great Britain by
Collins, Glasgow

COLORS

CHAPTER I

COPS.

The corridor smelled like cops, which was to say like two-dollar after-shave and hangover emissions. Danny McGavin had to sidestep carefully between two potbellied plainclothesmen so the powdered sugar from their jelly doughnuts wouldn't get on his blues, although he figured it really didn't matter: this was the last time he was going to work in uniform. From now on he was going to dress like Crockett and Tubbs. He might even hazard a couple days' growth—just like Don Johnson.

Joey Norton, a buddy from the academy and then Central Patrol, was heading toward him, walking with a knockout policewoman who did it with nobody in blues—ever.

"Hello, Marsha," Danny cooed.

She ignored him as she swept past, but Joey asked over his shoulder: "Hey, Danny—where the hell were you last night?"

"Busy." Hanging his tongue out at Marsha's back, Danny began masturbating the six inches of black baton that protruded above the chrome ring on his Sam Browne belt.

"You wish, McGavin. How about tonight?"

"Where?"

"Home Plate?"

"Okay. See you there." Still massaging his baton, Danny spun around and faced a secretary with hair the color of gunmetal bluing and bifocals on a leash around her neck. She'd caught his act—and was frowning as she studied his face. It was more strong than handsome with wide-set eyes and a lantern jaw. He grinned at her. His best grin. His world-class grin. *"Good* morning."

"Morning."

"Where's this gang unit hoopla, babe?"

"I'm not your babe."

He drew his face close to hers. "I know, but let me break it to the others in my own way. I've got my pride, too, you know."

"You're late."

"Right. Auditorium?"

She nodded gravely.

He thought of giving her a kiss, but she'd picked up her Bostich and he didn't feel like having his lower lip stapled to his gums.

Inside the auditorium about thirty cops were sitting in semidarkness, listening to a Sony burning bush from which the voice of the chief of police was booming, pompous and well-enunciated. Sliding into a metal chair, Danny had the weird feeling that the

COP really didn't exist, that he was like the Wizard of Oz and someday his minions would get wise and smash open the big tape recorder and discover him to be a naked midget.

As the chief's voice droned on and on, somebody in the back row started cutting up.

A wave of laughter worked forward to where the brass were seated.

"At ease there," a captain-type voice said.

Danny glanced around, wondering why everybody was sitting in near darkness. The only light was over a hokey plywood sign with silver letters, except that the first letter in each word was gold: Community Resources Against Street Hoodlums. CRASH.

So that was it—some deputy chief wanted to make sure everybody saw the acronym he'd come up with years before on his vacation to Nebraska or wherever deputy chiefs vacationed.

Danny yawned.

When his eyes finally adjusted to the room, he noticed a half-dozen badges glinting against the back wall. The men wearing them seemed a bit stiff in their blue monkey suits, as if they hadn't been forced to put them on in a while.

Finally, the chief shut up and the lights came back on.

One smart ass applauded.

The patrolmen in the chairs looked like what the United Nations would wind up with if it decided to form its own police department: blacks, Latinos, Asians, and—counting McGavin—about fifteen Anglos.

The crisply uniformed captain who'd turned off the COP's voice turned around but didn't smile. He was a stocky Chicano of maybe fifty years who probably had to get up an hour early each morning just to groom his full and lustrous mustache. "I, gentlemen," he said insincerely, "am Captain Melindez." If he was pausing for three cheers, he didn't get them. "Welcome to FLYING CRASH."

"What'd he say?" the guy next to Danny whispered.

"He said we can all take a flying fuck."

"Oh." The patrolman nodded as if to say that that's what he'd thought, too.

"The powers on high," Captain Melindez went on, "have finally noticed the gangs. Some white kids must've gotten hurt."

The black and Chicano cops laughed.

"Mau Mau, brothers!" Danny stage-whispered, lofting a clenched fist.

A few of the black cops looked affronted until they saw that it was just McGavin.

Captain Melindez let it slide, too. "We got over fifty thousand gang-bangers out there and you twenty-four new men . . ."

"His full name must be George Armstrong Melindez," Danny muttered.

". . . In Patrol or Juvenile you guys have all dealt with gangs before, right?"

"Right," some lone ass-kisser chimed in, immediately getting patted on the shoulder straps by a half-dozen hands.

"But the difference with FLYING CRASH is this: you'll each target two or three gangs and track these assholes all over town. They're mobile these days—and so are we. We're giving you brand-new unmarked cars, we got a deal on some righteous-looking Pontiacs"—Captain Melindez waited for some sounds of approval, but got only a couple of grunts—"so they won't read you a mile away. . . ." He paused again, and the way in which he did this gave Danny a sinking feeling. "But you'll be wearing uniforms."

Groans reverberated in the auditorium as Danny clapped his right hand to his forehead: "No, no, no . . ."

"Listen, gentlemen, we want a uniformed presence out on the street."

"No, no, no . . ." The nine-hundred-dollar jacket Danny had just picked up at Raoul's House of Leather was now about as useful as a saddle. "I'm going to be sick . . . sick . . ."

"Gentlemen, please! They're flying their colors! So we're going to fly *ours!* This is something they can relate to, so I want them to know who they're dealing with!"

At last everyone settled down—mostly because Captain Melindez was waving around a submachine gun. For the first time, he smiled a little. "I thought that'd get your attention. But on a serious note, gentlemen, the assholes have these. Know what it is? Anybody?"

The same geek who'd said "right" now stood. "Sir, it appears to be a nine-millimeter parabellum Israeli Mini-Uzi."

"First chance we get," Danny said, to no one in particular, "we cap him."

"Bingo, gentlemen. They've got Uzis. They've got automatic shotguns. They've even got fragmentation grenades. They're taking the neighborhoods down. They're turning this city into fucking Beirut. We're bleeding from open wounds, gentlemen. And we're jamming you twenty-four in—to stop the flow."

"Sounds like we're a bunch of Tampax."

"What was that?"

Danny felt the captain's eyes burning on him, but didn't answer.

"What's your name?"

"McGavin."

"McGavin . . . McGavin . . ." Melindez sucked on the name like it was a piece of stale candy. "You care to tell me what you were saying?"

"I said, sir—sounds like we're a bunch of Tampax." No one laughed this time, and Danny fully expected Melindez to explode. Yet, incredibly, the captain smiled.

"No, McGavin. Tampax winds up someplace good. Someplace warm and safe. You're going into the barrio . . . into the ghetto . . . into fucking West Beirut." He shared his self-amused grin with a sergeant, who was manning a clipboard for him. "Give this kid to Hodges. Go ahead and read off the assignments."

"McGavin and Hodges, Central *and* South bureaus on rotation. Allen and Stephenson, West Bureau. Young and Diaz, South Bureau . . ."

Danny craned around, searching for his new partner—and located him by the disgruntled way he rolled his heavy-lidded eyes. Hodges was leaning against the wall. He was one of the salts, a vintage Patrolman Three with two stripes plus a rocker on the sleeve of his dust-faded monkey suit. He'd segregated himself from the youthful company in the chairs. He looked like a balding Kansas farmer. His face had more lines and angles than a geometry book. And he appeared to be so drowsy it'd take a .357 to fully rouse him; even then he'd probably only blink and mumble, "Is it retirement yet?"

"Great," Danny said to himself, "just fucking great. I'm teamed up with a mummy."

Bob Hodges slumped in the shotgun seat of the yellow Pontiac, his bare elbow hanging out the window. It was mid-October, and the mellowing summer warmth meant that soon the department would be going to long sleeves and ties. In recent years it had been optional: a patrolman could wear long sleeves whenever he liked. But Hodges refused to be different, even though he thought long sleeves and ties looked more professional. There was a good reason for uniformity, he felt.

He rubbed his eyes and yawned.

If he lived in another part of the country he might mark the changing of the seasons by the maples going scarlet and the aspens going gold; but here in Los Angeles, the land of eternal spring, he only realized it was fall when one morning he found himself in long sleeves and a black tie. He had marked nineteen autumns in this way. And nineteen smoggy summers by going back into short sleeves with a triangle of white T-shirt showing at his throat.

"You win," McGavin said from behind the wheel.

"What?"

"You win."

"Win what?"

"Well, you're so much older than me—if we wait to see who talks first, you might be dead by then."

Hodges stared at the kid with the permanently insolent expression, then slowly shook his head. He reminded himself to mickey McGavin's coffee with Valium the first chance he got. "Where you from?"

"Central."

"No, I mean where'd you grow up? If you ever fucking did."

McGavin fished a Marlboro out of the crumpled pack he'd tucked in his sock. "El Monte."

That explained some of it. A tough, working-class town east of Los Angeles. Hodges sat back, trying to ignore the miasma of smoke that suddenly filled the interior of the Pontiac. It smelled delicious; he had quit only two years ago, reckoning that he'd forestalled the Big C longer than he probably deserved. He thought to ask McGavin not to smoke in the car or other confined spaced they shared, but he figured

McGavin would probably respond by lighting up a cigar. Hodges was sick to death of tough kids—particularly the ones on his side.

But Bob Hodges had the patience that is born of futility and exhaustion.

As they crossed the Olympic Boulevard bridge, he felt a tiny flutter in his guts that became a cramp as the Pontiac continued south on Central Avenue into a depressed commercial district of aged masonry warehouses, barricaded stores, and sidewalks sprinkled with aimless, plodding street folk.

Somehow he had deluded himself into thinking that, by going to Juvenile, he'd escaped all this forever.

In acrylic hues that were already being corroded by the smog, Martin Luther King talked about his dream from the wall of a community center. In his slick-sleeve days, when he'd been as bursting with hormones as McGavin was now, Hodges had despised King. Later, gradually, he had come to admire the man: he'd died for the right to take his kid to an Atlanta amusement park. It made more sense than the reasons for which most men were willing to suffer violent death. It was the only reason Hodges would be willing to die for—his family.

Hodges half closed his eyes and let the street run past in a blur: hubcap junkyards, rib shacks, chicken take-outs, clothing stores offering instant credit, and pawn shops charging interest rates that swiftly turned a hundred-buck note into something rivaling the entire Third World debt.

However, the most expensive thing south of the Olympic Boulevard bridge was still hope.

"Up ahead—take a right," he told McGavin.

"Whatever you say." McGavin spun the wheel like a dirt track hotshot, chipping the new tires in the sharp turn.

The stores gave ground to small frame houses thrown together in the 1920s, barren front yards shaded by an occasional date palm. Youngsters, future peewees, were running rusty bikes up and down the sidewalks.

McGavin slowed to decipher the graffiti spray-painted on a cinder-block wall. "Who—"

"Boomtown Crips."

"What are they doing out here?"

Hodges flicked his chin toward the next corner, where six youths were lounging against a school-yard cyclone fence, listening to a ghetto blaster they'd tied to the mesh. "Let's ask them."

McGavin tracked Hodges's gaze, then quickly accelerated. "Shit, we got them," he said eagerly. "Look at their colors—Crip de Ville, aren't they? The CDV. The Ville, man!"

Hodges rolled his eyes, then said in a quiet voice, "Stone-fucking killers. They'll walk into your house, blow you away, sit down, eat your dinner . . . then leave, champing on a toothpick."

"You know any of them?"

"Some." Hodges was first out of the car, smiling at the youths' reactions to a pair of blue suits emerging from a yellow Pontiac. "Wha's up, homes?" he said to one he knew by the moniker of Dog Bone.

"Hodges?" he asked uncertainly. "You back?"

"Better watch your back."

"Shee-it," Dog Bone chuckled, sweating slightly in his bomber jacket—his colors—which bore on its back the initials CDV. "Check it out, Killer Bee. Hodges's back. . . . Everything is everything."

Killer Bee strutted up to the Pontiac, stroked its front fender as tenderly as if it were a thigh. "Nice ride, man! I didn't make you. Hey, don't sneak up like that!"

McGavin had his fist on his baton, ready to slide it

out of the ring. "You want to get back on the side-walk?"

Killer Bee, with feigned meekness, showed his palms and obeyed. "Cool. . . . Everything is everything, my man."

Hodges eyed him from head to toe. He wasn't wearing colors, but the rest of his clothes were Crips regulation: black T-shirt, suspenders, jeans with rolled-up cuffs, and shiny leather shoes. "You all buffed out, Killer Bee! Them shoes hook?"

"Shit, no—they be no imitation. This *Italian* fucking leather, man."

"Been to the joint?"

"Just a bullet at County." One year in jail. "Missed you for a while, Hodges."

"Probation?"

"Sure."

"Turn around."

"Say what?" But Killer Bee had already started to pirouette. He knew the routine. He was an OG, an original gangster—what the Hispanic gang-bangers would call a *veterano.*

Hodges yanked a blue bandanna from one of Killer Bee's rear pockets. "What's this?"

He grinned, almost charmingly. "My Hopalong Cassidy rag."

Hodges frowned: it marked the youth as a Crip; it was as identifying as colors. "Get rid of it. Find a better class of friends. You're in violation."

Killer Bee continued to grin. "Just passing by. I live right over there. I'm retired."

Hodges laughed. "Shit, you won't retire. You'll graduate to the big time. From street gang to prison gang. Oh . . . this here is Killer Bee, McGavin."

"Got you in your blues!"

"Yeah, homes—just like you." Sneering, McGavin flashed the hand sign for Crips: his fingers fashioning

two facing C's as if he were holding imaginary binoculars. "I'm a fucking Crip, too."

"Good thing," Killer Bee said, his voice less conge-
nial than before.

Hodges could almost feel the electricity flow off the
two young men as they postured for each other.
Goddamn testosterone—the world's poison. Out of
the corner of his eyes, he kept watch on the five other
Crips, particularly a sullen one who was standing off
by himself, thinking up fierce expressions for the
benefit of The Man. "What's the matter with him?"
he asked Killer Bee, who was still eye-fucking
McGavin. "Don't he like it here?"

"Who, Rocket?"

A new one—Hodges made a mental note. "Yeah,
Rocket."

"He down for the hood."

"Y'all got any dope today?"

"Not us."

Hodges turned to the Crip who'd answered: "You
Shooter, right?"

"I know you, too, Hodges," he said grimly.

Hodges smiled. "How about you, T-Bone? You got
any Bo in your pockets?"

"Man, I don't smoke that shit."

"Well," Hodges drawled, wearily now as he pointed
at a ramshackle house across the street, "you can get
some right over there, homes. Go get some. I'll be
back."

As the two cops got into their car, the Crips fell
against the fence again, gripping the wire mesh,
making it undulate down the length of the schoolyard
as they laughed off the encounter.

McGavin pulled away from the curb, and Hodges
eased the back of his sweaty neck against the headrest,
closed his eyes.

He hadn't expected to feel this spent his first time

down the Central Avenue gauntlet again. But the sense was overpowering: this thing was older and more durable than he was. Hell, it had started in the 1920s with a black gang in Los Angeles called the Boozies, and some of the Hispanic gangs were even older than that. Most likely, it would be thriving long after Hodges was dead and gone.

"Fucking Melindez," he said, his voice low and resentful. "I worked CRASH for five years. I did my time. Enough overtime to justify two positions. I cannot believe I'm back out here. Emergency, my ass. The entire fucking world is an emergency. I finally made it up to Juvie six months ago, right? My own little desk with a cactus flower next to the phone. Home at night with the wife and the kids and the VCR—Christ!"

McGavin had stomped on the brake, hurling Hodges against the dash. "Jesus fucking Christ!" By the time he'd picked his aching knees up off the floorboards, he had the inside of the car to himself, McGavin having bailed out, leaving the driver's door open. "Hey!"

Hodges sprang the latch and tumbled out, scrambling on the pavement for his balance. He gathered in a split second what had happened: McGavin had interrupted a deal and was fast on the heels of a small pack led by a gangly black youth who had no intention of being taken.

Hobbling around to the driver's side of the Pontiac, Hodges groused, "This just isn't going to work."

They scattered like quail as soon as Danny hit the brake pedal, the seller and his main men on foot and the buyers in a white Chevy. Danny decided to zero in on the seller, pronto, while Hodges sat there rambling to himself about what a sad life he had.

"Halt!" McGavin shouted at them, holding his

revolver down at his side. He didn't throw in that he'd shoot because he knew he'd never get away with it, not while chained to a slouch like Hodges, who'd drop a dime on him to the Shooting Investigation Team. The Crips—Danny felt sure they were gang-bangers—kept on sprinting down the sidewalk until they heard Hodges barreling after them in the Pontiac; then they turned up a path into a courtyard enclosed by bungalows, the kind West Coast retirees slowly rot in.

"Freeze!" Danny cried, seeing the seller hesitate because there was no way out the back of the bungalow complex and the few open doors were now being slammed against him and his little band.

The Crips began showing their hands.

"I want you all in a line facing away from me—and keep your palms turned so I can see them!"

Hodges came huffing up. "Shit, a load of peewees."

"That big guy sure as hell isn't. All of you—hands behind your head! Down on your knees now! Cross your ankles!"

"Christ," Hodges said, staring down his sights at the row of kneeling youths, "you damn near threw me through the windshield!"

"What can I say that sounds sincere?" Danny growled, striding forward to search them, starting with the youngest ones, who were no more than ten or eleven.

When Danny was done with them, finding them clean, Hodges said, "You kids book."

They looked at the older cop in surprise.

"Go home. This banger creep you're keeping company with is a loser. Hear me? Go on home."

Reluctantly, the peewees left, strutting down the path all the way to the street before breaking into a run.

Danny seized the gangly youth's fingers where they were interlaced behind his neck, ready to twist them if he offered any resistance while his wrists were being cuffed together. "Where's the shit?" he demanded.

"What shit, man?"

He gave the fingers a squeeze, but the Crip showed no pain.

He, too, was clean. "Damn! He tossed it. The no-good fuck tossed it." Danny wrenched the Crip's fingers once again. "What the hell were you running for? Answer me! What's your fucking name, homes?"

"Let him up, McGavin." Hodges holstered his revolver, then slipped a field interrogation card out of his shirt pocket.

Danny glared at Hodges, then began hunting around the bases of some dusty holly bushes. Behind him, he could hear Hodges click open his ballpoint pen and softly ask, "What's your name, man?"

"Clarence Brown."

"Don't lie to me."

"Clarence Brown."

"How old are you?"

"Eighteen."

"What else do they call you?"

"Hightop."

"Hightop . . . Hightop. Where'd you get a name like that?" Hodges asked. "You wear sneakers all the time?"

"I don't know . . . no."

Danny ran his fingers through the bushes, disregarding the scratches from the spiky foliage.

"What set you from?" Hodges went on, probing the youth to find out which gang he belong to.

"No set, man."

"What's your address?"

"Five-five-one-one Hamilton."

"Blood House? You're a Blood, then. Hey, McGavin, this kid's a Blood! Tell me, Hightop, what're you doing over here? Don't these Crips have any pride? Letting a Blood come in to deal on their turf? Hood's all gone to hell, eh? Anything for a buck. Let's see your tattoos." Then, after a pensive silence, Hodges groaned, "Damn you, Hightop, you got House of Blood scratched all over you. I thought we had a rapport."

"We do . . . we do, man."

Then Danny's groping fingers found it—a crystalline mass of crack. "Oh, man, it's fucking Gibraltar!" Rising, he thrust it under Hightop's evasive eyes. "This look familiar, huh?"

"No."

Hodges plucked the rock out of Danny's grasp. "You on parole or probation?" he asked the youth.

"No."

"Well, I've got you on *my* file now." Hodges waved the F.I. card in his face. "And check it out—if I ever catch you here again I'm going to make you do squat-thrusts on my baton. You understand, Hightop?"

"Yes, suh."

Then, unbelievably, Hodges dropped the rock to the cement and crushed it underfoot. "Turn around." He unfastened the cuffs and handed them to Danny, who was speechless with rage. "All right, Clarence— I'm Hodges. Ask around who I am. And now you owe me one. You got that?"

"Yes, suh."

"Say it."

"I owe you one."

"And who am I?"

"Officer Hodges."

"Play straight with me, and I'll be straight with you. Get lost."

Danny watched Hightop diddybop out of the court-yard as free as a bird. Then the patrolman gaped down at the sugary remains of the biggest chunk of crack he'd seen in four years on the streets. At last he found his tongue: "What the motherfuck was that you just did?"

Hodges stretched like the small of his back was sore as he ambled toward the double-parked Pontiac. Old black people were beginning to peek out cracks in their doors. "Howdy, folks. Everything's okay. Just fine. Look at them, McGavin—poor bastards. What was that you asked?"

"I just made a righteous collar!"

"Oh, that."

"And if I do something, *partner,* I expect you to back me up!"

Wearily, Hodges got in behind the wheel, then flinched as Danny slammed his door. "Listen, McGavin," he said with a maddening reasonableness to his tone of voice, "you don't even know the neighborhood yet. Did you want to drag that kid in for some pissy little rock? Spend the rest of the shift doing paperwork?"

"Yeah, that was the plan. We get him for rock this time; then we get him for something else later on. And then when he does something serious, it's not a fucking first offense!"

They drove in silence for over half an hour, cruising the streets. Finally Hodges asked tersely, "Want a cup of coffee?"

"I don't care."

"What's that supposed to mean? You want some coffee or not?"

"Sure."

Hodges nudged the front bumper through the thick traffic and parked outside a chicken stand that had steel bars on each window.

Danny refused to meet Hodges's eyes as he said in that ultrareasonable voice of experience: "See, McGavin, you're not in a black-and-white anymore, chasing down Mickey Mouse crimes, giving people tickets for having no gloves in their glove box. The *plan* is to get to know these homeboys. Get them used to talking to us, so when something big comes . . ." Hodges sighed. "You listening?" Then he, too, saw her, a lovely Chicana inside the order window, her warm brown skin tones set off strikingly by her white uniform. "You gotta look at pussy right now?"

Danny smirked, but continued to gaze at the girl.

"You really know what this job is all about, McGavin?" Hodges paused. "You ever heard about the two bulls?"

"Not yet."

"See, these two bulls are sitting on a grassy knoll overlooking a herd of Guernseys, see, and the young one says, 'Hey, Pop, let's run down and fuck one of those cows.' But the old bull says, 'Uh, no, son. 'Let's *walk* down and fuck 'em all!"

Danny stared at him, refusing to laugh.

Hodges shrugged and got out of the car.

CHAPTER 2

Danny smiled up from the Ms. Pac-Man table console and, taking a nip of Jim Beam and then a swallow of Budweiser to wash it down, listened to a blitzed Joey Norton regale three admiring young girls with almost everything he'd ever done or seen pertaining to death: ". . . And so this guy is deader than Forest Lawn. I mean he's so dead the maggots have hired a skywriter to spell out 'Lunch' over him."

"Ooooh," one of the young women half-moaned, but her eyes were bright with expectation.

Danny went back to Ms. Pac-Man, although he was suffering from so many multiples of vision that he was losing badly. He hated losing, even to a machine.

". . . And all these coppers from Central and Newton are standing around and like making fun of the guy on account of he croaked with no clothes on.

Somebody asked what he died of, and Danny here like looks at the guy's business and says, 'Embarrassment.'"

Danny waved off the laughter.

". . . But then, all of a sudden, this guy's eyes snap open and he says, 'Give me a cigarette, for chrissake.' And all those fucking cops went screaming out of there like a bunch of Girl Scouts."

"What did Danny do?" a secretary asked Joey, a bit tauntingly. Danny had been keeping a predatory eye on her: a real squash blossom with yellow hair and all the right floppy places.

"Ask him."

Cradling her chin in her hands, she leveled her eyes on McGavin. "Well?"

"I gave him a smoke, what else? The poor son of a bitch was dying for a cigarette." He turned away from the game in disgust with his performance and polished off his shot glass of Jim Beam. "But that was nothing. There was this caper where a couple of Firestone deputies capped a six-time rapist—"

"You mean this rapist could do it *six* times in a row?" the squash blossom interrupted with a cunning smile.

"You wish, babe. Anyways, the deputies hit the prick square in center body mass, okay?" When the women looked confused, Danny illustrated by poking himself several times in the chest. "Well, an ABC camera team was in the area, monitoring police band, so they were there cranking away within seconds of the shooting. And to the limp-dick reporter it looks like the deputies are down on the asphalt giving CPR to the suspect. You know . . ." Danny joined his hands together and demonstrated on his chest. "Except the county mountie who's pumping this guy's chest is pumping his fucking blood all over Firestone Boulevard, pumping him till he's bone dry."

No one but Joey laughed. "Friend of yours, Danny?"

"Well, I'd shake his hand."

"If he'd wipe it off?"

The two cops laughed defiantly until the women smiled a little. The squash blossom excused herself for the ladies' room, but it was obvious that she intended to return to be titillated by the rest of the horror show. They all loved it—the horror.

The other two young women started talking about their work, so Joey lowered his voice and did the same: "How's this CRASH?"

"Fuck." The word said it all for Danny, and Joey nodded that he understood.

"Who's your partner?"

"Some cinder. They put us all with old-timers, in *uniform*. Some guy named Hodges, a real trip."

"Oh, God help us—Uncle Bob?"

"You know him?"

"He's a trip all right . . . in the sloooow lane. He tell you his story yet?"

Danny shook his head no.

"Time was he tore the gangs a new asshole. But then I guess the gangs tore him one."

"Whatever." Danny found himself not wanting to talk about Bob Hodges; it was enough of a trial to spend an eight-hour watch with the fossil. And he was still pissed about Hodges letting that gang-banger skate on a rock cocaine rap. Hodges wasn't waiting for "something big." He was waiting for retirement. But then Danny grinned: the squash blossom was coming back, all hips and red lips. "Jesus, she can really *walk*."

Joey chuckled. "I overheard her say she thinks you have interesting looks."

"Is that supposed to mean I'm ugly?"

"You *are* ugly."

"Good enough." Danny rose and at the same time gestured for her to sit down. "Don't go away." It was an order. Then, taking a few unsteady steps to find his sea legs, he made his way to the public phone in the restroom corridor. She answered on the first ring—no pride. Pretty but no pride. And in the background he could hear her two-year-old hammering the coffee table with something. "Yeah, Judy, it's me."

"Baby? Where are you?"

"Listen, we had a homicide."

"Oh, no . . . Is it bad?"

"They're all bad."

"Are you okay, Danny?"

"Sure—I didn't mean bad that way. But look, I'm going to be standing around chalk lines all night. Then I have court in the morning. So I'm pretty much out of commission."

"I understand," she said in her brave-little-trooper-hope-to-be-a-cop's-wife voice. Fat chance.

"I knew you would. I'll call. Okay?"

The Ford van cruised serenely like a green shark along the streets, some dim with houses whose owners didn't want to call attention to them and some bright with night life, the silhouettes of the ladies standing on the corners or near the bus benches. Killer Bee liked the brighter streets, but he wasn't driving the van. Shooter was, mostly because he wasn't fucked up, and Rocket was beside him in the shotgun seat—righteously so called because the silent cuz had a gauge laying across his lap. Rocket wasn't kicking because he had things on his mind; he always seemed to have things on his mind. Maybe it was because he worried more about holding down the hood, keeping the dingle-ball esseys in their low riders and the Crip-killers in their Buick deuce-and-a-quarters out of the turf, at an arm's distance.

But as far as Killer Bee was concerned, where he sprawled in the carpeted back of the van, everything was everything. Perfect. Out the back window and in the distance to the north, he could see the high-rise lights downtown, and he wanted to float on them. Tonight was going to be a trip, and he would float on the lights.

T-Bone, his teeth all shiny in a grin, was fumbling with a sherm, a short brown cigarette dipped in PCP. "Ooh, baby, come on . . . come on." He ran it under his nose and inhaled deliciously. "Oh, my, my, my . . ."

"Light the damned thing," Killer Bee said, but he was laughing from the hunger that was building in him. The good hunger that would soon be satisfied.

Dog Man flicked his Bic, and a squirmy little blue flame shot up and found the sherm. T-Bone sucked up a vivid coal, then held his breath and let the smoke push up through the top of his head and leak out from under his toenails. "Oooooohhh! Ow! Ow! Ow! Here, cuz. Get wacked on this."

Dog Man had his turn, then passed the sherm all pinchy-fingered to Killer Bee, who heard T-Bone rapping only when he finally exhaled: "Man, man, G-riding in the van . . . with the cuz, what it does . . ."

Dog Man joined in, hammering the beat on the metal sidewalls: "Some fucker gonna die . . . getting high . . . oh, my, my, my . . . man, man, G-riding in the van . . . with the—"

Rocket had swiveled his seat around and, keeping one hand on the gauge, busted T-Bone on the ear. He must have caught him across the nose, too, because a little blood was trickling down around his mouth. "Shut the fuck up!" Rocket screamed, showing how down for the hood he really was inside. "Chill, motherfucker!"

T-Bone had a trey-eight tucked in his waistband, part of the cylinder showing dark blue and gleamy, but he kept it there. He only whined, "What'd you do that for?"

Rocket didn't hit him again, but he red-eyed T-Bone, and his pupils were all silvery and strange from some headlights coming in through the back window. Then he turned forward again and said something low to Shooter, who made the next left, using the blinkers and doing everything legal like he was supposed to.

"The Shell station," Rocket said after five minutes or so in which everybody kept quiet. He laid the gauge on the floor mat and got out to use the phone—the final check with some hustler who was willing to drop the dime on his friends. After just a few seconds, Rocket got back in the van, looking like he was in a better mood, although he was still tense and down for the hood. "It's *on.*"

"He still out front?" Shooter asked, his voice kind of shaky because this was only his second time to ride on somebody, to cross the line into the strangeness of another hood and pop caps. He was imagining things, just as Killer Bee had the first time—and none of them was good. The fear made it go all to shit in your mind, Shooter reminded himself, although he now felt cool, floating on neon.

"Drive, Shooter, and don't be minding my shit," Rocket said, cracking back the slide a tad to see that he had a shell ready to light off. He did, so he closed the slide with a loud clack.

Dog Man started peeking out the tinted back windows for The Man, even though Rocket had already arranged for some hook call to Southeast about some gang-bangers bumping titties in a schoolyard—this to keep the beat car busy and away from the projects.

Then Rocket sat a lot straighter than he had before,

and Killer Bee realized that they were coming on the projects. Floating—he was floating. In and out of the passing shadows and lights went T-Bone's face; he was snuffling back the blood that still wanted to come out his nose.

When Shooter began slowing down, Rocket said, "Don't come in all cragered down like some fucking essey low rider, man. That a tip-off and a half. Speed up five or ten. Speed the fuck up."

Through the open side windows, Killer Bee could hear kid noises and a blaster wailing a song he usually liked but now cared nothing for—because he, too, now felt down for the hood and realized in a sudden, somber way that he was nothing without Crips and needed to prove it somehow. But Rocket was clutching the gauge tonight, and Rocket would do what had to be done.

Then Rocket did it: he swung the muzzle up lightning-fast and shoved it outside while he shouted, "Hey, Blood!" The explosion pounded the inside of the van and hurt Killer Bee's ears.

But he was still floating as Shooter jammed down the accelerator and the wind streamed in through the windows.

Some bitch's scream faded away like at the end of a song.

By the red light of his stereo console, Danny carefully studied the squash blossom's face. If only she'd open her tightly clenched eyes he might see the insincerity that would betray her soft moaning.

Maybe that was what he was searching for: insincerity. Hell, he didn't know.

All he knew was that his sheets were soaked with perspiration, that he was getting tired but knew he couldn't relent yet—not without losing some dignity —and that ever since she had stared up at him as if she didn't like what she saw, he'd felt empty and a little angry.

"Oh, God . . . please don't stop . . ."

He started to say something, but decided to hold his tongue. Instead, he began seesawing more vigorously, even savagely.

She stopped moaning. She watched him, her eyes cored red from the stereo lights.

Christ, he wanted to hit her—but knew he never would.

Still, the urge was there, a beast apart from the beast that had taken over the lower half of his body, raging at the delay her own demand for pleasure was causing it.

And then the phone rang.

Secretly he was glad. He rolled off her. "McGavin." He listened for a few moments, then said, "Yeah, okay . . . I'll be there." Hanging up, he smiled at her for the first time since they'd gotten into bed. "Sorry."

The violence was not really the worst part of the job.

It was the dizzying swing from comfort and safety to blood and outrage that had finally gotten to Bob Hodges. All within the same evening hour, he could be warm and cozy on the living room sofa, watching *Newhart* with his wife and then speeding south, anxiously, in an unmarked Pontiac with a sneering punk who smelled like he'd been rutting in a Tijuana cathouse.

As always, the emergency lights atop the black-and-whites were winking, giving a ghoulish cast to the scene, which had already been contained by Southeast Patrol behind a cordon of yellow tape. Parking down the street beside a fireplug, Hodges said, "Why don't you start humping for witnesses?"

McGavin shot him a killing glance, but then got out and ambled across the street to work the crowd outside the public housing units opposite the crime scene.

Sighing deeply, Hodges locked the doors before leaving the Pontiac—nothing like coming back to gobs of spit on the steering wheel or a pile of dog shit on the front seat—and patted his shirt pocket for his spiral notebook, which he wearily took out and opened to the first page. He'd already written down the victim's name as relayed to him by CRASH dispatch: Robert Craig. A son of the House of Blood.

Now a dead son.

Heavily, he began moving down the sidewalk toward the scene. He hadn't gone far when he could hear the woman keening. White women—at least the modern American variety—usually turned into zombies until the shock wore off, then asked a lot of answerless questions; but black women began letting it out right away. Maybe they had more to let out, especially down on this end of town.

A bony girl with cornrowed hair was trying to comfort the keening middle-aged woman, who was prevented from approaching the body by a patrolman: "Stop it. You can't help him . . . you just can't help him."

"Excuse me, Auntie, can I—"

The woman sput out of the hands grasping her and enveloped Hodges in a flabby hug. "No, he cain't die. . . . Don't let him die. Lord have mercy!"

Hodges closed his arm around her. His face took on a sick, strained expression, but he knew better than to try to say anything. After a moment, the girl succeeded in pulling the woman away and leading her up some concrete steps into the open door of her project apartment.

He was going to have a look at the body when

McGavin stepped over the yellow tape. "Bunch of guys in a van. Ford or Dodge. Blue or green. One guy hollered, 'Hey, Blood.' Then *boom.*"

From outside the cordon a boy, pointing to a neighbor woman, said, "She saw it."

Instantly, the woman's eyes went still in her face.

Hodges stepped over to her. "Excuse me, ma'am—"

"I didn't see nothing."

"If you could just—"

"Nothing!"

Then McGavin butted in, spreading on what he probably thought was his best community relations voice: "Auntie, if you witnessed this, you really can't—"

"*Who* can't? Leave me alone!" She started to turn but stopped when McGavin yelled at her.

"Hey! You gonna shut your eyes and shut your mouth every time these sons of bitches—"

Hodges gripped his arm gently. "Come on . . . come on. She has to live here."

McGavin was breathing angrily, but let Hodges guide him back to the corpse, where Homicide was stooping at work. One of the detectives, a hulking redhead, leered up at Hodges and smiled without affection. "Well, if it ain't Uncle Bob. And who's your sidekick? One of your reformed gang-bangers?"

"Rusty Baines . . . McGavin."

Neither man offered to shake, and McGavin glanced away disdainfully.

"What are you doing here?" Baines went on with the same insolent smile.

Hodges had locked horns with him before, but was in no mood to tangle over meaningless insults now. He looked past Baines at Robert Craig, whose black athletic T-shirt had been rolled halfway up his bloody, ash-colored torso. "Need anything, Baines?"

"Jeez, I don't know. Maybe your valuable expertise."

"Looks like shotgun entry wounds," Hodges said aside to McGavin, who nodded, expressionless.

Baines chuckled. "Hey, kid, stick with Uncle Bob and you'll wind up a deputy chief. He knows everything there is to know. Thing is, he never uses it."

"Any evidence of embedded wadding you can see?" Hodges asked, ignoring the gibe.

"What's it to you?"

Hodges shrugged good-naturedly.

"Why?" McGavin asked. "What would that tell you?"

"We'd know if the weapon was discharged within ten feet of the victim. And then the wadding itself can tell us the type of shot, the gauge of the gun, even possibly help us identify the gun itself."

"See what I mean, kid? A veritable storehouse of information," Baines muttered, examining the jagged exit wounds along Craig's back.

"I'm not a kid, pops."

"Coulda fooled me. You look like the typical shit-for-brains peewee they recruit for FLYING CRASH. So why don't you fly the fuck out of here and leave me to some real cop work?"

Again, Hodges grasped McGavin's arm, but Danny shook it off and grinned at Baines. "No sweat. This has been instructive. Real instructive. Now I know what happens to your brain if you start balling stiffs."

CHAPTER 3

ORDINARILY, HODGES HAD TO PUT UP WITH RUSTY Baines in small doses, a couple times a year at most. But all at once he wasn't so fortunate. It seemed as if, in coming close to completing a long and often stormy voyage of twenty years, he was being toyed with by the gods, who were dumping icebergs and hidden reefs in front of his bow. When he showed up with McGavin at the CRASH bureau at Southeast Station for a jam session with all the involved units, he found none other than Baines present to hold up Homicide's end.

They nodded at each other across the office.

One of the windowless walls was given over to a big pegboard on which were mounted brass knuckles, switchblades, butterfly knives, belt buckle knives, daggers, dirks, bayonets, swords, Saturday night specials, sawed-off shotguns, sawed-off rifles, defused homemade bombs, and other trophies of the neighborhood wars. Beneath this display stood Bill Young, his coffee-colored face screwed up into an expression of supreme concentration as he prepared to dunk a Nerf Ball into a trash can.

"You're going to miss, Young," Baines said, his lizard-skin shoes up on somebody's desk like it was his own. "You're going to miss."

"Fuck you, Baines." Gracefully, Young made the shot, then retrieved the ball.

McGavin was leaning against a file cabinet in a wooden chair, dozing, waiting like everyone for Lieutenant Wallace Reed to get off the horn with Parker Center and announce whatever it was that was coming down.

"Ten bucks, Young, that you can't do it again—but with one eye closed."

McGavin made a soft snoring sound—he'd probably rounded off last night by picking up some nymphomaniac triplets or God knows what.

Youth. Something infinitely precious the young unconsciously try to scorch out of themselves.

Hodges shifted his focus back onto Baines, who seemed, as always, to be gloating over nothing, his mouth set in a sarcastic smile.

Years and years before, Hodges had gone to fist city with the asshole. He'd had more of a temper then and was lucky the fight had been off duty behind a beer joint. A draw. After ten minutes of drunken roundhouses, it had been declared a Mexican standoff by both combatants. Baines was bigger, but Hodges had been angrier. Yet it had taught Hodges something: you can't pound the assholes out of existence with your fists. Like the poor, the assholes are always among you. So you just co-exist with them, ignore them if you can, and laugh them off if you can't.

A CRASH cop named Nakamura ambled in, peeling a banana. "What's this I hear about there being a witness to the Craig shooting?"

"Dozens of them." Baines yawned. "But you'd need that banana and a bunch more to coax them out of the trees to talk."

The office fell silent, and like everybody else, Hodges glanced at Bill Young, to see what the black cop would do.

Young's face went cold as he met Baines's sneer. In his early thirties, Bill still had a short fuse, and Hodges was afraid that he was going to fly into Baines, as he himself had so long ago.

But fortunately, at that moment the lieutenant stepped out of his cubicle and clapped his hands for attention like a schoolmarm.

Hodges could look from Bill Young to Wally Reed and see both sides of the same coin: two black men, one fresh out of puberty with all his juices undiluted, and the other out of energy after discovery of a heart condition that should have retired him. Reed and Hodges had gone to the academy together a couple of light-years before, had taken a liking to each other, boozed it up some in their rare off-time. Back then, they'd talked about beating the system. Now they just wanted to survive it.

"All right, listen up," Reed said in his molasses baritone. "I'll make it short and sweet."

"Good."

Reed red-eyed Baines before going on. "The kid was a Blood. Dealing, too. Whether it was drugs or some other gang shit, I don't really know. Really don't care. For now we're going to do one thing—hook and book, baby."

Nakamura whooped and Young overturned the trash can and drummed its base. Beaming, McGavin landed his chair legs on the linoleum with a click.

Hodges just rubbed his forehead. One more storm to weather. One final storm before putting into port. A major gang war was coming, that much was inevitable. But this just might trigger it sooner rather than later. And he preferred that it come later—much later, when he was getting sunburned in a bass boat on some lake far away from here.

"Be inventive," Reed went on. "Find your probable cause and use it. Get both gangs off the street, at least for a night or two. Let them cool down." Then the lieutenant added without much conviction: "See if they'll talk."

Hodges continued to massage his brow.

"Any questions? Okay, rock and roll, baby!" Then, as the men made for their cars, Reed noticed Hodges still slumped at a desk. His face showed concern. "You all right, Bobby?"

"Sure, Wally. Just a little tired."

"Ain't we all?"

"Yeah."

More than forty-eight hours later, Hodges crept down the street of identical stucco crackerboxes in his personal Chevy station wagon and turned into one of the driveways. His headlights rippled over the crabgrass, which was ankle deep because he hadn't cut it in ten days and probably wouldn't get around to it for another five.

Killing the engine, he sat behind the wheel for a few minutes before lumbering out.

The last two days had raged around him like a hurricane in whose eye he was marooned. The Motorola had squawked constantly with urgent traffic: "Roll me a back—I got five Bloods in colors at the McDonald's on Avalon."

"Control, my partner is in foot pursuit!"

"Adam Six, the peewee ducked in that alley right behind you."

"Any unit in position to back, report of a Crip with a gun at Green Meadows Playground. . . ."

Fumbling to insert the key in the front door lock, Hodges closed his eyes for a moment and could still see a hazy sunlight falling on colors of blue and red—yes, that was another sign of autumn in southern California: the light became softer, more slanting, and the wearers of those colors spread-eagled against graffiti-clad walls, chain-link fences, and the purring hoods of unmarked cop cars.

A shrieking voice: "Hey, what we done?"

"Shut the fuck up."

Another shrieking voice: "Hey, man, they rode on us!"

"Shut the fuck up."

One more strident voice: "The punk-ass motherfuckers hit us!"

"Shut the fuck up."

The world spoke only in strident voices, and Hodges shuffled into his own living room, muttering, "Shut the fuck up," although the house was quiet. Everybody was asleep. Everybody but Hodges, who would need hours to wind down before he might feel drowsy, because his ears were still snicking with the sounds of handcuffs closing around wrists.

The holding tanks had quickly filled up, one with blue and one with red—shouting and fists shaking in between the bars. Monikers. Bushels of monikers could be picked off the booking sheets: Snakedance and Ace Kool and Psycho and Double Deuce and Crab Man. They went on forever, the names these killer-children had dubbed themselves upon being reborn to the gangs, to hopelessness, to the American Dark Ages.

"Shut the fuck up," Hodges mumbled to himself again as he unloaded his revolver and hid it on the top shelf in the hall closet.

McGavin had gleefully tooled the Pontiac around South Los Angeles, every now and again looking sideways at Hodges's fatigue without understanding what it was all about. "We got damned near every last one of them," he said. "It's just about over, man!"

"Over." Hodges had laughed feebly. "No, this is just the lull . . . just the lull before they all bail out and it begins again. It will never be over, McGavin. Look at it as job security."

Now Hodges cracked the door to Tommy's room. Light from the street lamp streamed in across the five-year-old's bed, and Hodges was reassured not to see what he'd kept imagining during these last hours of incredible weariness: his own son in colors. He'd kept hearing that sweet little voice spouting jive, and it'd nearly driven him nuts.

Softly, he shut the door. "Jesus, I'm beat."

Danny duck-walked along the side of the chicken joint so he couldn't be seen from the windows. Grinning, he glanced back at Hodges, who was sitting in the Pontiac and slowly shaking his head at McGavin's antics.

"Can you see her?" Danny mouthed the words, pointing upward.

Contemptuously, Hodges nodded that he could.

Danny gave him the okay sign, which was ignored, then sprang up to the arched opening in the order window, wrapping his hands around the bars and making a grotesque face.

She was startled, her hand flying to the top button of her sleeveless white waitressing uniform. "What—!"

He disarmed her fright with a smile, although she

gave his blue uniform the once-over. "When do you get out?"

"Out of what?"

He rattled the bars. "Jail."

She didn't answer. Absently, she picked up a pen and began doodling on her order pad.

"Hey . . ."

She glanced at him again, the hint of a smile drawing up the corners of her full lips.

"I can put a word in."

"Who do you know that I know?"

"I was talking about Probation. I can put a word in with Probation."

She went back to doodling. "What would you tell them?"

"Only that you're too lovely to keep locked up in stir."

She blushed.

And damn but she was—perfect teeth, perfect eyes, perfect everything. He was even crazy about the way she combed her dark hair up at the nape of her neck. But then she half turned to talk to somebody and he saw it—a small butterfly tattoo on her shoulder that was nearly hidden by her bra strap. A *chola,* a gang girl, maybe, either now or at some time in the past. It didn't seem possible: there was something so angelic, so virginal about her. But he decided not to give up on the basis of some idle speculation.

A fat man with flour all over his dirty apron was asking her if everything was all right.

"She's fine," Danny answered for her, and the man went back to sprinkling flour over big trays of raw chicken.

She brought a light brown finger to her lips as if asking Danny not to get her in trouble with her boss.

He nodded that he wouldn't, and she relaxed a little. "What's your name?"

"Louisa."

"Danny."

"Hello." Her voice was shy—he liked that.

"You get time off for good behavior?"

"No."

He gathered from the way she said this that it was no picnic working for the fat man. "Ever been out with a cop?"

Her eyes became clouded, and he sensed an immediate shift in her feelings, which had been so good until now.

He told himself to keep bulling ahead. "Bet you don't like cops, eh?"

"No . . ."

"No, what?"

"No cream, no sugar." Hodges butted into his back. Danny rolled his eyes. "Perfect timing."

"How long does it take to get two lousy cups of coffee?" He winked at Louisa. "Or did he ever get around to the java?"

"No." She giggled.

"Watch this *gavacho,* honey—he's a player."

Her expression turned thoughtful but not suspicious. Then she busied her hands getting the coffees.

In addition to calling Danny an Anglo, Hodges had used gang slang to describe him: a player was a guy who was obsessed with girls. With his years of experience, did he sense even more strongly than Danny that she was a homegirl? McGavin hoped not, especially after he got a good look at her figure when she pivoted to face the coffee brewer.

Danny insisted on paying her, although most joints were happy just to have a cop on the premises and gave them freebies on everything but the waitresses. "Louisa, what time do you get—"

"No sale," Hodges interrupted. "Let's go."

"Yeah, sure." Danny's deep frown faded as soon as he turned toward her again. "We'll be back. Promise. I love your coffee, Louisa."

"But you haven't tasted it yet."

He just smiled.

"You jealous?"

Hodges glanced up from Brooklyn Avenue to smirk at McGavin, who was still smarting from his setback at the chicken shack. "Damn straight. And I've got a beautiful wife at home, whom I love, and three kids."

"Hey, that don't mean—"

"No shit, really. That's why I'm jealous, McGavin." Hodges chuckled, then paused to check out some Hispanic graffiti on a long wall and, a block later, the side of a mom-and-pop grocery. Flat painted surfaces were the newspapers of the barrio, advertising territorial boundaries, the advent of new gangs, the demise of others, changes in homeboy status, and the first inklings of war. "Listen, McGavin, you don't want to get laid."

"Oh, yeah?"

"Yeah . . . fucking leads to kissing and kissing to holding hands, and pretty soon you're *talking* to them."

McGavin snorted.

Cresting the Fourth Street bridge, Hodges suddenly realized that it was a relatively smogless day and he could make out the vague purple humps of the San Bernardino Mountains sixty or seventy miles to the east. Soon, any day now, the Santa Anas would begin to blow, reminding him that long sleeves and ties were not far away.

"Who are these jokers?" McGavin asked.

"Ah, yes . . ." Hodges smiled knowingly at the half-dozen homeboys and pair of homegirls perched on the bridge rail—the males in watch caps or stingy brims, Pendleton shirts buttoned to the collar, and khaki pants; the females in white tank tops and blue jeans. "White Fence. Oldest gang in L.A. Been in existence thirty, forty years longer than the United Nations. Will probably last a lot longer, too. White Fence is on to its fifth generation of homeboys."

"How bad-ass?"

"Came close to nailing a woman D.A. last year."

"They *rode on* an assistant D.A.?"

"Yeah."

McGavin whistled at the rash insanity of it.

Hodges parked on the far approach to the bridge, and they walked back to the gang-bangers. As they arrived in their midst, a *veterano,* a survivor of the wars who'd reached the grand old age of twenty-two and had two-hundred-year-old eyes to show for it, palmed off a joint.

"*Qué pasa,* homes?" McGavin asked, beginning to pat down the baggy Pendletons for weapons.

The *veterano* did not condescend to speak to the younger cop. All of his conversation would be with Hodges, a *veterano* of another sort, but a *veterano* nonetheless. "Again we meet."

Hodges squinched at him, but smiling. "Still smoking that PCP, Johnny? It'll make you stupid."

Johnny brought a cupped palm from behind his back and took a luxurious hit. The homeboys laughed. "This is weed, man. The peewees smoke that stupid shit."

"Haven't seen any gang members, have you?" Hodges said.

Everybody laughed—everybody except McGavin, who seemed busy imprinting faces on his memory.

"Heard anything about a drive-by? A Blood got killed a couple nights ago."

"Shit, Hodges. We don't bother with the black boys. Let them kill each other."

"Right. Easier to kill your own, huh? Don't even have to leave the neighborhood."

"Shit, shit, shit," Johnny said, weary with the world. "We just kicking back, man." Then a glint came to his eyes: "Give us some time, man—we'll fuck up." Then he laughed, a laugh made free and easy by the pungent *mota*.

After the Fourth Street bridge, Danny took the wheel and Hodges settled back in the shotgun seat. After a few minutes, the man closed his eyes, but just when Danny thought that he had dozed off, he said, "Make the next right. Head down into the hollow."

"Why?"

"I said so."

"Ain't good enough."

"Interesting group of homeboys I want you to meet."

As they entered a small barrio of ramshackle homes, shacks that had probably looked much the same at the turn of the century, Danny slowed to examine the graffiti sprayed in a style known as diamond:

TWO-ONE, RIFA!

Below this were the monikers, in fresh-looking black paint:

BIRD
WHITEY
SPANKY
LI'L BIT
SONNY

And off to the side, faded by years of sun and ozone and spring morning fog:

**LOONEY TUNES
FROG**

"Twenty-first Street boys," Hodges muttered, still without opening his eyes.

McGavin reached for his clipboard and began riffling through the gang-suppression handouts. "These guys on our list?"

"Nah, poor bastards. Professional victims. The Belgium of the L.A. gang scene. Get their asses kicked all the time." Stirring, Hodges began waving an index finger this way and that. "Got Diamond Street over there . . . the Ville, the projects to the west . . . gotta fight their way in and fight their way out . . . gotta fight just to stay home and kick back."

"Fucked, huh?"

"They *are* fucked, homes . . . but try to tell them that."

The two cops shared a somber laugh, and Danny wasn't sure why, but all at once he felt that he had a glimmer of what Hodges had been like as the blue hard-on that had ripped through these neighborhoods in the old bygone. "Why do they bother?"

"Why do they bother?" Hodges echoed reflectively. "Shit, I don't know. I don't think I'll ever know. Some say a kid joins for recognition. To be somebody. Others say it's for protection, so he won't get his skull caved in by some other gang. Brotherhood has to be a part of it—that's a big draw for the peewees, the fellowship. And hell, I've seen kids intimidated into joining, beaten bloody until they said yes." He watched Danny light up a Marlboro, and McGavin almost felt guilty, realizing that Hodges was aching for one.

"Want a smoke?"

"Nope." Hodges said resolutely. "As far as these Twenty-first Street bangers, well . . . everybody's got to be someplace."

And then it seemed as if the Pontiac's roof had exploded.

Instinctively, Danny reached for his revolver, sure that a bullet had just stitched the car.

CHAPTER 4

"COME ON BACK HERE!" HODGES CALLED TO McGavin, who was standing in frustration at a chain link fence, jiggling the mesh that barred him from chasing a band of little homeboys. The peewees were scrambling down into a ravine of dry brush that probably concealed their hideout. "Give it up."

"Fuck that!" McGavin shot over his shoulder, still thinking of going over the spiked top. "Let's—"

"What the hell do you want to do?" Hodges ran his fingers around the lip of the dent left in the Pontiac's roof by a chunk of concrete. "Stand in the street and shake your fist at them? We'll get them later. Let it pass."

McGavin spun on him, his face red. "That's your gig, isn't it, Uncle Bob?"

"What, what?"

"Get them later? The later the better, right?"

"Come on—"

"Let it pass, right?"

Hodges rested his hands on his hips, then laughed helplessly up at the heavens. But suddenly his lips tightened across his front teeth and he quit laughing. He could feel the cords go taut in his neck. He was pissed. Against his finest efforts, he was pissed. "So what the motherfuck should we do, hotshot? Nuke 'em? Yeah, that's the ticket—fry everything south and east of civic center! Clean it all out with a mushroom fireball!"

After a moment McGavin started smiling, which caught Hodges by surprise. Hodge's anger dissipated as quickly as it had erupted, and he found himself smiling, too. "Well, it was just an idea."

For the first time McGavin looked beat as well. He shambled back to the car, slope-shouldered, his black shoes kicking up dust. "Fuck it. Just drive, Pops. Kill the time . . . just kill the time."

Hodges drove McGavin up onto the heights, into neat Latino neighborhoods beyond the pale of the gangs, down streets with flawless lawns of dichondra and hibiscus bushes along the swept driveways and contented-looking old folks sitting on the porches, keeping an eye on toddlers in diapers playing with the water hoses.

The whole universe wasn't gangs and homeboys, and Hodges wanted these orderly, lower-middle-class streets to say it for him. He knew Danny McGavin's mentality. Christ, he'd lived it—and discovered it to be the loneliest trap in the world.

But they cruised the heights in silence while the sun descended toward the horizon, and Hodges eventually parked above the hollow the Twenty-first Street gang called home. Through the clear air, the Pacific was laid out in coppery sparkles behind the downtown high-rises.

"Shit," he whispered, turning off the engine, "you can look at that and almost delude yourself that this is the safest, prettiest place to live on earth."

After a moment McGavin drawled around the cigarette clenched between his teeth, "I'm hungry."

"Let me guess—chicken?"

McGavin hoisted an eyebrow, but he was smiling. "Any objections?"

"First I got a date of my own." Without further explanation, Hodges released the parking brake, and the Pontiac began rolling down the two-lane that snaked into the hollow.

McGavin sat up as the car gathered speed. "What's this? What's this about, man?"

Hodges just shrugged. The speedometer needle started bumping up around forty. The only sounds were those of the tires crunching softly on the asphalt and the wind gusting in through the windows.

"Hey! Are you fucking nuts?" Unconsciously, McGavin was pumping the floor where the brake pedal would have been if he were in the driver's seat.

Hodges had to use both lanes, banking madly but expertly, to keep the Pontiac out of the bottom of the canyon.

They coasted off the hill busting fifty, and Hodges bore down on the cluster of peewees he'd spied minutes before from the heights. They were still squatting at a retaining wall with spray cans in hands, not ten feet from the chunk of concrete they'd used to bash the unmarked car—oblivious so far to the silent car roaring down on them.

McGavin was now straining both feet against the firewall, staring at Hodges with fresh eyes. He uncrossed his arms and braced them against the dash.

At the last possible second Hodges leaned on the horn and stomped on the brake pedal. The Pontiac skidded sideways to a dusty stop, scattering the peewees in all directions.

He beat McGavin to the bailout. One small homeboy leaped up and grabbed a tree limb to swing himself over the cyclone fence, but Hodges shouted, "Hold it right there! Drop and you're dead!"

The others figured that this was probably meant for them as well, and they froze.

Hodges chuckled inwardly: not one of them had seen his thirteenth birthday.

Looking out the corner of his eye, he saw McGavin brandishing the Ithaca. "What's the matter with you? Put the fucking gauge away!"

Incensed, McGavin hesitated for a moment, then tossed the shotgun back inside the car through the open side window.

A few of the peewees got a kick out of this, and Hodges quickly regretted his harsh words, but a *twelve-gauge* on these runts, for chrissake. "Shut up!" he told them, and their faces went to stone. "Are you guys stupid, or what? Throw rocks at our car? You crazy?" He thrust a finger at a lummoxy-looking white kid. "Answer me, asshole!"

"I dunno."

"What do you mean, you *dunno?*"

"I dunno."

"What you called?"

"Whitey." If it was possible to have an Okie-barrio accent, this pug-nosed towhead had one. Hodges hoped McGavin was taking in the strange racial mix of this besieged gang, but the young cop was too busy being furious at the loss of face Hodges had just inflicted on him.

"Well, Whitey, we can have it any way you want.

You wanna have an understanding? Are we gonna have some rapport here?"

Whitey didn't know what to say. He was still at the concrete-chucking level of communication with The Man.

At that instant two full-blown homeboys came trooping off a side street, one *veterano* with a scowling mug like an Aztec warrior, the other an icy-looking black youth, handsome in a ruthless way.

"You still with that *rapport* shit, Hodges?" the Chicano barked. Frog was his moniker, Leo Lopez the name Hodges had booked him under a dozen times.

"You bet, Leo."

Then Frog looked up: "Hey, what's my brother Felipe doing in that tree? Thinks he's a monkey *vato*, eh?"

Hodges ordered Felipe to keep hanging there.

"You heard the *marrano*," Frog warned the kid.

"Little brother, eh, Frog?"

He exchanged a barrio handshake with Hodges. "Believe me, I was not consulted in the matter. Who's this?"

"My partner, McGavin. And Larry Sylvester," Hodges introduced the severe-looking black homeboy, appreciating once again that Sylvester's nickname didn't fit, "also known as Looney Tunes. What's the matter with your peewees, homes?"

"What?" Sylvester, too, had evolved a slight Spanish inflection. A regular Galápagos, this chain of barrios.

"Threw a damn rock on top my ride. My brand-new ride."

"Who did it?" Looney Tunes demanded, but nobody volunteered. "Who threw that shit?"

At last Whitey took a halting step forward, and Looney Tunes belted him hard across the ear.

"Ow, man!"

"You're one stupid little fuck. You know that? Tell Hodges you're sorry."

"I'm sorry, dude."

Looney Tunes let him have it again, but not nearly as hard, then tossed him back among the other peewees as if he were a fish under the limit.

Business completed, Frog turned sociable: "So, Hodges my man, out in the jungle again, eh?"

"This ain't the jungle. This is Disneyland."

Frog snorted. "I don't know about you, Hodges." He turned to McGavin: "They tell you about this *loco vato?*"

"Not much," the young cop said sullenly, but then Hodges cut short any talk zeroing in on him.

"Say, a Blood got shot the other night. Hear anything about that?"

"Me? I'm too old for that shit." Frog's face was quick with a variety of manly expressions; these had a subtle way of reinforcing his natural authority. With some education and polishing, many of these *veteranos* could become top-drawer politicians. They couldn't do much worse than the ones already in power, Hodges thought. "These little fuckers think it's nothing but a game," Frog continued.

"That's what you used to think, Frog."

"I learned, Hodges. This is what's wrong with this country today, man. Life's too cheap. Too fucking cheap. But me, I learned."

"So how we gonna teach them?" A sweep of Hodges's arm took in all the peewees, including poor dangling Felipe, who was beginning to moan from the pain building in his arms. "How we gonna bring the message home to these li'l winos?"

"I don't know, man. This fucking younger generation . . ." He glowered up at his brother. "You come down, Felipe, I kick your ass."

Grimacing, the kid nodded that he understood.

And the Marine Corps was supposed to build men—
Hodges smirked. "I heard you dropped out of junior
college, Looney Tunes."

"Yeah," he said gravely.

"Heard you knocked up the chancellor's daughter.
What happened, my man?"

"Wasn't for me."

"Knocking up coeds?"

Looney Tunes didn't smile. "You know what I
mean, man."

"So what is? Sitting back here in the hollow?"

"I don't know. I'll fucking know when I come
across it."

"Sure." Hodges turned to go. "Keep the homeboys
in line, gentlemen."

"*Ese,* Frog—what about him?" Whitey interceded
in Felipe's behalf.

"The little *pedo* stays up there till I say . . . till he
learns respect."

Inside the car, Hodges said quietly to McGavin,
"Listen, I didn't mean to jump in the middle of your
shit out there. It's just that you were blowing my
deal . . . my rap."

McGavin kept staring ahead, not saying a word.

After all these years, Joan Hodges could sense it
coming in much the same way she could feel an
earthquake rolling across the stillness of the night.

First there was an unnatural quiet. She'd been
conditioned by eighteen years of motherhood, and so
this was enough to awaken her.

His breathing changed, lost its rhythm, then became swift and shallow.

She almost wanted to wake him up now to spare
him what was on the way, but she knew better. It
would just have to run its course.

She inched over to the far edge of her side of the

bed. He whimpered—just like one of the kids when a baby. "Hold it . . . hold it there," he muttered.

He hadn't had one of these in months—being back on gangs was triggering it. But there was nothing she could say about his reassignment. Neither of them was a rookie anymore; she wasn't a rookie wife who could explode just to get the load off her own chest. And what could he really do? Only eight more months and he could put in his papers. She'd help him get through them. This time seemed impossibly hard only because it was so close to the end.

"He's got a fucking roscoe . . . that one . . . that one there . . . where's our fucking backup?"

Even without touching him, she could feel his body tensing, all the muscles bunching up as his terror, suppressed all day and cloaked in machismo—as the department shrink had explained to all the wives—crackled down his nerves like electricity, seeking its wild release.

"No . . . no . . . no . . . no . . ."

And then, at last, it happened—"God!" He sprang up from the hips, his fists flailing to protect his face, his fists protecting his face from bullets or God only knew what he saw coming at his eyes.

Then he stared forward for a few seconds, his eyes shining.

He went limp, hyperventilating, probably feeling ashamed—and she then knew it was safe to run her fingers up and down his bare back.

He laughed, still struggling to catch his breath. "Shit, baby."

"I love you," she said.

He reached desperately around for her hand.

Standing with Uncle Bob Hodges in the alcove of a southside Baptist church, separated from the bereaved family by a wooden screen, Danny made up his mind to get out of CRASH . . . ASAFP, As Soon As Fucking Possible. Not only did he have to put up with a total burnout of a partner, he now had to endure a lot of hostile black folk who didn't like The Man hanging around their house of worship even if it was at their preacher's request.

The door at the back of the alcove had been propped open with a brick, apparently so the family could have some air, but actually so the cops could watch the street.

Around the edge of the screen and over the tops of the mourners' heads, Danny could see the open casket and a slice of Robert Craig's waxy profile. An organ was whoofing. Flies were spinning above the pulpit.

Yawning, Danny checked his watch.

Hodges looked glassy-eyed this morning, preoccupied maybe.

Then, reflexively, Danny rested his right hand atop the grips of his Smith and Wesson. "Check this out," he grunted to Hodges— they were barely on speaking terms now.

The Bloods were streaming in the side door to the church, resplendent in their red colors. A long sinewy man led them past the casket. It wasn't the moment in which to pay last respects, but the Bloods did their act on their own schedule, despite the murmurings of the congregation.

"Snakedance," Hodges whispered, identifying the gang-banger in the lead. He was followed by a muscular, almost stumpy kid with a Grace Jones haircut on a rocklike skull. Looked like a real prince, which he then proved by reaching inside the casket and apparently shaking the dead hand.

"What the fuck did he just do?" Danny asked Hodges, hushed.

"Tucked a bullet into Craig's palm: *You shall be avenged, brother*. His moniker's Dr. Craze."

Ten more homeboys strutted past the body and toward an empty pew, and then the last banger in line raised a fist from which his forefinger jutted—number one.

Danny could see that the Craig family, especially Mama, wasn't taking to this at all. Between crying jags, she looked like she wanted a piece of the Bloods, bad.

A choir started singing, the best church choir Danny had ever heard, and Hodges slipped out the door to check around the back, almost as if the music bothered him.

The preacher, a white-haired patriarch with a fine look of indignation, mounted the pulpit. "This morning's scriptures are from Lamentations." He cracked his big Bible, skidded his specs higher up on his nose. "'For these things I weep; my eyes flow with tears; for a comforter is far from me, one to revive me, one to revive my courage; my children are desolate, for the enemy has prevailed.'" In case there were some who still hadn't gotten the message, he flipped the page angrily: "And . . . 'Lift your hands to Him for the lives of your children.'"

There followed some amenning from the congregation, and Hodges trudged back inside the alcove, expressionless.

"I want to thank Miss Loretta Thomas and her choir," the preacher went on, "and all the rest of you who have chosen to grace our church on this special day. What makes this day so special? What is so special now, you ask? Just another black child to bite the dust . . . the dust to which thou are all returned?"

"Amen . . . amen."

"I can't see the beat car at the end of the block," Hodges whispered, sounding a little worried.

"He must've gotten pulled off by a hot call."

Hodges bit his lower lip.

"I knew this boy, this Robert Craig—whose mama brought him up as best she could. It wasn't lack of love that brought this boy down. No, it wasn't, now. It was the scourge of drugs! It was the plague of gangs!"

The amens shot through the warm, heavy air like poisoned darts.

"And what makes this day so special, brothers and sisters, is that we have now declared war on this plague! Yes, now—*war* until gang violence is driven from our streets!"

"Amen!" Craig's mother said more fervently than anyone, then turned her face and red-eyed what Danny felt sure were the Bloods, although he couldn't see their pew from where he stood.

Hodges looked like he was trying to pick some sound out of the vague roar from the traffic on the nearby Harbor Freeway.

"We have been bullied by these sawed-off gangsters far too long, brothers and sisters. These gang-bangers, as they so proudly proclaim themselves, these enemies within our midst who desolate our children! And now is the time for decent folk, for the people of God to start banging back!"

Danny had to hand it to the preacher: he more balls than most, what with the Bloods sitting and probably stewing within easy pistol range of him.

"Are we afraid, brothers and sisters, of these hoodlums?"

"No!"

"I said, are we afraid of these terrorists holding us hostage with their—"

What happened then did not make sense at first: the preacher spun around and ducked behind the wooden pulpit as if a locomotive were bearing down on him. Shards of red and yellow and green and blue showered down on him, and the congregation started hollering and screaming as the stained-glass window disintegrated out of its casement. Only as the bright slivers were dancing around the pulpit did Danny hear the *rip-rip-rip* of automatic gunfire. But in the echoing, vaulting spaces of the church he couldn't tell where it was coming from.

He was half convinced that the Bloods had turned on the preacher when Hodges yanked him outside by the arm. "It's a hit! Crips are hitting, goddammit!"

"Where?"

Hodges rushed before him to the street, lofted his revolver to eye level, hesitated, then lowered the weapon as a car, yet unseen by Danny, could be heard accelerating away. Hodges hand-signaled for McGavin to take the wheel while he bounced himself into the shotgun seat and immediately reached for the microphone.

"Did you see the bastards?" Danny cried, slapping the stick-on code three light on the roof, hitting the yelp siren, and gunning the engine all at the same time.

"Stomp on it—left next corner!" Hodges keyed the mike with a tremulous thumb, yet his voice was cool and detached as he communicated his emergency traffic to control.

Danny took the corner almost up on two wheels, and Hodges winced. "You been through the defensive driving course, McGavin?"

"Twice!"

Hodges brought the Ithaca out from under the seat and made sure a round was seated, although he kept the red button behind the trigger on safety. "Wait—nobody goes through defensive driving twice."

Straining ahead for a glimpse of the Crip war

wagon, Danny hiked a shoulder. "I like wrecked a car the first time through."

Hodges chuckled. "They turned right onto Avalon." He broadcast an update to Control, which then hit an alert tone, and the female dispatcher calmly intoned: "Attention all units . . . attention all units: One CRASH Thirty-two in pursuit southbound on Avalon approaching Slauson of a two-forty-six vehicle, early seventies, black sedan with chrome wheels, possible Crip involvement, suspects armed with automatic weapons. Repeat: Suspects armed with automatic weapons. No further details."

"Ha!" Hodges chortled—and he really seemed alive for the first time. "Pucker factor just went to ten! I can hear the assholes slamming shut! *Auto*-matic weapons, mama! Whoa—he's turned, homes!"

As Danny threw the Pontiac into four-wheel drift, the locked tires screeching, Hodges purred into the mike: "Control, we're now eastbound on Nine-fourth. You got a chopper local?"

"Roger," a voice said before Control could answer. The rotor was making a warbly whine in the background. "That you making tracks in the yellow Firebird?"

"Roger," Hodges said. "See our black sedan?"

"Up ahead. Be advised he's now south on Clovis, being slowed by traffic."

"You belted in?" Hodges asked Danny, without turning his head.

"Naw, I don't like—"

"Fucking *do* it!" Hodges held the wheel while Danny strapped himself in. "Now left here quick, man."

"He's turned left onto One hundred seventh, CRASH Thirty-two," the chopper pilot said.

"What'd I fucking tell you?" Hodges asked triumphantly.

At last, Danny could see the Crip car, but then a Southeast black-and-white careened in off a side street and buffered them from their quarry. "Shit!" A new siren from behind made him glance up to the rearview mirror: a Firestone sheriff's unit was horning in on the action, too.

"Jesus!"

Hodges's shout made Danny peer ahead in time to see two Crips in colors whip their upper bodies out the rear side windows of the black sedan and let go, one with a pump shotgun and the other with an Uzi. The black-and-white's windshield exploded, and the unit started weaving in slapdash pattern all over Compton Avenue, as if the patrolman was drunk or blind—or dying.

Hodges shouted over the airwaves for the first time: "You okay? You hit?"

"Just something in the eye. Get them . . . get them!"

"Roger, brother." Hodges growled as he hung up the mike, but by the time Danny got around the disabled cruiser, the black sedan had bolted up an alley, hurling garbage cans and even an old refrigerator aside like broken tackles.

Hodges eased the Ithaca out his window and was squinting down the barrel when the sedan made a lightning left onto 108th Street and then another up Santa Ana Boulevard.

"Shit!"

The steel rod spires of Watts Towers loomed into view just as Danny came up on the sedan's rear bumper, Hodges keeping the heads of the Crip trigger men low by waving his gauge from side to side.

A foot apart, the two cars raced through a busy

intersection, a wail of horns building and then trailing off behind.

"Come along him on my side!" Hodges shouted, snugging the shotgun's stock in the pocket of his shoulder and preparing himself for some nasty gunplay at arm's length.

Danny started to flank the sedan, but the Crip driver decided he didn't like this—and spun out, burning rubber with a horrible screech as he came around one hundred eighty degrees. Instantly, Danny duplicated the maneuver, the vehicles banging together so ferociously Hodges nearly lost the Ithaca in the sliding collision.

"Careful, will you!" he bawled as both cars continued the game northbound.

Then the Crip driver, no doubt rattled by Danny's persistence, looked away from the white line long enough to drift sideways, catch the curb, and flip in front of the Pontiac.

Certain injuries for the homeboys, Danny realized with a fleeting sense of glee.

Then, wildly, he jinked the wheel to avoid the spinning sedan. "No!" Danny felt his side of the car lurch up as it caught a fender on the smoking undercarriage of the caroming black vehicle.

And then everything turned to vibration and sparks and blears and Hodges yelling to beat the devil.

When it ended, they were upside down, held in only by their seat belts.

While his partner crept forward with a carbine to check out the Crip war wagon, a deputy trotted up to the Pontiac, asked if everything was okay.

He was ignored.

Hodges's bald head looked swollen and redder than usual, probably because all the blood in his body was draining into it. He blinked for several seconds; then his puffy inverted lips moved—it looked strange because his chin appeared to be his nose: "My wife thinks I should invite you over for a fucking barbecue or something."

Danny just hung there, speechless.

"She said you can bring a date."

CHAPTER 5

BECAUSE LIKE HELL HE WAS GOING TO BE THE ONLY ONE to have his evening ruined, Lieutenant Wally Reed put the arm on Bob Hodges to attend; and because like hell Wally and he were going to be the only ones to have their evening ruined, Hodges put the arm on McGavin to attend. McGavin grumbled over the phone, but he showed up—he was already skating on thin ice with the CRASH brass for having squared off the Pontiac's aerodynamic lines and buckled the roof, although miraculously the Firebird was still roadworthy. But Hodges had to roll his eyes when McGavin came through the recreation center door in a big leather jacket that made him look like a depilated Hereford. "Man, don't you look buffed up in that thing."

"Fuck you, Uncle Bob." And he took a chair at the side of the hall without bothering with the coffee and pastries department community relations had sprung for.

Hodges sat in the nearly empty front row beside Wally, who looked tired but was trying to jack his energy level up with a third cup of coffee and was making up for another skipped dinner with a strawberry bearclaw.

Glancing around, Hodges suspected that the same people attended these things wherever they were held in the city. A good number of them worked for government, like Rita Gallegos, a hefty probation officer who was accused by the Juvenile detectives of spending her off-hours arm wrestling at truck stops for cheeseburgers. Jesus, maybe *all* of them worked for government, even the alleged concerned citizens. The thought was freaky, Orwellian or something. Proles fed and clothed to lodge complaints—within limits; other proles fed and clothed to handle those complaints—within limits.

"Well, here goes shit, Bobby." Wally set his Styrofoam cup on the waxed concrete floor, knotted his tie, then took center stage. "Folks, I'm Lieutenant Wallace Reed and I want to thank you all for coming tonight."

Hodges made himself sit straighter: Wally had developed a public relations voice different from his ordinary one. It was so warm and pleasant it could bring on drowsiness quicker than Seconal.

"Our community has kids out there who're dying over colors. I mean, actually dying over red or blue. And the thing is, we need help . . . your help, ladies and gentlemen."

Rita nodded this way and that at the audience and, when she felt that this wasn't enough to get things rolling, clapped her hands together once, sharply, startling Wally, who didn't care much for sudden noises.

A cheerleader in her Catholic high school days, Rita still loved to get the spirit snapping.

"So," Wally went on, "we need you decent people to testify when you see something go down out there. We are outnumbered. We are outgunned—"

"You mean you cops don't have enough guns? Shee-it!"

And here it begins, Hodges muttered inwardly, resisting the urge to jerk back his sleeve and check the time.

Wally folded his arms across his chest and let the commotion swell.

"You wanna know why the kids pull this shit?"

"Ain't no jobs, baby!"

"You got that shit straight, jack!"

"What's a motherfucking thirteen-year-old need a job for? And that's who shot my brother's ass—a motherfucking thirteen-year-old punk. Shot his ass *dead!*"

Folks were caterwauling at high pitch when a huge black man stood and immediately quieted them down. He spent his days holding up five-ton I-beams so other construction workers could weld them into place on high-rises. His name was Harold Brown, and he attended all of these things rain or shine, usually in a dirty T-shirt, but tonight in a dirty polo shirt.

"I know what being outgunned is about, Reed," he rumbled. "I was in 'Nam."

"Yeah, Harold?" Wally asked, because Brown's dramatic pause was going on a bit too long.

"It's not what you got in your hand! It's what the people want!"

Hodges had no idea what this was supposed to mean, nor did anybody else inside the recreation center, but that didn't keep the others from applauding like mad.

McGavin sneered as the hubbub began to build again, then closed his eyes and leaned his chair against the wall to catch some more z's.

"People . . . people," a patient but weary black voice said from the back. "People . . . people . . . people . . . ."

"Let me guess," Hodges whispered to himself. "Ron Delauney."

And he didn't have to swivel a look to know that Delauney was swaggering toward the front. He could hear the taps on the man's shoes striking the concrete: click . . . what a dick . . . click . . . what a dick . . . click . . .

Delauney took one last drag from his cigarette, then crushed it underfoot with the grace of Fred Astaire. He was wearing a guacamole-colored leisure suit, if that's what they were called nowadays. Wally sat down, probably relieved to be off the hot seat, and McGavin was sneering at the lean and smooth young black man as if he'd enjoy strip-searching him in a blizzard.

"I ran with a gang," Delauney said, making sure everybody saw the two-pound gold ring on his pinky when he lowered his shades to peek confidentially over the frames at the audience. "I'm *working* with them now."

What a scam: professional gang-banger on both the city and county payrolls, not to mention the private charities that grubstaked his operations. Yet in another sense, Hodges had to admire him. He was no dummy. Who else but Ron "the don" Delauney could convert a twenty-page rap sheet into a cottage industry with three secretaries—his sisters—and five *liaison specialists*—his brothers and cousins?

"Lemme to try to make a point here . . . a point

about the reality on the street," Delauney went on. "See, the dope dealer's got the Mercedes-Benz. The fast money. The fast women. These kids got eyes. They look around and *see*. And that is their socialization. It's the values they respect. We—the community, now—we don't educate them, get them jobs . . ."

"Right on, brother," a middle-aged woman called out.

"Hell, man, we all know that!" somebody shouted, not buying Delauney's slippery ration of caca. "We want some damn *protection!*"

"Then," Wally said, twisting around in his chair, "you gotta get involved!"

"People . . . people, lemme try to clarify this thing." Then Ron Delauney showed that he had retained at least some of his street smarts, because he shut up: Harold Brown had risen again.

"Why the hell do you think we're here, Reed? 'Cause we fed up! Sick of this shit!" Brown's head hung off his powerful neck in a moment of mute protest. "But the po-lice will never get nowhere. Not when you shake people down. Shine your fucking light in our face. Treat us like shit. Treat all us like Crips—because of where we live! Right in front of our kids!"

"Quiet, people!" Rita leaped up from her chair. "Hold on! Wait! Will you just—*quiet!* Pleeease!"

Hodges saw McGavin check his wristwatch, then did the same himself.

Two excruciating hours later, Hodges thought he was making a clean getaway when Ron Delauney called his name across the parking lot.

McGavin, who was unlocking a meticulously restored '66 Mustang that had his El Monte upbringing written all over it in glittering red metal-flake, laughed sarcastically at Delauney's click-clicking approach. "Buddy of yours, Uncle Bob?"

"Yeah, sure."

"Hey, Hodges, my man." Delauney offered the cop some hand jive, which was ignored. "Lynch mob, eh? Good thing they forgot the rope."

"Pure fucking horseshit," McGavin said through the rolled-down side window from the Mustang's front seat, where he was busy deactivating the alarm system.

Delauney appraised him with a cautious smile. "Don't think I've had the pleasure."

"My new partner," Hodges said. "McGavin."

"And ain't no pleasure involved." McGavin got the six cylinders firing thunderously. "I was getting paid to take it in there. On my own time now, bro."

"Hey, baby," Delauney chuckled, "my motto is—everything is everything."

"Your motto is—everything is cash, check, or plastic. See you tomorrow at your place, Hodges. Am I supposed to bring anything?"

"Nope."

McGavin backed up, his front left tire passing within inches of Delauney's shoes, and burned rubber out of the parking lot.

Delauney shrugged. "Something I said?" He cocked up his arms and sniffed his arm-pits.

Hodges smiled at him as if to say, *I've got your number.* But the simple truth of the matter was that the former gang-banger could be useful from time to time. Not often, but now and again. "You feel like talking, Ron?"

"Anytime, homes. Talking is the name of the game."

Hodges smirked. "Sure is, ain't it, though?"

Delauney let the dig pass with a smile.

"Who shot Robert Craig, Ron?"

Delauney took his time shaking a cigarette out of the pack and feeding it between his lips. It was hard for Hodges to imagine that this might be a relative question, but maybe it was. "If I knew, Bob," he said on a smoky breath, "and I told you . . . well, I'd never get near them again."

"Now, wouldn't that be a crying shame."

"You got your job and I got mine." He narrowed his eyes at Hodges. "You think us gang workers are just a bunch of fucking cons, don't you?"

Hodges hiked a shoulder a little.

"Think we're making out like bandits on this thing, right? It's all a joke, right?"

Again, Hodges didn't answer. He was too weary to argue. He needed energy to argue, and his energy needle was on empty.

But then Delauney let go with a low, sultry laugh. "Ain't no thing, Uncle Bob. Didn't mean to make you uncomfortable."

Turning, he started tapping off toward his white Corvette with the name Youth Gang Intercession, Inc. on a magnetic sign on the door to keep it all tax deductible, when Hodges stopped him.

"Hey, Delauney, you want to do something useful?"

"You think I'm capable, baby?"

"Sometimes."

About-facing and clicking back, Delauney chuckled. "Fair enough."

"Go check out Twenty-first Street."

"Twenty-first. Two-one . . . Two-one . . ." Delauney ran the gang through his mental file. "You mean old Frog and Looney Tunes got problems?"

"Sorta. They've got some peewees up there ready to cross over. Maybe they don't really have to."

"All right. Those homeboys always been shaky in the self-perpetuation department. I'll give it a try."

"Thanks," Hodges forced himself to say.

"Shit, man, you don't have to thank me." Delauney made his way to the Corvette and got in, showing Hodges a telephone receiver. "See this cellular phone, baby? This, Hodges, is your *raise* this year!"

CHAPTER 6

DANNY COULD HAVE DESCRIBED HODGES'S RESIDENCE even before he arrived at noon with Louisa. Eleven hundred square feet built in a week right after World War II. A crumbling asphalt driveway with a forty-year-old oil stain at its center. Some camellia bushes framing the bay window, dripping their spent pink petals onto the uncut grass. A paycheck-to-paycheck palace.

Danny McGavin had grown up in one just like it.

Joan Hodges was attractive, but tended toward the plain side in both looks and dress. Decent knockers, though. And, thank God, right off the bat she tried to make Louisa feel at ease, which was no easy trick. It had taken a lot of coaxing to make her come along in the first place. She'd even insisted that Danny pick her up at the chicken shack instead of at her little cottage in the barrio.

She looked dynamite today in a light blue blouse and skirt that brought out the warmth in her skin tones.

Everybody was stumbling through the introductions and the usual awkward bullshit—about what a nice place you have here and don't you look nice and ain't the weather fucking nice—when a kid around five years old came ripping into the living room on a trike. He would have looked exactly like Hodges if he'd been bald.

Hodges gently scolded him for having the tricycle in the house, like the kid never rode his trike inside, which was obviously crap. But everybody let it slide with a lot of smiling and ha-ha-ha-ing, and Joan led the way through the stuffy little kitchen, where everybody picked up a Lite beer off the drainboard, out to the backyard, laying the chitchat on Louisa without pause: "We've got Linda. She's eighteen and away at college. Her first semester. And Tommy here. And then Bob said, 'Hey, let's try it one more time.' I really thought Tommy would be our last. But these things do happen."

"They better not," Danny said under his breath. The two women heard and shot him withering looks in unison.

The patio cement was still wet where Joan had no doubt ordered Uncle Bob to hose it off. Danny picked out a rusty lawn chair and eased himself down, praying that Hodges would get going with the eats so Louisa and he could get the hell out of here as soon as politely possible. Thank God the briquettes were already smoldering in a cheapo K-mart barbecue.

"And how long have you been in the department, Dan?" Joan asked.

"Four years, Mrs. Hodges."

"Oh, call me Joan, please. 'Mrs. Hodges' makes me feel so old."

"Sorry."

"Just kidding, Dan—you'll get used to me. Where did you work before CRASH?"

"Central Patrol."

"And where did you and Louisa meet?"

"At the restaurant where Louisa works." Danny teased her with a smile.

But apparently Louisa didn't see the humor in it and hurriedly changed the subject: "Where's the baby?"

"Oh, nap time. I'll get her up in a few minutes."

Just as Danny realized that Hodges hadn't followed them out from the kitchen, Uncle Bob backed through the screen door in a greasy apron, a tray clenched in both hands. "Jumbo shrimp. There's a goddamn contradiction. And fourteen ninety-five a pound."

"Bob," Joan said, smiling. But her voice was brittle for the first time.

"Hey, what's money?" He winked at McGavin. "My partner and me—two highly paid professionals."

"Are you going to start the shrimp now?"

"Thinking of it, honey." He started tossing them on the grill.

Joan got up, but then said, when Louisa followed suit, "Oh, sit down, girl, and relax."

"No, let me help."

"Absolutely not." Yet, with this little female ritual out of the way, Joan said nothing more as Louisa trailed her into the kitchen.

As soon as the screen door knocked shut, Hodges said, "You dog."

Danny took a thoughtful sip of beer. "What do you

think?" He could see it in Hodges's eyes—the *chola* question—but Uncle Bob then surprised him.

"Whatever—she's a good girl. And you'd better treat her right."

Danny smiled slyly. "Why?"

"Because if you don't, her Mexican mama gonna chop it off and do this . . ." He plopped one of the pink shrimp onto the hottest part of the grill, where it immediately began sizzling.

"Nice."

"Hey, I didn't make the rules." Hodges groaned as he lowered himself into a chair. "I'm still aching in places I didn't know I had."

Danny ignored this reference to the collision, but Hodges wouldn't let it lie.

"Pretty fancy driving the other day, my man."

"We didn't have to try to catch them," Danny shot back at him. Guest or not, he wasn't going to take any shit.

Hodges rubbed his chin for a moment. "You saying I wouldn't have?"

"If I was you . . . less than a year to go to pension-ville . . . a wife, kids . . ."

"That's bullshit."

"What?"

Hodges repeated himself irritably, then took a long swallow of beer.

"You sure you wanna get into this now?"

"I just don't get you."

"Gonna psychoanalyze me now, Uncle Bob?"

Both men paused and glanced up as the droopy green fronds of Hodges's banana palms began rattling. Abruptly, a breeze had risen, a warm and dry one out of the north.

"You know, I used to get all jacked up, too. Figured I needed the edge."

"Maybe you don't. Maybe I do. Maybe we're just different."

Hodges conceded this with a nod.

And now Danny was pissed, asking himself why he'd bothered to say yes to this barbecue in the first place. Maybe it had had something to do with how *righteous* Hodges had been during the pursuit after the Crips, how wired in the way a good cop should be. But now, back in the safety of his own seedy nest, that proficient and fearless enforcement machine had reverted into good old Uncle Bob.

"But let me tell you one thing about the edge, McGavin."

"Please do."

"No, I'm serious. Know what I remember most from that time in my life? The regrets. Nothing but the fucking regrets." He flicked his chin toward the kitchen. "I regret the raw deal she got so I could maintain my fucking edge."

Danny sighed, his aluminum beer can making a crinkly sound as he crushed it. "Well, that's—"

"Let me tell you, McGavin—you can't prove anything out on those streets. It's bozoland, What you can do out there is your job. You can try to be a professional. Granted, you can't achieve that very often. But you can sure as shit try. That's the best you can fucking do!" For a moment it seemed as if Hodges was going to calm down, but then another thought jacked him up again and returned the glaze to his eyes: "In nineteen years I've learned one sorry lesson: if you fight every jerk on the street, you'll be one sad, sorry son of a bitch at the end of each and every day. You'll never last twenty years. And God forbid you ever get married and take it out on your wife. She will *walk*. Fucking walk as soon as she realizes what a tub of hatred she's tied to. She will leave you. Maybe alone is fun at your age, homes. But it's the fucking pits at mine. So why make it worse on yourself all the time?"

Danny shook his head. "Is that what you call *one* thing?"

"Yeah, one thing . . ." Hodges fingered the bridge of his nose, coming down off his anger at last. "It's all one thing."

"Uncle Bob have a couple beers before I got here?"

"Couple," he admitted, almost smiling.

After several long seconds of silence, Danny said, "Now, my turn. . . "

Hodges waved for him to proceed.

"First of all, about the other day—"

"Ah, Christ, this has nothing to do with—"

"Shut up."

"I just want to—"

"*Shut up!* My fucking turn! Listen to me, will you?"

"Okay, okay."

"Jesus, do I get to talk?"

"Talk." Hodges got up, quickly turned the shrimp, then sat again. "Talk!"

"I'm sorry about the car, because I know the heat came down on you as much as me. We wiped out. What can I say? You want me to say it won't happen again?" He paused, mostly to see if Hodges would keep his promise and keep quiet. He did. "Look, I understand what you're trying to say . . . and what you try to do on the streets. But I didn't volunteer for CRASH to play jive games and be pals with these assholes. Do you honestly think you get respect? No offense, man, but they just laugh at you and then go out and fuck people over right and left like you don't even exist. I can't deal with that. And if you don't think you can deal with me . . . well, I can understand that, too."

Hodges took another drink, then stared down the hole in his beer can before jiggling up some foam.

Even though Joan kept smiling and pretending that nothing was going on in the backyard, Louisa found herself feeling more and more nervous. She wanted things to go well with the Hodgeses. She wanted this to be a pleasant and memorable day, her first with Danny. And then, when Danny hollered for Bob to shut up, Joan's smile trembled a little and she said, "Time to wake that baby."

Alone in the kitchen, Louisa exhaled and watched Danny.

She didn't like him like this. She barely knew him, but she realized that she didn't like *this*.

Once again she asked herself why she had come. And once again, she told herself that there was something appealing and good beneath this *loco vato* act of his, something that shone now and again through the cracks in his crusty machismo. She believed that she understood men like Danny McGavin, that they behaved as they did only because they were ashamed of the goodness within their hearts.

Joan returned with the nine-month-old girl in her arms. The baby was sweaty and cranky from her sleep.

"Oh . . . let me have her, please."

"Are you sure, Louisa?"

"Yes, yes—please."

The baby didn't resist her clutch, as Louisa had trusted she wouldn't. Smiling, she began cooing in Spanish to the child, but then grew self-conscious—needlessly, for Joan was hurriedly trying to catch the rest of the meal up with the shrimp, which were already done.

Louisa's eyes dimmed as she looked back out at Danny, who was now sharing nothing but silence with

Bob Hodges, both of them looking as miserable as a couple on the verge of divorce. This only proved what she had suspected all along—there was a painful but strong bond between these two *vatos*.

Then the baby squirmed, and she realized something else.

She glanced around the kitchen, briefly fixed her eyes on Joan, who looked contented in her little chores.

Yes, this was something she would hide from Danny McGavin. Otherwise, she risked having it flung back in her face.

Louisa Gomez, born to the White Fence gang, coveted this house, this baby . . . this life in which the women knew nothing of the drive-by, of falling to the floor as the bullets started flying.

The wind really kicked up around four-thirty, unexpectedly answering Danny's prayers by whirling the dirty paper plates and empty cans against the wooden fence. "The Santa Ana," Hodges declared, seeming grateful, too. Louisa and Danny said their good-byes, and getting on the freeway felt like pure freedom. Even Louisa had smiled at this reprieve from tension.

And now, with the sunlight fading fast and the Santa Ana flowing off the desert and opening up fifty-mile vistas, she was still smiling. Up north in the communities tucked against the Verdugo Hills, and south along Boyle Heights, the lights were starting to wink on, clearer and more glittering than usual.

As Danny veered down the off-ramp into a thicket of oleander trembling in the wind, Louisa reached out to catch the satiny air in her hand.

"You and me, babe . . ."

She tilted her head toward him, a long strand of brown hair catching around her soft throat. "What?"

He shook his head—nothing. A mural on an

apartment-building wall in some projects—crucified homeboys caught in the last light—sobered him a little. "You'll have to tell me where you live. I don't read minds."

"I noticed."

"What's that supposed to mean?"

But she just brought her hand back inside and pressed two fingers against his lips for a moment. They were cool from the Santa Ana, which always seemed to lose its Mojave Desert warmth at dusk. "Keep going straight."

"Only way I know how, babe."

"I noticed that, too."

"You noticed one helluva lot."

"Yeah," she said a bit sadly.

As they started across the Fourth Street bridge, a file of low riders whooshed past one by one in the opposite direction, a string of gleaming Chevy Impalas, their undercarriages lowered to the absolute legal minimum above the asphalt. He knew that few low riders were gang-bangers, that most were too terrified their expensively modified vehicles might get bullet holes in them, but he nevertheless flipped off the last car in line, whose driver wisely ignored him, making Danny feel like a fool.

"What'd you do that for?" Louisa asked, looking genuinely baffled.

He didn't feel like explaining that he was beginning to despise it all, the entire corny barrio scene—everything about it except her, of course. "I don't know."

She told him to stop at the far side of the bridge.

"Listen," he protested, "I'm sorry I did it. Want me to go back and apologize? I'll do it. I'm perfectly serious. I'll tell the loser I'm sorry."

"It isn't that," she said, quietly, smiling at the sudden hint of desperation in his voice.

He told himself to get back in control. What the devil was going on here?

"I get out here, Daniel."

He checked around for houses—none was close by, only a gas station with a pay booth more heavily fortified than a Nazi pillbox. "I don't get it."

"I had a nice time." Her hand found the door latch, but he stopped her from opening it with his next words.

"Come here—look at me, will you?"

She did so. "What?"

He let out a long breath, exasperated. "Nothing."

"What?"

"Looking pretty good."

"I like you, too."

"I didn't say that," he nearly snarled, tapping in the cigarette lighter and reaching for a Marlboro.

"Don't be a tough guy with me, Danny. Everybody's a tough guy around here, you know? That doesn't get to me."

"What does?"

"Be *nice.*"

"Okay, I'll be nice . . . I'll be world-class nice."

"I mean it." She turned to take in the sunset for a few seconds, the peach-colored glow of it glancing around her cheek, and he almost reached over and brushed the perfect smoothness of her face. "You want to tell me what you were thinking?"

"I was thinking about the butterfly on your shoulder."

She said nothing for a while. "I was only eleven."

"Hey . . . I don't mind. I don't even know why I brought it up."

"Someday I'll get the money and have it removed. But there's always the scar. The damned things always leave a scar."

Catching him unaware, she sprang out her door. "I'll go, then."

"No, no, no—I'm gonna drive you. This neighborhood's like dangerous."

She leaned back in though the open window. "Daniel, I live in the barrio. I'm a homegirl. I'm safe, okay?" She paused. "They see me with you and maybe I'm not."

He sat there glumly, passing the unlit smoke back and forth between his fingers.

"Good night," she said.

"Yeah, right."

"Daniel?"

"What?"

"Come here."

Then, with her legs kicking up behind her, she leaned halfway across the front seat and planted a little kiss on his cheek. He grabbed for more, hungrily, but she tilted back out the window, laughing. "Tomorrow, eh?"

The wind cut like a *filero,* so Felipe and the other peewees knotted their *moco* rags tight around their heads and were trying to keep out of that *filero* of a wind by staying low behind the power station wall. And they were squatting there with a little *grifa* going from hand to hand, saying like *que gacho* on the bad scene day—when Bird ran up and told them to stay cool because a big *rata* was on the way and Frog said nobody was to say shit.

After a while, with the wind making this like whistle in the power lines, the *rata* showed up with Looney Tunes on one arm and Frog on the other. This *rata* was *tinto* like Tunes, and the peewees didn't say shit when he, who Frog and Tunes called Ron the Don, said to them, "*Qué pasa,* my men?" When nobody said shit, he went back to what he'd been saying to Tunes, but none of it made sense to Felipe because he didn't know the dude they were talking about: "Not kidding you, man. That dude was *fly*. He so fly he *gone!*"

Frog laughed, even Tunes laughed a little, but then Bird stopped laughing and got this *pendejo* look in his face. "Made his own from the curb, man—that dude. Over and *out.*"

And then the *rata pina* got the same *pendejo* look in his face and started twisting a big gold ring around and around his finger. Felipe counted like ten times, and still the *rata* kept doing it. "You could get out, too . . . all of you."

"How?" Tunes asked. "Maybe I go up to Hollywood —be Eddie Murphy. But you think America's ready to love two niggers at the same time?"

Felipe and the other peewees laughed, laughed as hard and as long as the *veteranos*. It was good to laugh the same as the *veteranos* and nobody smack you.

"Maybe," the *tinto* answered Tunes. "No future in hanging around here." He shut up for a minute. He had a way of looking around the hood that made Felipe see the dust and the trash and the rusted *ranflas* and the big *nada* at the heart of everything—like for the first time. "No future nohow."

"Shee-it," Whitey said.

But like he'd warned everybody not to speak up, Frog smacked him one good, and Whitey's eyes got wet and he didn't say anything else.

Then the *tinto* went on, "No future but what you make it."

"Shit," Tunes said, but Frog didn't smack him. Not *him*. Nobody fucked with Tunes, because when he got *loco* he was like Rambo or something.

"No, man, this gang-banging—"

"Hey, listen, man," Bird spoke up, eyes all squinchy because of the dust, "that's the way of the world. Always gonna be gangs. Always gonna be fighting. Always was. Always is. Nobody gonna stop it. That's life." An idea made him quiet for a second. "Shee-it, United States just a big gang. Russia, too. And when push come to shove, they ride on each other, man. Ride on each other with like ships and airplanes. Nobody gonna stop it. That's life."

"Well, I don't know about no Russia," the *tinto* said. "You can stop it for yourself . . . if you got the balls."

Then Bird got hot. "Fuck you."

The *tinto* stopped twisting his ring. "Fuck you, you little asshole."

"Yeah, man?"

"Jesus—what the fuck do I do with you guys?"

"Orale!" Frog told everybody to quit fooling around, then red-eyed the *tinto:* "What do you mean? What do you do? You don't do nothing, *vato.* Come around here, talk trash. Okay . . . okay . . . okay. We talk trash all the time. But as for what you *do . . ."* Frog looked away to like think a little. "You got your job. You happy, man. You can tell them you were here. Maybe you want me to like sign your hall pass or something?"

"Who told you to come by, anyway?" Tunes asked.

"Hodges sent me."

"Shee-it . . . Hodges."

"He's worried about you guys."

Everybody had a laugh at that one.

"He thinks maybe you're smart enough to turn away from this bullshit—but too stupid to realize it."

Then the fire came into Bird's eyes. "What's Hodges know? Fuck Hodges! Where's Hodges come from, anyways? These here are my homeboys, *vato.* Our homies all we got! I love them and they fucking love me! *Mi barrio es primero!* Do I walk away from that? How, man? For what? Tell me!"

Bird's words made Felipe feel real good and proud inside, but then he looked at Frog and he didn't feel so good. His big brother was getting that *pendejo* look, all sad and confused. He kept looking from the *tinto* to Felipe and back and forth again. "Hodges sent you?"

"Yeah."

"Goddamn." Tunes clapped his hands on his knees and stood up. "We must be stupid."

The *tinto* grinned. "We ain't exactly talking no Einsteins here." Then he said to Bird: "I know what you're saying, man. I know what you're feeling. I banged. I banged twelve fucking years, baby. But there's more—"

"I don't see it. Where?" This time it was Bird who looked all around the hood, and the way he did it made Felipe see that this was all theirs, that this belonged to the Two-one, Rifa! The rule of the Twenty-first Street homeboys! "You tell Hodges to come down here hisself and look."

"Felipe . . ."

He looked at his big brother. Frog's mouth was set like all fierce.

"Yeah?"

"Get outta here."

"What?"

"I said—outta here."

Felipe glanced at the other peewees. "Just me?"

"Just you."

"*Donde?*"

"I don't care. Just get, man!" And then he balled up his *mano* and walloped Felipe in the lips, hard.

CHAPTER 7

ONCE IN A WHILE THE BRASS ADHERED TO THE philosophy that the punishment should fit the crime —no more, no less. So the city mechanics simply pulled out the collapsed front fenders, hammered the roof back into a semblance of its pre-crash shape, popped in a fresh windshield—and Hodges and McGavin were back on the road in the yellow Pontiac.

"Bullshit," McGavin said when Hodges told him to jump behind the wheel.

"What do you mean, *bullshit?*"

"I'm not going to be seen driving this rasty son of a bitch. They can give me days off without pay. I don't give a shit."

"Then you'll miss the raid," Hodges said offhand-edly.

McGavin hesitated in the midst of his indignation. "What raid?"

"The one I'm going on right now."

"Where?"

"You'll have to drive to find out."

McGavin glared at him a few moments longer, then opened the driver's door, which was warped and groaned. "You prick."

Twenty minutes later, on Hodges's instructions, McGavin turned off the Harbor Freeway and followed a winding two-lane up into an industrial park that overlooked San Pedro from the east slope of the Palos Verdes Hills. To the west were the ritzy estates on the peninsula, their swimming pools like platinum nuggets under the afternoon sun. Funny, Hodges thought, but he had no desire to join all those folks in a life of luxury. And he wasn't even sure why. *Oughta have my head examined . . . again.*

"Where now, for chrissake?" McGavin asked.

"Next right."

"What the fuck and am I looking for?"

"Got me, brother . . . you honestly got me there."

"I'm *serious.*"

"Yeah, far too serious, homes."

"Fuck you. Believe it or not, with the right company, I can be quite fucking funny."

Hodges yawned. "Okay, here's the command post. Pull in."

McGavin stiffened as he saw the scores of cops in blue LAPD windbreakers and baseball caps, and as if their presence didn't promise enough humiliation, among them stood thirty or so deputy sheriffs in green jumpsuits and riot helmets.

"You set me up!" McGavin hissed between clenched teeth. "When this is over, I'm going to kick your ass, Hodges—do you hear me?"

"Hey, I'm riding in this lemon, too, man."

"But you're not *driving* it!"

"One of these days we've got to sit down and talk about your values." Then Hodges started chuckling as the catcalls began in earnest.

"Hey, boys—nice ride!"

"Thank you, thank you . . . my partner does his own body work."

"Who's that in there with you, Hodges—Pac-Man?"

"Who?"

"The Pac-Man."

Hodges looked questioningly to McGavin, who had just set the parking brake with a yank. "What's he talking about?"

"That's what they called me at Central," McGavin mumbled.

"How come?"

"I used to play a lot of Pac-Man."

"Used to?"

"Okay—I like fucking Pac-Man, so what?"

"Down, boy . . . down."

A black deputy sergeant with a voice like a marine D.I.'s thrust his face through Hodges's open window. "Got any registration for this?"

With his thumb and forefinger, Hodges fashioned a circle and began jerking the tip of his nightstick through it. "I'll give you some registration, Bailey."

"Take all you candy-ass bluecoats to hold me down, first."

"That's what you said last time, then bent over before any of us could grab you."

"My ass!" Bailey barked, laughing.

"That came next. Bailey, this is my partner, McGavin—Pac-Man, I just find out."

"Come on, Pac-Man, get out of this thing before it

catches fire or something. We can take my sled." The deputy sergeant led them over to his black-and-white, which was parked on the edge of the hillside lot. Below them was the harbor: warehouse complexes along the docks, the superstructures of container ships jutting up over the corrugated roofs.

"What's this all about?" McGavin asked, sitting on the trunk lid. "My partner won't tell me shit."

"Your partner don't know shit. He was just told to be here at zero-now hour. Speaking of . . ." Bailey checked his wristwatch a bit impatiently. "The sheriff thought it'd be a good idea if somebody from your gang unit was in on this. And I asked for Uncle Bob."

"How'd you mounties become involved?"

"*Become* involved? Shit, Hodges, we're the ones called *you* in. Sheriff's got the G-two, man."

"What intelligence?"

"Had all these gang-banging assholes driving fire extinguishers off the docks."

"These docks in city or county?"

"Right on the fucking line, baby. Why do you think we're bothering with you pogues? Anyways, I couldn't for the life of me figure out why these homeboys were suddenly so concerned about putting out fires. Well, the long and the short of it is, these are Taiwan fire extinguishers from Colombia via a Panamanian boat."

Hodges chuckled: "And the only thing you can snuff out with one of them is your *mind.*"

"You got it." Bailey pointed down at a big building along the main channel. "A hustler's sitting on a warehouse full of the things."

"And that's what we're hitting?" McGavin asked eagerly.

"No, Special Enforcement will crack that nut. We drew the living quarters for some of the hired help."

He patted the young cop's shoulder. "Don't worry, baby—there's plenty for everybody. Were we ever like this, Hodges?"

"Never."

Suddenly, a chopper banked down off the hills and looped above the parking lot. Bailey's radio crackled to life: "Eleven George, you ready?"

The deputy sergeant reached through the window for his microphone, which he'd laid on the dashboard. "Eleven George. Yes, sir, Big Bird. Let's do it to it."

"Attention all units . . . attention all units: Operation Port Wine is commenced. Repeat: Operation Port Wine is under way. . . ."

The idea, of course, was to hit all the targets at the same time, because the organizers of this cocaine ring probably had alert procedures on a par with the Strategic Air Command.

This much Danny figured out on his own. He had to, because Bailey and Uncle Bob were up front, ignoring him as they jawed about some joint raid they'd both taken part in during the Peloponnesian War or some shit.

"Excuse me, dudes," he interrupted through the waffle mesh of the prisoner screen, frowning at the two balding heads. "Mind telling me what I'm getting into?"

"In time, Pac-Man—don't want you to worry." And with that, Bailey turned back to Hodges, keeping only an occasional eye on the string of blinking amber lights ahead—the long caravan of police and sheriff's vehicles streaming down the hill and beginning to peel off at intersections along the way, headed for targets all over the harbor area. "Damn . . . damn . . . name's on the tip of my tongue. He retired just a few years back because his wrist wore out on him

. . . worked Firestone all them years with my cousin James—"

"Neuro!"

"Yeah, Dr. Neuro!" Bailey cried, convulsed. "We called him Dr. Neuro 'cause he opened so many fucking heads!"

"Remember that certificate the underhog gave him?"

"Yeah . . . yeah . . . American Diplomate of Baton!" Bailey had to wipe his eyes. "Shit, I miss those days . . . yes, indeed I do."

"You bet," Hodges said warmly. "We'll never see guys like that again . . . guys who joined because it was a *calling* to be a cop, like being a priest or something."

Unseen by the two veterans, Danny crossed his eyes.

And then it got quiet inside the car.

"All right," Bailey said, his voice serious, almost strident again, "we drew a little house two blocks off the waterfront. Couple heavies who work their enforcement detail. These boys are good for packing heat. But, Jesus, they could hunt Bigfoot with a switch if they had a mind to. Sons of Samoa."

"Oh, shit," Hodges whispered, then tried to laugh it off.

Bailey's eyes flickered to the rearview mirror.

Danny turned: a one-man sheriff's car was close behind. "That's our backup?"

"The one and only—everybody's going to be busy today. Bob, how about sealing the back door with a gauge?"

"You got it."

"Pac-Man, there's a solitary window on the west side. You mind making sure nobody crawls out it?"

"You want me to effect an entry?"

"Negative." In the mirror, Bailey's eyes turned stern.

And Hodge's head spun around. "You hear the man, McGavin?"

He nodded glumly.

"Other deputy and I will take them down," Bailey went on. "Clear enough?"

"Right," Hodges said.

"Yeah," McGavin said.

"Good—because we is *there.*" Bailey seized a shotgun he'd laid under the seat, leaving Hodges the one in the rack, and led the way up the sidewalk, jacking a round into the chamber as he ran.

The other deputy fell in behind Danny, moving crouched like everyone else. "How do," he greeted them under his breath, sucking one last hit off his cigarette before spinning it away.

Needlessly, Hodges motioned for Danny to follow him down the windowless side of the house, a white clapboard job that had faded through the decades to the dingy gray of bread mold.

Hodges knelt beside the crumbling cement porch, directing his shotgun squarely on the middle of the back door. Danny passed him at a sprint, coming to the west window in ten strides, holding his revolver muzzle skyward, listening over the hammering of his pulse for Bailey and the other deputy to maybe play by the rules and announce that they were executing a search warrant.

After three seconds came the sounds of a doorjamb splintering apart, closely followed by some unintelligible words screamed by Bailey as he charged into the dwelling.

Close enough for government work, Danny decided.

Showing only an inch of his face, he peered inside

the open window and realized that it was to the bathroom.

"Freeze, motherfucks!" Bailey bawled in the living room.

Yet, despite this warning, footfalls were thundering in rapid approach down the hallway, and it took only a split second for Danny to put two and two together: one of the assholes was headed for the toilet to flush the goods.

Fumbling for his pocket knife, Danny slit the rusted screen, boosted himself up off the gas meter, and wriggled through the window, arriving in the bathroom at the same time as the most massive human being he'd ever seen—topped by a pitted, monolithic face that looked like it belonged propped up on Easter Island.

"You there," the Samoan said like it was grace or something. He gaped at Danny and his pistol for all of two seconds, then calmly started dumping the powdery contents of a large plastic bag into the toilet bowl.

"Touch that handle and you're a dead man!" Danny thumb-cocked his hammer for single-action fire—and immediately wished he hadn't. It was a rookie thing to do. Either you shot somebody or you didn't. You didn't play fucking games.

Jesus, it came to him with a chill, *I'm going to blow somebody away . . . I'm honestly going to kill another human being.*

But just as the idiot's hand moved toward the chrome handle on the tank, Bailey appeared from behind and coldcocked him with the butt of his gauge.

The Samoan's eyes started fluttering, then ballooned up into his head until only the junkie-jaundiced whites were showing.

He collapsed squarely on Danny—it felt like being hit by a landslide.

"Help me!" he groaned, honestly afraid that he might suffocate under this mountain of flab, "Fucking help me, man!"

But the deputy sergeant was howling with laughter. "Uncle Bob, come on down!"

"What you have?"

"A Samoan Crip and an overage homeboy cuffed in the living room—and in the lavatory I caught me an elephant fucking a flea!"

"Did that little bastard make an entry?" Hodges shouted.

"It's cool." Bailey chuckled, picking up the half-full bag of coke. "Your boy Pac-Man did good . . . real good."

Under ordinary circumstances, the Chicano who called himself Oso would have seemed a giant of a man, but compared to his silent Samoan compatriots he looked like small change.

Yet Hodges knew that of the three he would be the first to talk.

Bailey must have sensed the same underlying lack of fortitude in the man, for he sent the Samoans—one with thirty-eight sutures in his scalp—off to the holding tank inside the Carson sheriff's station and concentrated on Oso, who waited uncomfortably in the interrogation room.

For starters, Bailey just stared and stared until Oso looked away and scratched his pudgy cheek.

Hodges smiled at Bailey: piece of cake.

The prisoner regarded McGavin's cigarette longingly—but that would come later, and only if he traded something of value.

"*Oso* means 'bear' in Spanish, don't it?" Bailey asked.

"I guess so."

"Well, ain't this a fucking bear, eh, Oso?"

"Yeah." He laughed unhappily.

"You know what we want from you?"

Oso shook his head no.

"Five names."

The man considered this for a moment, then scratched his face again, harder now, leaving red streaks that only faded after a few minutes.

As if in total disgust, Bailey reeled away from the seated prisoner. "You ain't shit. We can fuck you. Ex-con with a gun. You played that rap under the new laws the folks of this state voted in, man?"

"No"—a peep.

"It's a whole new sentencing trip, baby. Believe me. One big bummer. Or do you want to walk?"

"D.A. deal?"

"Naw, maybe I can do better than that. You know I got no control over what the D.A. does. I'm talking a you-and-me deal."

"Is that . . . you know . . . *proper*, man?" A regular civil libertarian.

Bailey winked aside at Hodges before saying, "Sure —from where I stood maybe *both* guns was in arm's reach of that Samoan sack of lard."

Oso glanced up hopefully.

"Five names."

His hopeful look faded. "I don't know nobody."

"And then again, Oso, maybe that fucking forty-five was right under your nose. And didn't your *compadre* palm that sack of snow off on you to throw down the can?"

"I . . . I didn't resist arrest, man."

"Neither did Charlie Manson—and he's doing life, Oso."

The man sighed miserably. "What if I like . . . talk?"

"And it's righteous? You walk. From right here . . . as soon as it checks out." Bailey inhaled, then exhaled expansively. "You notice what a gorgeous day it was out there? No fucking smog? Fucking little birds twittering their little asses off? My, oh, my . . . what a beautiful day."

McGavin started humming the tune, but then Bailey cut him short with a glare. "What's it going to be, Oso?"

"Fuck it, man," he relented, his shoulders seeming to cave in as he gave up the burden of loyalty. "You Carson sheriffs? You got Chango, Mosca, and Train."

"That's good . . . real good. I know those assholes as well as my own. Now, who takes it up the city—for the sake of my friends here?"

When Oso hesitated, Bailey shouted in that Marine Corps style of his, making the man flinch like a raw boot: "Let's go! Let's go! Who takes the coke outta the hose? Who is Smokey the Bear?"

"Cat named Winky."

"I know him," Hodges said. "It's possible . . . old Winky's a possible."

"No, man," Oso said hastily. "It's righteous."

Bailey leaned on the table with his knuckles, his grim black face inches from the prisoner's. "Go on . . . five's the magic number."

"And . . . and Hightop."

McGavin came up out of his chair. *"Hightop?"*

"Am I like lying to you? I don't give a fuck about them dudes."

Silence.

Bailey looked to Hodges, who nodded. The deputy sheriff took the prisoner from the room: "Come on . . . you been a good bear, Oso . . . a regular honey bear. You go hibernate a little or shit in the woods or whatever it is you bears do . . ."

As soon as the door clicked shut, McGavin seethed, "Hightop!"

"Yeah, Hightop."

"And I *had* the motherfucker!"

"Had what? We didn't have squat on him. A piece of rock—"

"The Rock of Gibraltar!"

"Big deal . . . the first fair-sized piece you've seen. How many you seen? You keep count for court testimony, right?"

McGavin just worked his jaw muscles.

"And did we know Hightop was tied in here?"

Suddenly, McGavin laughed sarcastically. "What? Hey, boys and girls, did Uncle Bob make a fuckie-uppie here?"

"Get off it."

"No way—not this time. I wanna go back and bust him!"

"What are you gonna do? Pull a fire extinguisher out of his ass?"

"I'll plant one there if I have to. Then *you* can pull it out, okay? It'll give you something to do instead of dicking around Southeast, shucking and jiving with the natives!"

Hodges inclined his head toward the door, meaning Bailey. "Keep your voice down, for crapsake."

CHAPTER 8

*F*REEZE!"

It had come out of nowhere, an invasion in the
early evening dark against Crip de Ville's little gig.
Killer Bee sprang off the chain-link fence, thinking to
break—when he saw The Man with the shiny blue
roscoe, aiming it with both hands like the cops do on
TV, shifting it from Crip to Crip so everybody had a
peek up the muzzle with the help of the school-yard
light. The hole in that gun looked big.

"Drop it! Put up your hands!"

Killer Bee was more scared for Spooky than for
himself. Spooky was carrying the rock, and sure as
shit The Man was going to conclude this put-up-your-
hands jive with a pat-down. That rock was near the
size of a golf ball, and Spooky wasn't wearing his
bulky colors tonight on account of later they all

planned to walk the boulevard and he wanted the ladies to see how buffed up he was in his T-shirt.

Another cop walked out of the dark and into the faint throw of the yard light—but over on the side, so nobody could book that way either. After a couple seconds, the features seemed to fill in his face, and Killer Bee saw that it was Hodges. He didn't have his roscoe out of the holster, but was resting his right hand on top of the grips, like he was thinking of getting down. And he looked like he had nothing to say, which was weird: Hodges always had something to say.

Then Spooky lost his cool and popped the rock inside his mouth.

Which wasn't cool at all.

The young cop saw him do it and jammed Spooky right away: "Spit it out!"

Now Hodges whipped out his roscoe—to keep all the cuz from moving in when this smack-ass younger cop put away his own heat and wrapped his hands around Spooky's throat and started shaking Spooky like he was a dog or something.

McGavin—Killer Bee recalled The Man's name now, with hatred.

"Spit it out!" McGavin screamed, really losing it now. "Spit out the rock, asshole! Spit it out! Out!"

"Fuck, man . . ." Killer Bee felt sick for Spooky because he could see him trying to chew down the rock while McGavin was trying to strangle him and like snap his head off his neck. Killer Bee was kind of glad he wasn't packing tonight. If he had been, he would have busted a cap on this McGavin; he would have lit up Hodges, too, although he had nothing special against Hodges—but Hodges was standing there not doing shit, either.

His lips tossing spit and his eyes too big and dark for his pale face, McGavin reeled and shouted at all the cuz: "Your friend here's gonna die! You know that?"

Then he slugged Spooky in the pit of the guts.

And again, harder, lifting him right off the pavement.

Still, Spooky wouldn't give up the rock, and Killer Bee felt like standing tall.

"Spit it out, motherfucker! Now! Now!"

McGavin was winding up his fist again when Hodges said, quiet-like, "That's enough."

McGavin stopped swinging, but then laughed crazy-like and spun Spooky around. The Man flattened out his hand so it was on the same line as his forearm and gave Spooky a blow between the shoulderblades before letting go of him.

Choking, getting ready to puke now, Spooky staggered over to the curb, where he braced his arms on his knees and gave up the rock, his Burger King supper—everything.

Killer straightened up because McGavin was stomping his way and he figured he was next. He hoped he would do as good as Spooky had done.

"Shit," McGavin said, like something was funny—but not really. He was fighting to get his breath back, too, and his face was all red along the bones. "You fucking gang-bangers are a trip." He lifted his chin toward Spooky, who was still retching, bad. "When he starts turning blue and dying and shit . . . you can take him down to the hospital . . . if any of you gives a shit."

Then McGavin and Hodges backed out of the lights, vanishing as quick as they'd come.

Joan Hodges awakened early, perhaps because she'd sensed that the other side of the bed was empty, something she always associated with danger, the possibility of sudden and crushing loss in the form of a deputy chief and the department chaplain showing up at the front door.

But he was home, not on the streets—sitting out in the pink dimness of the living room, watching the sun come up through the bay window.

He hadn't made himself any coffee, probably not wanting the percolator to disturb her or the baby.

When he turned his face toward her, she saw that it was haggard, although his eyes were tender and moist.

"You get any sleep?" she asked.

He shook his head no, then said after a few moments, "What the hell was I really like back then?"

She looked away.

"How bad was it for you, baby?"

Friends don't lie to each other. Lovers can get away with it. But in these past few years, they'd become as much friends as lovers, so she let her silence, her sad hint of a smile answer for her.

"Sweet Jesus," he sighed. He started to ask her forgiveness, as he had before when oppressed by this mood, but his voice broke and he couldn't go on.

She went to him, curled up in his lap, and he enveloped her in his warm grasp.

Retirement wouldn't come soon enough.

All at once, she was scared to death of the next seven and a half months.

After they crossed the Fourth Street bridge and began cruising the back streets of the sprawling barrio, McGavin got out of the battered Pontiac and walked in front along the sidewalks—like a skirmisher advancing in front of a Sherman tank, Hodges realized with a tic of a frown.

He was reaching for McGavin's pack of Marlboros on the dash when remembrance seized his hand, and he was left wondering if he was capable of lighting one up unconsciously after all these years.

"Christ," he muttered, checking his watch. Only a little after ten. Hours and hours to go. A lifetime and several reincarnations to go until quitting time.

Suddenly, McGavin slid his baton out of his Sam Browne ring and started sprinting up a narrow side lane.

"Shit!" Hodges flattened the accelerator against the firewall and barreled around the corner, overtaking McGavin, who was making for a peewee who'd been busy until that moment spraying some new *placa* on a green metal dumpster.

Immediately, the kid realized that he'd been had, what with cops coming both by car and on foot. He didn't try to run, although the spray can slipped out of his hand and clattered against the pavement.

Hodges was first to reach him. "Hands up. Hold it." He patted down the peewee's Pendleton and the pockets of his khakis, but found no weapons.

McGavin huffed up, but let Hodges so ahead with his rap.

"What you doing here, Picasso?" Hodges scanned the graffiti. The peewee was obviously connected to White Fence and was defacing declarations of the rival homeboys. "Crossing out the names of your friends? They're not gonna like that, are they?"

The peewee said nothing; he was too preoccupied trying not to look scared.

"What's your name?" Hodges waited, smiling. "Come on, you can tell your goddamn street name, can't you?"

"Gato, man."

"Gato . . . the cat. You're not a pussy, are you?"

The eyes flashed in the small brown face, but Gato held his tongue.

"I didn't think so," Hodges went on. "Because we both know what this means . . ." He pointed to the

C/S marking White Fence's enemies had added to their *placa: Con Safos,* loosely meaning "anything you do to this writing, twice to you." "We both know that if it'd been them instead of us to find you doing this, your fucking ass would be dead meat right now. You at war with these guys now or something?"

Gato gave a meaningless shrug.

Hodges reached for a field interrogation card, but found his shirt pocket empty. He turned to McGavin, who'd retrieved the can of spray paint and was absently rattling it in his hand. "You got any cards?"

"I don't fuck with them."

"You don't *what?*"

McGavin tapped his temple with a finger. "I keep it all up here."

"Ever think of sharing with the rest of the unit so we might keep updating the intelligence on this shit?"

"Nope."

Shaking his head, Hodges started for the Pontiac. "Keep an eye on the peewee."

"You got it."

While rummaging around in the glove compartment and under the seat for a card, Hodges could hear McGavin talking to the kid.

"You know, this is a misdemeanor . . . a fucking misdemeanor, homes." Then, without warning, some bite came into McGavin's voice. "Destroying fucking property! Does destroying fucking property mean anything to you?"

Hodges thought about telling him to take it easy, but then decided against it—five-thirty, he reminded himself. Besides, McGavin had lowered his voice again.

"I can take you in for this, homes. But maybe we can work this out. Yeah . . . ever heard of Earl Scheib Auto Painting, amigo?"

Then a distinctive hissing sound backed Hodges out of the Pontiac and spun him around. "Hey!"

McGavin was spraying Gato's immobile face. "Enough!"

McGavin started in on the kid's hair, then his Pendleton and khakis.

"That is *enough!*" Livid, Hodges batted the can out of McGavin's grasp. He could see that McGavin was thinking of throwing a punch. "Go right ahead, homes. Let's get it on. Let's settle this thing right here and now. Because—check it out, baby—I can't hack this shit anymore!"

But McGavin slowly grinned—with menace, although he was no longer flexing his right arm.

Hodges turned to Gato, who'd begun sneezing madly from the paint up his nostrils. "Get out . . . now."

The peewee ran halfway down the lane, then wheeled to hoist a finger: "Fuck you, Pac-Man!"

Then he was gone.

"You hear that?" Hodges asked, struggling to keep his voice under control.

"Yeah . . . maybe I shoulda put masking tape over his eyes."

"They're beginning to single you out."

McGavin gave the can a vicious kick. "So fucking what?"

"They've even got your moniker down pat."

"Yeah, Pac-Man gobbles up the assholes—I *want* that news out on the street. What are you getting at, Uncle Bob?"

"Just this—you've come down to their level. And they're the first to know it."

Back at the station, Hodges fell into a desk chair and immediately closed his eyes on McGavin's impertinent face.

"I'm not going to eat lunch out of a fucking vending machine again, Uncle Bob."

Cracking an eyelid, Hodges unclipped the Pontiac keys off his Sam Browne and tossed them to McGavin. "See you in an hour."

When McGavin was gone, Hodges groaned, rose to his feet, and poured himself a cup of a muddy-looking coffee left over from the morning briefing. It went down like fire, and he wound up pouring most of it down the water fountain.

A blue shadow bleared past his absorption and tossed off a hello, but Hodges didn't answer.

He was staring at the lieutenant's closed door. In nineteen years, Robert Hodges had never dropped the dime on a brother officer. He'd never even remotely felt the need—until now. And he had no doubt that it would feel shitty and low to snitch on McGavin. All the older guys in the unit would appreciate why Hodges had been compelled to talk, but they would treat him differently from then on, treat him like somebody who'd beefed a brother officer.

Snitching put an entire new cast on a man's network of trust. And cops subsisted on mutual trust. It was all most had left, what with three or four divorces behind them and their own kids insolent strangers.

"Shit." Hodges turned his back on Lieutenant Reed's door and headed for the vending machines down the corridor.

Danny rounded the corner inside the projects at fifty, taking the older Crip and his three peewee bagmen by surprise. The little kids scattered and ran, one of them shouting, "Pac-Man"—which gave him a grim sort of satisfaction.

He let them go, scampering into the maze of run-down complexes.

The Crip dealer, satisfied that his goods were now

being ferried out of law enforcement's reach by his servile peewees, pasted on a smile for the squeal of brakes that announced the Pontiac's arrival.

The dealer's smile dimmed when he saw that it was Pac-Man, even though The Man had come alone—perhaps *because* he'd come alone.

Grinning widely, Danny got out and ambled up to the dealer, who was kicking back on his apartment porch. "Where your itty friends going, Dealer Man?"

"What friends, dude?"

"Using ten-year-olds to carry your dope? Haven't you heard about the child labor laws?"

The dealer chuckled, but was cut short when Danny seized the front of his black T-shirt and hauled him to his feet.

"Say, man—"

"Shut the fuck up or I will put your dick in the dirt right now. Do you understand me?"

The Crip fell silent, his eyes wild with confusion and even fright—he had no homeboys at hand to impress, not even some peewees standing around on the edges of this jack-up.

Danny frisked him hard, coming up with a beeper and squashing the Crip's nose with it. "What the hell's this? You a surgeon on twenty-four-hour call, man?"

"That hurt, dude!"

"You Dr. Feelgood, huh? Got a stethoscope down in your scuzzy drawers? Or did your mama use the rubber cord to tie herself off again?" Danny backed off a pace, pointed to the porch. "Empty your pockets there, right down to the lint balls."

The Crip balked for an instant, then sized up the glint in McGavin's eyes and began dumping wads of cash onto the cement.

"Check it ouuuut," Danny cooed. "Where'd you get all this probable cause, homes?"

"My auntie give it to me."

Danny snorted.

"Hey, I'm just kicking back here," he nearly whined. "What the Pac-Man on *me* for?"

Then the beeper went off. Danny smiled down at the tiny flashing red light. "You in?"

The Crip gazed off indifferently.

"Who you call when this beeps?"

He shrugged.

"Who's the nice man who buzzes you up, homes? Give me a name."

"I don't know this shit, man."

"Who's your connection? Hightop?"

The Crip's eyes shot back to Danny's—with a vengeance.

"Don't you red-eye me, homes!"

"I ain't eye-fucking nobody, man."

Danny's baton flashed out of its ring, its rounded end catching the Crip in the solar plexus, doubling him over. The Crip was still bent down when Danny clenched a handful of his lustrous hair and dragged him toward the Pontiac.

Hodges was almost caught up with FLYING CRASH's activity logs when Nakamura sat down on a corner of the desk. "Your li'l brother sure don't let no moss gather."

"What do you mean?" Hodges asked drowsily. His sleepless night was catching up with him.

"He's in booking."

Hodges tilted his wrist to read his watch. "He should be on his way back from lunch."

"*That* he is," Nakamura said somewhat mysteriously, which Hodges didn't care for.

Pitching his stale half-eaten tuna fish sandwich in the trash can, Hodges strode down the corridor toward the booking counter, nodding at Captain

Melindez and Lieutenant Reed, both returning rather glumly from a staff luncheon up at the academy.

"Bobby," Reed said, unsuccessfully trying to snatch him by the short sleeve as he swept past. "I want to chew a bone with you when—"

"In a sec, Lieut." Hodges kept hurtling toward booking, his face feverish with anger, although he kept pressing his lips together as if trying to hold something corrosive inside.

McGavin had his back to him, jiving with the prisoner on the other side of the screen: "Okay, Dr. Kildare, where were you born?"

Hodges laid a hand on his shoulder and spun him around. "One question," he said, his voice low and tremulous.

"Uncle Bob . . . have a nice lunch?"

"Okay, okay." Hodges visibly attempted to calm himself. "Whatever it was, it went down in the restaurant where you were eating, right?"

"No," McGavin said blandly. "It went down in the projects off Central."

Hodges seized him by the shoulder straps and manhandled him through the interrogation room, slamming the door shut with his shoe.

Sneering, McGavin broke free of his clutch, losing a blue strap, which dangled from Hodges's shaking fist. "Easy now, Pops . . ."

"Think you can handle me? Huh? You think I'm over the hill? You wanna a piece of me? Huh?" He taunted McGavin with a light slap across the jaw, but the young cop only smirked. "You think you invented this hard-ass shit? Huh? You think I'm not crazy, baby? Well, think again . . .Shit, they even tried to certify me once! When I was young and dumb and full of come as you, *loco!* So try me! Try me, you nasty little fuck!"

McGavin only stared at him.

Hodges pivoted and drove his fist into the wall, his breath surging out of him as he did it once again. Then he leaned into a corner of the tiny room.

After several moments in which the only sound was Hodges trying to recover his breath, McGavin asked quietly, "What are you talking about?"

Hodges laughed, but it was more like a sob than a laugh. "That's what I thought. Get outta here."

"Hey, Hodges . . . Uncle Bob . . . I don't have any problems with you as long as—"

"Oh, no? You got problems with the whole fucking world, kid. And I'm in it."

McGavin's eyes hardened for the first time. "Yeah, well, why don't you just chill out a bit—decide which side you're on?"

"I would if I could . . . believe me." Hodges tried to smile, but it came to his lips as a scowl. "You know, you're just like them. Nothing but a gangster, Pac-Man." Hodges dragged himself to the door, but then turned again, his expression incredulous: "You rock-and-rolled without your partner . . . your *backup,* for chrissake."

"I figure that was my call."

"No!" Instantly, Hodges went hot again; he kept stabbing his forefinger only inches from McGavin's face. "How many of us do you think there are? Jesus, man, you ever bother to count the blue uniforms around this dump? And we all try to survive, help each other survive, by following certain rules. We don't do it for the fucking brass. We do it for *ourselves*. And now you showed the bangers that the chain is—!"

"The *what?*"

"This chain . . . this brotherhood!"

"Oh, man, brotherhood *now.*"

"You showed them this chain's made of individual links! Weak links like you!"

"This is a bit over my head, Hodges."

"Listen to me, dammit! You just delivered a message to the assholes out there that the cops in this unit fuck up from time to time—royally! You just begged them to hit us! I just hope it's you who pays the price for sending the message—"

Insistent knocking on the door made Hodges shut up.

Lieutenant Reed stuck his head inside. "Everything code four in here, boys?"

"Yeah, Lieut," Hodges said, his voice raspy from all the shouting. "We're just squaring away a procedural thing between us."

Then Hodges sidestepped out without another word.

It was too warm inside the chicken shack, and the flies buzzing and the smell of dead poultry were driving her mad. It was so bad this afternoon that Louisa actually looked forward to the distraction of customers, even rude ones.

Her eyes kept darting to the fly-specked clock above the Pepsi sign, wondering what she would say to Danny when six rolled around. She was almost tempted to tell her boss that she was feeling sick so she could leave early and be safely home when Danny arrived at the chicken shack.

Some illegals came up to the window and ordered shyly in thick Mexican Spanish; she threw in extra portions without the boss seeing—the Indians looked hungry. And then some homeboys dropped by for Cokes to impress her with their posturing. Later, a *gavacho* truck driver pulled in, uncertainly—probably lost or he wouldn't have stopped in this part of town.

At last the hour hand was pushing six.

She saw his Mustang slowing to make the left turn

into the parking lot. She expected him to look across the traffic and wave, as he usually did. But then, still gazing straight ahead, Danny switched off his signal and continued down the boulevard, speeding up as he got farther and farther away from the chicken shack.

Louisa's eyes burned with tears, but she tried to tell herself that she was relieved.

Joey Norton slid into the seat across from Danny's at the Pac-Man table. "Hey, long time no see, dickless. What can I get for you?"

"Some space."

Joey smiled as if he thought Danny was joking, but then saw that McGavin wasn't. He rose. "Understood, guy . . .Whenever you feel like talking."

"Thanks."

Looking a little hurt, Joey drifted over to some rowdies from Wilshire Vice who looked like they'd spent the last week here in a pup tent.

The cocktail waitress brought Danny's order: a triple bourbon, no ice. Tonight he would dispense with the beer back.

He didn't check out her terrific fanny and even more terrific black-netted legs as she withdrew, as he normally did. Instead, he fed more quarters down the slot and hunkered over the screen, its light making his face look waxen.

He smacked the start button with the heel of his hand.

Ms. Pac-Man began zigzagging through the maze aimlessly as Danny stared right through the screen into some middle distance only he could appreciate.

The convolutions of the maze brought to mind the narrow dogleg streets and the cul-de-sacs of the projects, any of the countless housing projects in the city. And Ms. Pac-Man became a battered yellow Pontiac weaving from dead end to dead end.

From the heart of the maze popped the monsters, blue and red . . . wearing colors of blue and red . . . spreading out across the screen like a blue and red blight.

Finally, at Lieutenant Reed's personal insistence, he'd sat down and scanned yesterday's gang-related activity log: a shooting between rival war wagons on the Santa Monica Freeway in which an innocent motorist was wounded; a dope double-cross and triple murder in East L.A. involving two cadres of homeboys under the conflicting protection of the Mexican Mafia and Nuestra Familia, the prison gangs to which the most vicious and dedicated homeboys aspired; the knifing of a black kid, an honors student, by a white fascist gang in a disco parking lot—the kid was expected to die; a smash-and-grab at a jewelry store with suspected Filipino gang involvement; an elderly woman driver rammed while waiting for a red light on Manchester Avenue, then mugged and beaten when she crawled out of her vehicle to inspect the damage —possible Crip involvement; six drive-in shootings with two injuries resulting, one serious, one critical . . .

The monsters roamed the screen at will.

Danny sat transfixed, his hands frozen on the controls, Ms. Pac-Man immobile.

And the bastards laugh, he thought, taking a swig of bourbon, then another. *They sit in the fucking holding tanks and laugh because they know that there is no punishment that fits what they do day in and day out. . . .*

All at once his hands flew into action, and Ms. Pac-Man went on the offensive, began gobbling up the monsters. But they were no sooner consumed than fresh and vigorous ones sprang from the heart of the maze:

Play Boys, Budlong Gangster Brims, Eastside

COLORS

Crips, Water Gate Crips, Lap Boys, Colonial Watts, Exposition Park Boys, Sotels, Temple Street Gang, Barrio Twenty-fourth Street, Trey-five Block, Bounty Hunters, Rolling Sixty Crips, White Fence, Marvin Gangsters, West Side Brims . . .

Danny pounded the side of the machine.

Then he emptied his glass and held it up for a refill.

CHAPTER 9

IT WAS NOTHING LIKE *GRIFA* BY ITSELF, THIS SMOLDERING sherm—and Felipe spent most of the night more pissed than he'd ever felt before, stronger than he'd ever been before, so strong it scared him a little.

Bird was mellower, but he was older, too. He just grinned whenever he began to feel hyper and would shake his head and chuckle, *"Ese vato!"* Hey, dude.

Now and again, Felipe wanted to hit his stupid face, but was afraid that the stupid *cholo* would hit him back, squash his own face numb like a rotten melon.

Bird had promised he would look after him. And Felipe had believed him.

He'd believed Bird.

But then the sun came up like this nervous yellow fire all over the sky, and two *marranos* walked out of

its painful yellowness all dark blue and tall, tapping
their sticks against the sides of their legs and asking
what was going on.

Bird just said, *"Ese vato!"*

And the cops laughed.

Acknowledging the dispatcher's return-to-station
call, Hodges took the next exit off the Golden State
Freeway, crept across the congested overpass, and
then built speed on the southbound on-ramp. He
glanced sideways and smirked.

McGavin slumped in the shotgun seat, the pale
bloat of his face as much an indication as his silence
that he was devastated by a hangover.

Good, Hodges decided—yesterday's confrontation
had been as upsetting to McGavin as it had been to
him. He started weaving in and out of the moderate
traffic.

Dumping a partner required a certain delicacy. Oh,
it was nothing as grisly as a divorce, but it did require
the same careful maneuvering as, say, evicting a shack
job. One didn't want to ignite an unholy row in which
one's most prized possessions might wind up smashed
against the walls.

One did not simply see the lieutenant and demand
a new partner. Why not? Well, the lieutenant would
then lean back in his swivel chair, prop his hands
behind his head, and ask what was wrong with one's
current partner. Answering that question was the
same as dropping the dime on one's current partner—
and Hodges had already decided that he didn't have
that kind of ruthlessness in him. He might as well ask
McGavin to wear a sign that declared: "Pariah—Kick
Me."

No, groundwork had to be laid in such a subtle
manner that it would be self-evident to the lieutenant

that this conglomerate of oil and water personality traits would never meld—and that it was time, figuratively, to split the blue sheets.

Fortunately, the wheels were already in motion toward this end.

While it wasn't kosher for Hodges to bring McGavin's shortcomings and boners to the attention of the lieutenant, it was quite all right for someone else, a party to the dispute, to bring them to administrative light.

Nakamura had apparently done just that. And Hodges could have kissed him for it.

An hour before the end of yesterday's watch, Reed had barreled out of his office and dumped the activity log on the desk at which McGavin had been brooding. "Read it," the lieutenant had grunted, turning on his heel and slamming the door behind him.

This, in the era of the Peace Officer Bill of Rights, amounted to a verbal warning. A bona fide verbal warning, in which Reed would haul in McGavin by the ear and tell him precisely how he'd fucked up royally, would have to be documented, which meant that the verbal warning then became a written warning. *Documentation* is just a fancy word for putting all the shit down on paper, and everything written about a cop winds up in his personnel jacket. For anything even remotely smacking of disciplinary action, McGavin could request a hearing and bring along legal counsel to sit in his corner and shout down the brass as needed.

Still, all in all, Reed's action added up to an ass-chewing.

Groaning softly, McGavin now donned his sunglasses, even though his eyes had been closed for the last half-hour.

"Want some air?" Hodges asked.

"I'm fine."

"You sure? I'll put it on vent."

"I said I'm fine."

With the wheels in motion, there remained one thing for Hodges to do: buffer any hard feelings arising from the dissolution. Telling a woman that you no longer wanted her for your wife was the same as saying that you didn't think she was much of a woman—at least, that's how she'd take it, deep down. Why should it be any different between two cops? So, when the right moment came, Hodges would have to convince McGavin that it was just a personality thing and McGavin was still one helluva cop and one of these days he was going to make some lucky blue-suiter a wonderful partner.

Hodges sighed as he entered the station parking lot. Having settled these things in his mind, he was feeling much, much better.

"We're there, homes," he said to the dozing McGavin.

Awaiting them were Ron Delauney, impeccable this morning in white seersucker, and Frog. Both had visitor badges clipped to their shirts.

Frog had the whore-in-church look all gang-bangers assumed in police facilities. "Hey, no shit, man," he said with a tense grin, 'You did it . . . you came in."

"Yeah, yeah, I'm a regular fucking prince." Hodges felt McGavin brush past him on his hurried way to the men's room. He turned back to Delauney: "What's up?"

"Well, Leo here called me because—" "Felipe's fucked up on PCP," Frog butted in. "The kid got whacked bad, man."

"So?"

"But he's straight, Hodges! He goes to school, you

know. And I kick his ass when he don't show. But now they got him down in the gang file, man—and the kid ain't banging. He's not in the gang!"

Hodges glanced to Delauney, who confirmed this with a slight nod.

"The barrio don't fucking need him," Frog went on, twisting his navy blue watch cap in his hands. "Hodges, I'm *telling* you this. Get him off the computer, man."

"I don't know, Frog." He flopped into a chair. "I just don't know."

"I'm begging you, man to man."

Hodges let no softness leak into his eyes. "Felipe might have to go to Juvie hall anyway. Might even do him some good. Scare him a little."

"He's scared, man. He's scared what *I'm* gonna do. Hodges, man . . ."

He yawned. "What?"

"Just get my brother off the file. The file will fuck up his life."

"And you don't want his life fucked up?"

"On my mother's grave, man. My father's, too." He crossed himself for good measure.

Hodges now believed that Frog had squirmed enough. "I'll talk to the kid. See what I can do."

"What did I tell you?" Delauney said. "Hodges is cool, ain't he, though?"

"No, Hodges ain't cool," Hodges said sternly, red-eyeing Frog.

"Okay, okay . . . I know the routine. I *owe* you one. That's what makes this country great. You take VISA, man?"

By three that afternoon, Danny's hangover had faded enough for him to imagine the taste of bourbon without puking again. He coasted by, pretending to work on an incident report until quitting time, then made for his Mustang, realizing that a beer might go down all right.

Yet as soon as he sat down behind the wheel, he knew what he was going to do. And it didn't involve beer.

It involved chicken.

She was closing the back door bars on the grimy little shack when he walked up behind her, startling her.

"I'm sorry." He tried to embrace her, but she pushed him away. "Hey, I said I'm sorry."

He went on smiling, but sensed already that this was more serious than having stood her up last night. "What's wrong with you?"

"Nothing. I'm fine." She didn't sound fine, and he felt his temper flare as he caught the fire in her eyes.

"Then what the hell do you want from me?"

"Nothing. Just go away!"

"This is stupid." He noticed the hordes of flies swarming around the dumpster. "It stinks back here."

"Oh, thank you . . . I didn't know that."

"Hey, let's start this from the beginning. You're Louisa. I'm Danny. Now, Louisa, tell Danny what he did wrong."

"They hate you, McGavin," she said, taking a step back from him.

"It's McGavin now, huh? Why don't you just say *marrano* and then spit on me!" He took out his black basket-weave wallet and flipped it open to his badge. "See this? I wear it, so what do you want? And this . . ." He swept back his windbreaker, revealing the revolver snugged tightly against his flank in a rawhide off-duty holster. "I wear this, too, so what's the big deal?"

"The other day, you caught this boy. Sprayed paint all over his head and clothes. He was my cousin."

Danny laughed disbelievingly. "Your what?"

"That's funny?"

"Well, I had no idea you had such a big family."

She spun around to go, but he caught her gently by the arm.

"Please, Louisa—I'm sorry. I wouldn't do anything to hurt you. . . ."

Her eyes moistened, but then quickly cleared again. "I don't know about that."

"Jesus—do you know what your cousin was doing? He was crossing out names on some Sixteenth Street *placa*. You know what that means when somebody does that?" His lips thinned. "Sure you do . . . they start killing people. That's what. So I sprayed him a little. Hey, I'm sorry. Maybe I saved his life that way, but I swear, I didn't—"

"Are you a member of One-Six, McGavin?"

"Christ." He shook his head, exasperated, then snapped: "Are you a *chola?*"

Immediately, he regretted asking her if she was a gang girl, for defiant tears came to her eyes. "I was once . . . some time ago. But that's none of your business. My *life* is none of your business."

"I'm sorry. I didn't mean to say that, Louisa." He tried to cup the side of her face in his hand, but she swatted it away.

She was really crying now.

"I don't care about your reasons. What's done is done. But you're mean, Danny. You're sadistic."

"They threatened you, didn't they? The homeboys are leaning on you because of me, right? That's what this is really all about—"

"No, no one knows I saw you."

His voice was almost a whisper: "Then what?"

"*You* threaten me. At first I saw a goodness in you. I thought you act tough because you aren't sure yet what it is to be a man. But now I know different. You have a mean heart, Danny. Good-bye."

He didn't follow her. Leaning against the dirty stucco wall, he watched her walk away.

CHAPTER 10

IT COULD WIND UP BEING THE LAST HOT SATURDAY OF October, if not the year, and the oceanfront was mobbed.

Adult—if Hodges could call them that—roller skaters were slaloming through the crowd, competing with younger skateboarders for the attention of the season's last batch of enthralled European, Japanese, and North Dakotan tourists, who'd probably never seen so many nuts assembled in one semitropical basket: a guy with a Malcolm X beard and Charlie Manson eyes happily pedalling along in a scooter he'd fashioned from a zillion-amp speaker; break dancers alarming the Japanese, who seemed on the verge of running for medical assistance; and the usual religious zombies chanting in Sanskrit or early Bob

Dylan or whatever. And so far, only a handful of gang-bangers.

Smiling, Hodges turned away from this scene and looked seaward. At that instant a big comber curled over, the wall of water a pretty translucent green, then exploded into suds and spray.

McGavin watched the same wave in grim silence.

His color had returned, but he seemed as down as he'd been yesterday.

Maybe the message was beginning to seep through that thick skull—Hodges hoped so.

He began strolling again, unconsciously twirling his wooden baton between his fingers and across his knuckles as he wended through the crush of human flesh.

McGavin gave him a barren smile, his first all day. "Where'd you learn that?"

"What?"

"That drum majorette shit you're doing there."

"Oh, first six months outta the academy—walked a foot beat downtown."

"What happened? Was the posse short of horses back in those days?"

"Funny, asshole." Hodges suddenly hurled the baton at the sidewalk. Striking on one of the tips, it swiftly bounced back toward him, then appeared to freeze in midair, at which time he simply closed his hand around it and went on twirling as if nothing special had happened.

"Jesus fucking Christ," McGavin had to admit. Then, waiting for the foot traffic to thin out a little, he tried it himself, but his baton went bounding and skipping along the pavement like a Chinese gymnast. "Shit."

A kid recovered it for him: "Thanks."

"Only works with hickory sticks," Hodges said.

Frowning, McGavin slid his stick back into his ring. "Well, I'll take my black polycarbonate. It sure as hell won't break on a hard head."

Hodges was going to say that hickory usually snapped before it really did someone in, but then he realized that another argument was brewing. He let it slide. "First guy to show me," he went on easily, "tossed his baton down and it flew apart into kindling. . . .Glad that didn't just happen to me."

Again McGavin smiled a little. But then, abruptly, he looked his usual pissed-off self again. "What's the purpose of this gig? I haven't seen enough bangers for the brass to turn out the whole unit. Who's out working the hoods today?"

"Oh, Christ, McGavin . . ." With a sweep of his arm, Hodges took in the sunlit skies, the Pacific, the breeze-tossed palmettos. "You'd rather be humping up and down the projects right now?"

"Maybe."

"You oughta have your fucking head examined."

"I'm surprised you haven't tried to arrange that, too."

Hodges's immediate thought was *Who shot his mouth off?* This was delicate business, and somebody could blow it by jumping the gun and mouthing off to McGavin. "What are you saying?" he asked carefully.

"Nothing. Never mind."

"Listen, McGavin . . ." Then Hodges fell silent: across a litter-strewn grassy area and in front of a sidewalk café, four Bloods were being shaken down by a pair of Pacific Division patrolmen, a salt-and-pepper team.

Hodges and McGavin approached within thirty feet of them, providing what was called a "soft back," because the two cops already had a public relations problem. The average civil liberties–conscious citizen thought four blue-suiters at one problem to be a Nuremberg rally—unless the problem happened to be his own.

"What's going on?" a platinum-wigged biddy asked from one of the round, umbrellaed tables, apparently having killed the better part of a carafe of mad dog over brunch. "What's this all about?"

The black cop, covered by his white partner two paces to his back, was methodically patting down the bulky colors of an indignant-looking Blood for weapons.

"My husband happens to be an attorney, Officer!"

"So is my wife, ma'am." The cop went on frisking.

Hodges chuckled, but he saw that McGavin's jaws were tightly locked.

A skinny little accountant type with a gray sweater tied by the arms around his shoulders poked his nose in: "I'd like to know what they were doing, Officer. They were just sitting here, as far as I could see."

"Would you people move back?" the white patrolman said.

But a well-dressed brother with an earring stood his ground when the white folks scampered for safety as quickly as their dignity would allow. "I'm staying."

"Stay," the black cop said, reasonably enough, making sure one Blood's belt buckle wasn't a buckle knife. "Just move back."

McGavin started to bolt forward, but Hodges held him back. "They're doing just fine. And they know we're standing back here if they need us."

"What's wrong with these fucking people?" McGavin hissed, looking as if he'd prefer to see them standing against a bullet-pocked wall with blindfolds on. "What's with them?"

"Nothing you or I can fix." Hodges chuckled again. "This is America and it's in the Constitution—you got to fuck with police . . . I forget which article right now."

The black guy with the earring had raised his voice to full pitch: "Man, you shake the li'l brothers down? This ain't South Africa, bro!"

By this time, the black cop had hit the mother lode and was digging an object out of a Blood's front Levi pocket. "You're right, bro," he said triumphantly, as the switchblade jutted from his fist with a resounding click, "because in Soweto some poor nigger would go to prison for six, seven hundred years if caught carrying one of these. We're just going to keep this errant lad overnight in Juvie—and let him go in the morning."

Laughing loudly, patting the black cop on the arm, Hodges passed directly through the middle of the scene and continued on his way, McGavin trailing behind, red-eyeing the bystanders.

Diaz and Young from FLYING CRASH were strolling toward them, looking bored.

"Hey, Hodges," Young said, brightening as he put on a pair of novelty glasses with a hook nose and bloodshot eyeballs dangling on wire springs. "Check this out."

"Check what out?"

"Come on, man!"

"You change your hair or something, Bill?"

At that moment an old woman tapped Young on the lower back. "Excuse me, Officer—"

He spun around, and she quick-marched away, clutching her purse. "What's with her?" Young asked, folding up his glasses for the next occasion.

"We're supposed to pass the word," Diaz said. "Keep an eye out for half of East L.A.—Eighteenth Street . . . Happy Valley." When McGavin suddenly sidled through the milling throng for a snow cone, Diaz changed the subject: "How's hotshot doing?"

"We'll see . . . we'll see." It was all Hodges felt comfortable saying, even though he knew his gripes would fall on sympathetic ears.

Young smiled at him. "You know how you always say—he reminds me of me way back when? This dude don't remind me of me at all. He don't remind me of any of us."

"Well . . ." Hodges let his voice trail off.

"Say no more," Diaz said. "We understand perfectly."

McGavin sauntered back. When not slurping at his lime snow cone, he looked slightly hunted, as if he suspected that they'd been talking about him. For a second or two, Hodges felt sorry for him: McGavin was freezing himself out of the camaraderie, the only thing that made this job bearable. But then, Hodges just had to picture a peewee with a spray-painted dome to lose those feelings of pity. "Got my Blood House boys right here today for some sun and fun."

"Why, shit—" At that moment Young's elbow accidentally rubbed the squelch button on the radio handset attached to his Sam Browne belt, and he had to turn off the burst of static. "We not only got the Blood House boys, we got their fucking royalty, too."

"Who?" McGavin tossed his half-eaten snow cone in a can. *"Who's here?"*

"Well," Young said a little uneasily, looking to Hodges, "I saw Li'l Big Man, Big Man, and Snakedance."

McGavin's eyes widened at mention of this last name. "Where are these fucks?"

"'Round and about, Dan."

"Where?"

"Down by the volleyball shit, man."

McGavin took off at a trot.

"Hey, hold up!" Hodges barked, he and the other two cops hustling to catch up with McGavin.

Simply amazing, the young Hispanic in the white long-sleeved shirt and blue cords thought to himself.

It was simply amazing, the lengths to which some people would go to get attention, whereas he himself cared nothing for being in the spotlight. On the contrary, he preferred to blend into the background and watch the activity around him—such as a guy with a spooky patch of white in his otherwise chestnut hair—had he been struck by lightning in his youth or something?—who was calmly juggling three twelve-inch chain saws, deftly catching the grumbling, lethal machines, and spinning them back up into the air.

The Hispanic man saw the delight his four-year-old was taking in these antics. He gripped the small, bony shoulders with an almost desperate affection, and then was gratified to feel his wife's hand cover his as he continued to hold the child.

Then the little boy asked if he could have a Coke.

The man glanced around for a snack stand of some sort—and suddenly a small jolt of fear passed through him like a chill.

A take-out place was only a few yards distant on the far side of the walkway, but lingering close by were some gang types with crimson headbands. They were perched like vultures on a picnic table, eyeing those who passed by as if they were dead meat.

The man took a lot of tiresome ribbing at the electronics plant in Thousand Oaks where he worked about being "a *pachuco.*" He was nothing of the kind—never had been. In fact, gang types embarrassed and frightened him.

"Daddy, can I have a Coke?" his son asked again.

His wife looked to the stand and understood his hesitation at once. "You want me to get it, honey?"

This shamed him. "No, that's okay. You want anything, babe?"

"I'm fine."

The Hispanic man started resolutely across the walkway.

Diaz caught McGavin by one arm, and Young snagged him by the other. McGavin whipped a glance to both sides, surprised to find himself in their firm but gentle clutches. "What—"

"Let Uncle Bob handle this, Dan," Young said. "He knows these boys from way back when."

McGavin's face turned cold, but he shrugged as if it meant nothing to him.

Hodges approached Snakedance and his sidekicks, who were grinning at the cops. "Well, well, well . . . what's happening, 'Dance?"

"Just kicking back."

"Gonna do a little surfing today?"

"Yeah," he laughed. "That's it, my man. Gonna hop on one of them motherfucking boards." Snakedance's gaze flickered across McGavin's face, moved on to Young's, then came back to McGavin's, a look of deep hatred following the instant of recognition. "Love to *ride* on them boards, homes."

With Diaz's help, Hodges began patting them down. "You didn't happen to bring roscoe along today, did you?"

"Shit, I *never* bring roscoe along. Old roscoe and his six itty babies, they get you killed, man."

Hodges harrumphed. "Yeah, sure. How'd you get here?"

"We come on our dime speeds."

"Twenty-five miles on bicycles?"

"That's a fact, man. What you fucking with us for, Hodges? We just kicking back."

"Where'd you park your ten-speeds?"

"Back a ways . . .We walk some."

"I certainly hope you used bicycle locks. Bike theft's a major problem in this town, you know."

"We done it . . .Everything is everything, man."

"Say it again," Hodges said, a sudden edge coming to his voice.

"Everything is—"

"No, you lying sack of shit. Tell me you rode your goddamn bicycles down here!"

Snakedance clammed up, then sneered as he wearily shook his head.

"I thought so. Where's your friend, 'Dance?"

"What friend, man?"

"Hightop."

Snakedance glanced over Hodges's shoulder, then quickly back again into the cop's face. "Back in the hood."

"Oh . . . his auntie must be sick, then. He musta said no to going to the beach on this lovely day because his auntie be sick."

Snakedance swallowed hard. Again he glanced inland toward a large municipal parking lot. Hodges noticed without turning around. "The 'Top, he didn't say. He just back in the hood, that's all. What you on me about the 'Top for, man?"

"It's just that I feel sorry for him, stuck in them projects on such a nice day."

"Yeah, well, maybe he don't like the motherfucking beach, homes . . ."

The Hispanic man had been standing quietly in line for some minutes, thinking perhaps that he was home free, when one of them slunk off the picnic table and strutted up to him. A Saint Christopher medal glittered against his bare hairless chest. "Hey, *vato* . . ."

The man clenched his fists only to keep his hands from shaking. "What?"

"Where you from?!"

The man faced forward again, hoping against hope that, if ignored, the insolent punk would just go away.

"Answer me, *puto!* Where you from?!"

Then it dawned on the man: he was being asked which gang was his. What the hell could he say? Hudson Electronics, Rifa? "Hey, I'm not part of that bullshit."

"Fuck you!" the punk spat. His *compadres* were beginning to rise from the table.

The man experienced a sinking feeling, an inevitability of violence, but he knew that he could never run, not with his wife and son watching. People began to clear away, and that only intensified the icy feeling in the pit of his stomach. "Hey," he said hoarsely, "fuck *you*, punk. Why don't you go leave decent people alone?" He could sense movement to his back, but didn't want to suffer the humiliation that would come from wheeling around and coming face to face with no one.

"Oh, *puto*," the punk said with a terrifying grin, "you shouldn't gone and said that."

"I'll say whatever the—" The man went to his toes. He had actually felt the blade slide in between two ribs. And now, as his attacker viciously jiggled the hilt to widen the wound, the man experienced a dazzling and suffocating pain in the middle of his back.

"One-eight, Rifa!" a voice cried far, far away, and this was followed by much screaming and finally shouting for the police to come.

It was agony to take even the slightest breath, and the man felt his strength gushing out of him as if he were one of those air-filled toys being deflated.

Reeling drunkenly and then collapsing to the pavement, causing a bicyclist to spill in a clatter, the man looked up from the walkway for his wife, his son—but everything had muddied to a gray blur.

"How come I haven't seen Hightop lately?"

"Yeah, well . . . he around, Hodges. Can we raise, man?"

"Stand right where you are until I'm done with you."

An alert tone issued from Young's handset, and the cop swept the radio up to his ear, trying to listen over the surf and crowd noise. "It starts," he said after a moment. "Somebody just got shanked at the snack bar. *Cholos* with red *moco* rags. Perpetrator's bare-chested. Fernando and I'll back!"

"Go," Hodges said.

McGavin started to fall in behind Diaz and Young.

"Where do you think you're going?" Hodges asked.

"Help out."

"Bullshit! You're helping me right here."

"For chrissake, Hodges, somebody just got *shanked*. What the fuck are we doing *here?*"

"Getting ready to take down Hightop. Watch these assholes." And with that Hodges turned and started running toward the parking lot.

"Hey!" McGavin hollered after him uselessly.

Within two rows of sun-baked cars, Hodges had zeroed in on the gangly youth, who was reclining in a jade-green El Dorado, immersed in the vibrations flowing through his headphones.

Glimpsing movement fast in approach, Hightop glanced up. His jaw went slack—but only for a split second. Then he ripped off the phones and dived out of the Cadillac through his open window, landing like a cat and quickly sprinting north through the parking rows, maybe hoping to pull an end run on Hodges and make his way back to his cuzzes on the walkway.

"Give it up, Hightop!" The air already burning in

his lungs, Hodges knew he had little hope of overtaking the eighteen-year-old. "Freeze!"

"My ass!" He didn't even crane his neck to see if a revolver was trained on him—sheer, stupid balls.

Hodges began to gain on him. He ignored the fiery pain in his chest and gave his leaden legs everything he could, realizing that, while this supreme effort would never help him catch Hightop, it would put the fleet Blood within throwing distance.

Grasping his baton by one end, he hurled it at Hightop. Lazily almost, the stick looped through the air, then dropped suddenly and entangled in the youth's lower legs, pitching him to the asphalt.

But Hightop rolled like a paratrooper and sprang up again, seeing an opportunity in the form of an old man putting past in a Honda Fifty.

Before he knew what had happened, the old man was toppled over and groaning in pain. Hightop righted the bike and took off through the cars, scraping paint and tearing off chrome trim with the handlebars as he fled toward Pacific Avenue.

Hodges was furious now. Recovering his baton, he kept running from the pure anger he felt with each plodding step.

Keeping an eye on the Bloods, Danny sensed it first from their restlessness. One rubbed his nose so hard it was a miracle it didn't flake off. Another became so antsy he began jogging in place, and all were trying to whisper to one another on the sly.

Hodges was righteously closing in on Hightop. But where?

"Anybody move and I'll bust his fucking kneecap!" Danny growled, drawing out his polycarbonate nightstick to make good on the promise if need be.

The Bloods quieted down sullenly.

And then, out of the corner of his eye, he glimpsed

Hodges running as he probably hadn't run in fifteen years: head tucked low, arms pumping, legs churning out high-stepping strides.

Hodges was in honest-to-God foot pursuit. Bob We'll-Get-Them-Later Hodges was honestly trying to run somebody down.

Impossible.

"Stay put!" Danny shouted over his shoulder at the Bloods, knowing damned well they'd split as soon as he looked forward again.

From the edge of the parking lot, he could see sunlight glinting off Hodges's bald pate as the man streaked after—Hightop!

Incredibly, Hodges was actually closing the gap—although Danny could hear him huffing, even at this distance—when he spun his stick at the gang-banger, dropping him in the blinking of an eye.

"All right!" Danny cried.

But then Hightop executed a somersault on one shoulder and came right back up, only to knock some old poop off his motorbike, which he then commandeered and sped off on toward Pacific Avenue.

Miraculously, Hodges kept ground-pounding after him, zigzagging between the cars.

Danny backtracked a few rows and leaped into the yellow Pontiac parked beside a fire hydrant, jamming the shift into reverse the instant the cylinders caught fire.

He scowled: a parking ticket was fluttering under the windshield wiper on his side.

Not bothering to wind around the big lot to one of the exits, he roared off the curb onto Pacific, where Hightop was locked into the traffic awaiting a green light.

"Way to go, Pops!"

Hodges's frantic hoofing had once again brought

him within range of beaning the gang-banger with his baton.

Hightop took no chances and acclerated around the vehicles in front of him, blowing the signal to an elongated blast of horns from the dense and swift cross traffic.

"You just missed your fucking chance, God!" Danny wailed, slamming the dash with his fist. "Let's keep awake up there!"

Then he was faced with the same jam of trucks and cars that had delayed Hightop. Tapping his horn impatiently, Danny veered two wheels up onto the curb and squeezed down the right side of the avenue, making tourists and bathers cringe against the storefronts until he'd passed and bounced back down off the curb into the intersection. He blared across it without benefit of a green light.

"Same to you, asshole!" he screamed at a horn he found particularly obnoxious, then began scanning the alleys on both sides. For the moment, he'd lost sight of Uncle Bob, but still trusted that Hodges was hobbling along somewhere in the crowd.

On a hunch he took the next right. Someone being chased this hotly would invariably choose right over left—it was usually a quicker maneuver.

Then he whipped the wheel right again.

Round the corner, he caught a lightning glimpse of Hightop leaning into yet a third right turn.

"Bingo!" Danny decided on another ploy and, with tires screaming, performed a full christie in the middle of the side street—the pedestrians spinning past his eyes melting into long blears like sixty-second exposures. He went back to a one-way three-lane he'd just forsaken and plowed down it the wrong way, advancing cars parting like the Red Sea for him.

"Thank you . . . thank you . . ."

Danny broke out of this caterwauling of horns onto North Venice Boulevard and stomped on the brake pedal with both oxfords, coming to rest in a pall of his own Goodyear smoke—directly in the path of Hightop, who had to lay down his motorcycle unless he liked the idea of piling into the passenger side of the Pontiac.

"Wow!" Danny cried, waiting an instant before bailing out so he wouldn't miss anything.

Tossing up a roostertail of sparks, the small Honda angled into the curb, dragging Hightop behind it at a speed Danny realized was too slow to result in any real injury, although the front wheel popped off its axle and took out the window of a trendy little joint crammed with brunching yuppies.

Limping, the gangly Blood crawled through this jagged hole in the glass, bowling over tables as he thrashed out of McGavin's line of sight.

By the time Danny made it inside by ducking through the same opening, Hightop had taken a hostage to hide behind, a frail-looking blonde with pearls around her pale neck and crepes all over her dress.

"Freeze!" Danny shouted, his Smith and Wesson drawn.

Making the young woman follow by wrenching her arm, Hightop moved back and forth between the tables and the heads of the stunned yuppies, who moments before had no doubt been talking about their *humanity* but now were wishing that the cop would dust this little piece of vermin so they might get on with brunch. Danny despised them; even as he waited for his opening, he found himself despising the rich bastards. *Jesus, what a crazy thing to feel right now.*

Hightop was grinning. He knew all too well that

even Danny would never risk a shot in a room filled to fire law capacity.

"It's over, 'Top. Let me take you *alive!*" This would sound good to the Shooting Investigation Team.

"It's over when Hightop say, fool!"

"You got no weapons!"

"I got hands!" Then he dragged the woman through the swinging door into the kitchen, where he was bound to find all kinds of weapons.

Danny hurtled in after him, seized the woman by the wrist, yanked her back out without closing the door, and flung her into the tables.

But this quick rescue cost him his wheelgun—Hightop batted Danny's right hand with a heavy copper skillet, and the revolver slid across the floor and under a large refrigeration unit.

A follow-up blow could have caved in the side of Danny's head, but he hugged Hightop like a punch-drunk boxer waiting for the bell, and the blow was glancing—smarting just enough to make Danny pummel him three times in the belly, fast and furious.

But the young Blood had a hard abdomen, and he came back up without pause, using his elbow as a piston to try to drive Danny's chin through the roof of his skull.

"Shit!" Danny belted him low again, but realized that it was going to take a lot of these punches to wear him down. For the first time in his life he sensed what a vigorous, mindless thing youth is—and that he no longer had it in first raw blush, as Hightop did.

The Blood wrapped a hand around Danny's throat. It felt like an iron claw.

Danny relented for a split second, just long enough to draw him off balance and roll chest-to-chest with him along a butcher-block counter onto the grill.

One of Hightop's long arms came to rest on this sizzling surface, and he screamed.

"Yeah!" Danny shouted. "Yeah, baby!"

But the pain only incensed Hightop, rejuvenated his awesome wired strength. "Motherfucker! Motherfucker!" And suddenly Danny was being swung around to be pressed like a patty against the grill.

A taste of scorching pain on his elbows made him resist, frantically, but Hightop was inexorably pushing him down toward the searing metal plate.

Fumbling behind him, Danny grasped the pumice scrubber and smashed it into Hightop's nose, which instantly bloodied.

But like a robot programmed to do one thing, Hightop continued to drive Danny down toward the grill.

Then, quickly and quietly, an arm wrapped around Hightop's throat, and Hodges's flushed face rose like a red moon over the Blood's shoulder. Expertly, he used the crook of his arm to pinch shut the carotid arteries running up the sides of Hightop's lean neck.

The Blood's expression became confused, then sleepy as his eyelids fluttered. Finally his pupils began lolling this way and that, and his brown skin took on a gray cast.

Quietly, he collapsed, and Hodges laid him out on the floor to cuff him.

Danny stood erect, then staggered away from the grill as quickly as he could.

Doubled over now, Hodges lost his breakfast, then wiped his ashen lips with his handkerchief and continued to breathe as if he'd just completed a marathon. In the relative terms of fitness, he probably just had. Two of them.

Danny started to say thanks, but couldn't do it. It seemed too little. And then again, he was frightened

that Hodges would tell him to get fucked or something.

"You okay?" he asked instead.

Hodges waved him off—and puked again.

Officer Fernando Diaz crouched beside the ambulance gurney and touched the young man's agonized
face. He did this without self-consciousness, as if he
were brushing the face of a child—his own, even.
"You're going to make it, 'mano. I've seen plenty of
these, and you're going to make it."

Even with an oxygen cannula attached to his nose,
he was having trouble breathing, yet he tried to speak.

"Don't talk, 'mano. Everything's okay."

"Wife . . ."

"She's here. She's right here. Your *hijo,* too. Everybody's okay."

"Lemme touch . . . son."

Diaz joined the tiny light brown hand to the larger
one, then looked away.

"We're going to move him now," one of the para-
medics said, he and his partner releasing the catches
and lowering the gurney.

The man tried to rise against the restraining belts.
"She . . . can't drive. How . . . ?"

"Don't worry, 'mano. I'm going to drive her over to
the hospital in your car. We take care of our own."

The man probably didn't mean to sound so bitter:
"Yeah . . ." He lay back down, and the rear doors
swung shut.

Diaz put his arm around the man's wife and said, "I
already got the keys from him. I'll get your Malibu—
Row D, right?—and pick you up here. Then we'll
meet him at Saint John's, okay?"

She nodded tearfully. "Thank you."

Diaz was hurrying toward the parking lot when Bill

Young tried to stay him for a moment: "Hey, any word on how Hodges and McGavin did?"

But Diaz kept walking, his eyes damp and skin looking clammy.

Young understood at once: his partner needed some privacy, fast.

CHAPTER 11

THE DAY AFTER NEARLY BEING FRIED ON A GRILL BY A pubescent short order cook called Hightop, Danny decided to get serious again about his weight training program. He'd temporarily suspended it some time before in favor of bourbon and beer backs and three hours of sleep a night. He even considered giving up cigarettes, or at least switching to one of the hernia brands—smokes so low in tar and nicotine that a serious smoker could give himself a hernia trying to draw any satisfaction out of one.

Maybe he should just go cold turkey off both booze and carcinogens.

Whatever—he just couldn't get it out of his mind: the helplessness and fear he'd felt as his back slowly sank toward that blistering grill.

In his own mind, he had always been stronger than

any conceivable threat—until Hightop, who was really nothing as far as bad-asses went, just a gangly kid. Wasn't he? What was going on? Had this thing with Louisa rattled him more than he thought? Had the anger blazing in her eyes somehow sapped his vitality just as he needed it most? Was she his Delilah?

Sucking in three staccato breaths through pursed lips, he addressed the weight machine in the station basement, steeled himself against the good pain that would restore his strength.

Then he began executing tricep builders.

The sweat trickled down between his flexed pectorals, and he closed his eyes as the fire swelled along the backs of his arms.

A few weeks of this and he'd be back where nobody on the streets could touch him. Teeth clenched against the growing strain, he grinned at the thought—the ideal of invincibility in which he could never be threatened, in which he would never feel fear.

It had been the most distasteful and humiliating thing to come his way in a long while—the terror Hightop had inflicted on him. Recalling it, Danny suddenly decided to do two more repetitions.

His face began trembling, and then he groaned—loudly enough for him to be grateful that he was alone in the weight room.

Hodges shuffled past the open door, headed wearily for the locker room, and Danny eased down the bar.

"Hey, Hodges—"

In the hallway, shoes scuffled to a halt, and then Hodges came back, his face a little drawn. "Yeah?"

For an instant Danny couldn't think of anything to say. "You on your way home?"

"Every night."

"I mean, you up for a quick one?" There went the booze resolution.

"Some other time, maybe. I'm bushed."

"Sure." Danny said nothing for a few seconds, and Hodges began to look restless. "That was some hot shit yesterday, eh?"

"You bet," Hodges said blandly.

"I mean, you hauled my chestnuts out of the fire. And I appreciate it. I really do, Bob. You really came through."

"Well, thank you."

"For an old man." Danny saw his attempt at a joke bring a slight rise to Hodges's eyes.

"Yeah, right. Every dog has his day. Of course, it was my own fault, right? I was the asshole who let old Hightop go in the first place, right?" Hodges stared at him briefly, then turned to go.

"Hey, wait up—for chrissake."

Thrusting his hands into his pockets, sighing, Hodges stepped into the room, curled his nose a little at the smell, but then looked surprised at what Danny had to say next.

"I want to apologize."

Hodges gave an uneasy smile, then sat on a weight bench. "What for?"

"I don't know," Danny said, feeling foolish as hell now. "A whole lot of shit, I guess."

"Go see a priest. Say a couple Hail Marys."

"Come on, man—"

"Listen, McGavin, I'm not the one who—"

"You know, if you would just cut me half as much slack as you cut those other assholes, I might just owe you one."

"I have. And you do."

"Well"—Danny laughed grimly—"that fucking settles that, doesn't it?"

"Not quite."

"What do you mean?"

"I had a talk with Melindez this morning while you were in court—"

"You spoke to the captain?" Danny interrupted, blinking rapidly now, surprised by how betrayed he felt. "The *captain?*"

"Yeah, well . . . Lieutenant Reed's on days off . . . and Melindez and I go way back."

"What's the bitch?"

"No bitch, McGavin."

"Then what the fuck's going on, man?"

"I get a new partner . . . start of the month."

"You mean you're going back to Juvenile?" Danny asked, a bit hopefully.

"I wish. No, I'm staying with CRASH, probably until my time's up."

Danny nodded thoughtfully. "Okay . . . okay . . . sure." He couldn't think of another thing to say. The silence was ghastly; Hodges must have thought so, too—when he spoke again his voice was soft, even kind.

"Ever had a bad relationship with a woman? Fight all the fucking time? Even when you love them, you can't help but fight all the time?"

"I suppose."

"It's like having two heads on the same body. One says red, the other's sure to say green."

"Right."

"Well, once you've had one that *wasn't* like that, you can't take going back to the fights again. If you see that it's going to be like that . . . well, you leave it before feelings get hurt. You don't point a finger and blame the other one. You just shake hands and go your separate ways . . . you know?"

Danny knew his eyes had clouded. It infuriated him because he wanted them to look flinty, even cold, but there was nothing he could do about the sudden smarting. "Yeah . . . good point, Bob." He moved on to his next exercise station: leg lifts. "Well, anyways, the apology still goes . . . ."

Now it was Hodges's turn to look as if he'd been slapped. "This is all I told the captain. This is all I had to. He doesn't think any less of you for what I said. Melindez knows how these things go."

Danny nodded distantly, then fell into a plodding rhythm as his legs worked the weights.

"See you in the morning," Hodges said at last.

Danny gave him a wave, but refused to meet his eyes.

Maybe law enforcement was the ultimate gang, and cops the ultimate gang-bangers.

Hell, a cop had his initiation rite: six months of torment and aching muscles at the academy. Then he got his colors—dark blue for most police departments, tan over forest green for most sheriff's offices. At least during the honeymoon period of his first two years on the job, he openly declared his loyalty to his "brothers" and the "hood." He defended his own agency, which was of course better at holding down its turf than any other agency of comparable size. Physical courage was what he prized above all else in himself and in his brothers; that it might one day desert him was what he most feared. He would rather die than turn and run, and chickening out under the eyes of his brothers was unthinkable. He would always treasure the first time, after the bullets had flown or the shit had otherwise hit the fan and some *veterano* with a rasher of service stripes on his sleeve said over coffee in some greasy spoon, "You did okay, McGavin . . . for a dick-lick."

And when it was time to kick back, cops didn't adjourn to some country club or quiet little place with a piano bar. They either congregated in the grimiest and sleaziest dive in town or, like gang-bangers, held their gig at some public hangout, setting warming fires in trash cans if it got cold, intimidating all who dared to barge in on their fraternal gathering. This evening's engagement was of the latter kind: alfresco, on the top level of a concrete parking structure across from the LAPD heliport. This aerie was affectionately known as "the Penthouse," and gigs here were usually marked by a lot of loud talking, or hoo-rah, as a Crip would put it.

Danny sat alone on the parapet, drinking Jim Beam and spitting down five stories when he felt like it.

It was a tradition, something that was completely understandable to all: a brother by his lonesome on the fringes of the gig, the warrior at war within himself—not wanting to talk, but not wanting to be entirely alone either.

Of the eight cops drinking at the Penthouse, each had had his hour on the windy parapet.

A chopper, which had been idling for some time on the pad, finally took off and tilted into the rapidly dimming sunset, its running lights winking like small arms fire, a Valkyrie on some fatal mission across the night.

Joey Norton, ripped beyond immediate repair, was staggering across the oil-stained lot toward his car. "Gonna get me . . . some Two-eighty-eight-A," he had announced some minutes before, jiving in California penal code that he intended to seek some oral sex.

"Give or get?" a brother from Rampart Division asked.

"Fugg you," Joey growled, an ankle turning on nothing and making him wobble. Amazingly, he stayed on his feet. "I'm gonna get some, then come back and kiss your ass . . . all you."

"Do you think maybe he means something else?"

"Sssh—don't blow a good thing."

Even McGavin had to smile.

Joey rooted in both front Levi pockets for his keys,

which he eventually located and drew out, sprinkling the concrete with what sounded like several dollars in loose change. Then, shutting one eye, he tried to insert the key in the lock with little success.

"Hey, Joey!"

"What?"

"Would it help if we put a little hair around that hole?"

"Shuddup."

At last he saw that the door was unlocked and climbed inside, immediately confounded by a second lock.

"You think he should drive in that condition?"

"He's got a fucking badge, don't he?"

"Jesus, he could kill somebody."

"Shit, they're trying to kill *him,* aren't they?"

A patrolman from Newton laughed knowingly, bitterly: in the past month, his partner had barely survived a .32 caliber wound to the abdomen. He was still ingesting his food through a tube and shitting into a plastic sack.

Us against them— Danny wondered what the devil had happened. Had it ever been different? Had the cops always been a gang apart? The street gangs had been forged by the pressures of the barrio and the ghetto. Maybe cops had been shaped, even warped, by their own special pressures.

Eventually, Joey did everything in correct sequence, and his car's engine roared to life.

"No capping, Joey!" the Newton cop hollered in warning.

"Nah, hah . . . straight arrow . . ." Joey backed up and started jerkily for the exit ramp. "Straight arrow."

Yet, before he descended to the next level, he lofted his revolver out the window and fired two loudly reverberating shots into the air.

"Crazy motherfucker!" They laughed, chucking empty beer bottles after him. "Asshole!"

After Joey was gone, Danny stayed ten minutes more, then pitched the nearly empty pint of Beam over the side and strolled to his Mustang.

Returning a few waves with a quiet nod, he skirted the sprays of caramel-colored glass on the concrete and started down the ramp toward the streets below.

He drove eastbound on the San Bernardino Freeway with the vague intention of dropping in on his old man. But with each passing mile, the idea lost some of its luster, and long before El Monte he gave it up. It was almost eight, and by now the old man would be too far gone on Colt malt liquor to hold any decent sort of a conversation. And then there would be the old man's boozy shack-job to endure, a part-time palmist who'd once given in to wishful thinking and predicted that Danny, like his mother, would die relatively young. The old man had laughed like hell and said that, like him, Danny was too full of piss to die young. He'd called Danny a regular scorpion. His shack had had an interesting occupation prior to palmistry. His father knew nothing about that. How could he? Only a cop has ready access to a rap sheet: Margene had nineteen solicitation priors in the San Diego area. And how could Danny tell dear old Pops that, before the bottom had fallen out of her looks, his beloved had been a service-town hooker?

"Shit," Danny whispered to himself, getting off and then back on the freeway, heading westbound this time.

The Los Angeles night was glittering around him, lights on every hill and big, smog-fuzzy clusters of them concentrated around Pasadena to the north, the civic center and Hollywood to the west. Yet, he couldn't think of a goddamn place to go, a single thing he felt like doing.

Hodges had really blown him out of the saddle with that new partner business. Until that moment, Danny had figured he was making progress with Uncle Bob—especially after Hodges had thrown himself heart and soul into taking down Hightop. Sometimes it worked the other way: instead of a salt toning down a rookie, the rookie reinfected the mummy with a new fever for the job. Danny had glimpsed an inkling of this in Hodges's performance yesterday. But today it was back to Uncle Bob and *is it quitting time yet?*

He realized that he ached to talk this over with somebody. Not with another cop—one of the guys would simply say that Hodges was a useless old fart and that was it, next subject please.

But that wasn't all the truth about Hodges; there was more to the guy than that. As strange as it sounded to his own mental ear, he wanted to discuss Hodges with somebody who *liked* Bob. Only that would help him put today in perspective, because—deep down—Danny felt that he had somehow failed miserably. And telling himself that Hodges and CRASH were all bullshit did little to alleviate this rotten feeling. "Shit, I feel low," he said out loud, trying to shake the sensation off as if it were a cramp.

Then, a few miles later, he whispered, "Ain't going to work, Dan-o . . . Forget it . . ."

He left the freeway despite this warning to himself and soon found himself crossing the Fourth Street bridge.

Waiting for a red light near the heavily fortified gas station, he smiled. Had she actually thought she could keep her address secret from a cop? It had taken him all of a few seconds to cross-index her name, race, approximate age, and city of residence and come up with her driver's license number. This gave him her house digits and street, which he now turned down into a shanty-crammed arroyo, reducing his speed to look the neighborhood over.

"Definitely *cholo* country," he muttered. "Six thousand Chevies to the acre. Our Lady of the Enchilada Catholic Church on the corner. Bingo gig in progress in the quasi-adobe parish hall behind. Peewees standing watch outside the crack houses for the narcs. Yes, indeed . . ."

Stop it, he warned himself. *Do you want her to slam the door even before you get a word out? She'll see this bullshit in your eyes—she has the ability to see your anger no matter how carefully you wrap it in a grin.*

On a sudden thought, he unholstered his piece and tossed it under the front seat. He would bound up her front steps armed with nothing more than a smile. He would come in peace. Shit, he might even try some jive on her father and her brothers—if any of them had survived the White Fence gang wars.

Looking back up toward the bridge, he saw orange flames wriggling out of a fifty-gallon drum among the pillars—the homeboys' answer to October's first serious chill. He could see the slick brown faces topped by watch caps, a bottle and a joint being passed from hand to hand as they partied.

He started searching for a house number, but few of the places showed a porch light. Few dared. While working patrol, he'd been inside places like these, which had one-inch marine steel plate fastened to the insides of the street-facing walls: something solid for *la familia* to wait behind whenever junior's rival gang-bangers roared past in a cragered-down Impala, loosing a volley at the windows.

What a fucking life . . . and it's her life . . .

Resorting to flashlight, he at last found the house, a

tidy but timeworn clapboard with a rusted Biscayne up on blocks in the gravel driveway. The lawn and a single row of shaggy survivors from a turn-of-the-century orange orchard were enclosed by a white picket fence. One light was burning within the house.

He parked at curbside and sat awhile, smoking, thinking.

What if she refused to see him? That would make two rejections in one day. Not a pleasant prospect.

A head showed briefly inside the glowing window; then the light went out.

This wasn't the neighborhood in which McGavin would choose to sit in front of a house for hours. So he got out and was approaching the swinging gate when somebody stepped out of the shadows.

His first thought was that the boyish silhouette was a member of her family. "Excuse me," he said. "Señorita Louisa Gomez *esta en la casa? Por favor—*"

"Hey, Pac-Man," someone said from behind, a dark figure on the far side of the Mustang, "nice ride you got here. Lemme take a ride in your car, okay?"

A half-dozen homeboys had materialized out of nowhere, and in the background stood that many more *cholas* in a ragged line, giggling at what the *vato* beside Danny's car had said.

To protect his back, Danny spun around and pressed against the fence. Instinctively, his right hand darted to his off-duty holster—and then telegraphed the message along stripped nerves to his brain: his revolver was fifteen impossible feet away inside the Mustang. He had even failed to lock the driver's door as he usually did.

He clenched his fists, but kept them low, waiting for the first blade to flash toward him through the dim starshine.

The *cholos* formed a semicircle around him. Yet

they didn't close in for the kill, which convinced him that they wanted to shoot their mouths off a little before making their final move.

"What do you *pedos* want?" he demanded, knowing that he had to sound utterly fearless if he wanted to come out of this alive. At the first hint of panic in his eyes or voice, they would lunge for his throat like wolves.

"Oooh, Pac-Man, you got your *quette* tonight?" He tried to pat down Danny's windbreaker, but McGavin batted the prying hand away and hooked his fingers into claws to dig at eyes should any of the homeboys advance farther. They had to believe that he would resist maniacally, down to gouging out eyeballs. Yet, at the same time, he couldn't appear to be desperate.

"You touch my gun," he said ominously, "and I'll kill you."

"Oooooh!" they wailed mockingly—the homegirls, too.

But none gave an indication that he believed Danny to be unarmed. Still, despite this hopeful sign, they continued to press him—one flick of a knife and it would be over, his guts spilling out of him. A horrible way to die, often with full consciousness right up to the screaming end. A way Danny had seen before.

"Hey, Pac-Man, you know who I am?"

"Why should I care, homes?"

"I'm Flacco. I just wanted you to know."

"What're you looking for?" someone else asked. "This your fancy car, man? You on duty?"

Some peewees had trickled out of the darkness and taken up stations behind the ring of *vatos* trapping Danny. One of them now squirmed forward and spit at McGavin's shoes. "What the fuck you doing here, Pac-Man?"

He was Gato, Louisa's cousin, whom Danny had spray-painted.

"Leaving, right?" Flacco said. "Do a ghost, Pac-Man. You don't belong around here, man."

It proved to be a conflicting signal. No one budged, and the semicircle remained intact, a human wall in front of him.

"Puto!" Gato cried, then spat again.

With this, their hostility tightened a click—Danny could feel it. For the first time he considered making a dash for the Mustang, flailing his arms and risking whatever slashes came his way until he could get his hands on his revolver.

His first shot, even one aimed skyward, would probably scatter them. But he doubted that he would survive those fifteen feet.

They were waiting for him to try to break. It was the signal they were watching for in the flickerings of his eyes.

Then hope came unexpectedly from Flacco, the oldest of the lot and possibly a *veterano,* who showed some sense—killing a cop would bring intense heat down on White Fence, and this kind of police attention would cut deeply into the gang's drug and protection rackets. "Go, Pac-Man." He took a half-step backwards. "Come back some day like on duty. We'll smile and play nice, okay?"

But Gato would have none of it, and he had the support of the *cholas,* who weren't ready to see Danny leave in one piece. "Wait, Flacco," the peewee said, the homegirls slinging catcalls at Danny from behind Gato. "Don't let him go noplace yet, okay?" He inclined his head toward the Mustang. "This new, *vato?"*

"Restored," Danny said because he was out of arguments and didn't want to stir up anything fresh, what with Flacco offering him a way out.

Gato whipped out a can opener, the church key kind, and laughingly ran its point down the length of

Danny's thousand-dollar metal-flake paint job. The screech set his teeth on edge, but he said nothing.

"The payback," Gato hissed with this sudden and ugly maturity to his voice, "is always a bitch. *Always.*"

Now the homegirls were ragging on Flacco to do something, *anything* other than let the cop walk away with only one scratch—and that on his car.

Then it came. The snick of a butterfly knife being jerked open.

Danny raised his forearms to fend off the fiery strikes he expected within seconds. His heart was tripping so ferociously he knew that he would feel the pain only as fire.

Suddenly the amber light from a porch fixture flowed around him like honey.

"No!" Louisa cried, running down the cement walkway.

"Get out of here, lady!" Danny cried, hoping that they wouldn't connect her to him, forgetting in his desperation that he had already asked for her by name. "This doesn't concern you!"

"He's here to see me! Move out! All of you!" Her eyes darted to her cousin. "Gato, you, too!"

Even before the homeboys began shuffling backwards, she broke through the ring and, taking Danny by the wrist, pulled him toward his car. "Danny, get in."

"I can't leave you with them!" he whispered, pausing with his door half open.

And then he realized the danger she had put herself in when she slid across the front seat instead of going back inside her house. "Come on," she said evenly. "Let's go."

Even before he turned the engine over, he reached down and grasped his wheelgun, holding it out of sight against the door panel while he drove away from the curb at idle speed. To run one of them down would mean that Louisa Gomez might never be able to go home again.

Fists drummed the Mustang as he and Louisa made their escape toward the Fourth Street bridge.

CHAPTER 12

THE PROFANITIES AND LAUGHTER OF THE WHITE FENCE homeboys soon faded beneath the throaty rumble of the Mustang's exhaust. Danny kept checking the rearview mirror even after he'd gotten back on the freeway, looking for the headlamps of a war wagon in pursuit, but Louisa said, her voice small, "They won't follow . . . It's over."

Everything except the rage, he realized.

Now that he was free of the danger, he despised them, wanted to drive back and humble them. And he was angry with himself as well, humiliated by the tightrope the homeboys had forced him to walk during all those excruciating minutes. And he wanted a piece of Gato—for spitting, Danny would paint his *entire* fucking body next time, in Day-Glo red with the Pac-Man face in black on his skinny little ass!

He glanced aside: Louisa was slumped in the bucket seat, her head angled back against the rest. "You shouldn't have come outside your house—"

"You shouldn't have come at all!" She bolted upright, her eyes flaring at him.

His voice turned soft. "I wanted to see you."

"You're lucky I was even home!"

"Why? You working more hours now?"

"I'm going to Sacramento." She pressed her fingertips against her temple and stared out the side window. Her hair billowed in strands around her bare arms and shoulders. She was wearing a yellow halter top and white slacks tonight. Again, he noticed the faint blush of the butterfly tattoo.

"You got somebody there?"

"Yeah."

When she said nothing more, he shifted uncomfortably in his seat. "Who?"

"My sister."

"Oh." He relaxed again. "Well, those assholes weren't going to do anything. Not to a cop."

"Fine. Take me back."

He studied her for an instant, then gazed ahead into the streaming files of red taillamps: the freeways were moderately jammed tonight, the traffic moving along at about fifty. "Listen, if I messed things up for you, I'm sorry."

"I can take care of them. You worry about yourself. You can't even deal with yourself!"

"That's probably true." The tone in his voice made her look at him quizzically, but she held her tongue.

Instead of taking her home, he continued east on the freeway, feeling exhausted from the confrontation with White Fence, but also free . . . strangely free. His mind was brimming with possibilities, and it seemed that—if they only stayed on this elevated magic carpet of concrete—Louisa and he would wind up in

Paris or Kashmir or some other exotic place neither of them would ever see.

But before they ever glimpsed the Eiffel Tower, he turned off onto Santa Anita Avenue and headed north through El Monte, his old stomping grounds, which seemed more run-down than he'd remembered. "I needed to talk to you, see . . ."

Again she glanced at him, but kept silent.

"Something happened today . . . Hodges—"

"Is he hurt?" she asked, eyes frantic for a split second.

"No, he's fine . . . Bob's fine."

Waiting for a traffic signal, he watched a low rider pull alongside in the adjoining lane. For once, his face registered no contempt, and both vehicles crept forward with the green light without incident. "See, Hodges is like dumping me."

"What do you mean? Are you two going with each other or something?"

He laughed under his breath. "Cute, Louisa."

"I'm sorry," she said more gently. "Tell me what's wrong."

"Nothing earth-shattering, I'm sure."

"No, Danny—*talk* to me."

His eyes were glassy in the headlights of an oncoming bus. "There was this collar yesterday down by the beach. A Blood gang-banger who took off like a fucking rabbit. Hodges did great. We both did . . ."

"Yes?"

"Well, I thought he was coming around, you know. I thought we might make it as a team. And then this afternoon he springs this shit on me . . ." For a moment, Danny couldn't finish.

"What kind of shit, Danny?"

"He talked to the captain. . . . He's getting a new partner first of the month."

"What reason did he give you?"

"We fight too much. Don't see eye to eye about the job. The old clashing personalities B.S." He took the next left off Santa Anita and, after several blocks, drove out into the racetrack parking lot, a dark lake of asphalt rimmed by city lights and, to the north, the coppery green backside of the grandstand. He flicked off his headlamps and killed the engine. "The other guys, they're taking his side in this."

"What do you mean by his *side,* Danny?"

"Shit—I don't know. All I know is that they're all walking on pins and needles around me."

"And what does that tell you?" she asked a bit too eagerly to please him.

"Not a fucking thing—except that Hodges belongs to the right clique at CRASH and I don't."

She clasped his forearm; her small hand felt warm. "*Who* do you think you are?"

"Is this a charade?"

Her voice turned sharp. "Let me tell you something, Danny . . ."

"Do I have a choice?"

"Shut up!"

He lowered his head with a stung smile.

"Those homeboys who just shook you down may be fucked up—but they have each other. What do you have that's better? Huh? Your car? Your badge? Your bullshit? What do *you* have, Danny?"

His hand moved toward the ignition, but she seized it before he could turn the key. "I don't want to go. . . . I don't want to leave you, Danny."

He began drawing her toward him, but she refused to let go of his hands. She grasped both of them fiercely. He found her mouth, moist and open, and kissed her.

"Oh, Danny, why do you make everything impossible? I could love you, Danny, oh, I could love you . . ."

"I do love you," he whispered. "I guess that's what I wanted to talk about, too."

He rolled over for the twentieth time in that many minutes, grunted, then took a deep breath.

Finally, Joan Hodges could take it no longer. "Bob?"

"Hmm?"

"What's wrong?"

"Oh . . . the damned *jale* . . . that's all. Go back to sleep."

"What about the job?"

"Same old shit. I'm okay."

"You know," she said, carefully measuring out her words, "there was a time when you wouldn't tell me a thing about the job. I was kind of hoping those days were behind us."

Sighing, he sat up and reached for the beer on the nightstand, drank the foamy heeltap in the bottom of the bottle. "Little ruckus down at the beach yesterday."

"Is that why you were so exhausted last night?"

"Yeah," he said, almost bitterly.

"And . . . ?"

"I don't know, maybe it was enough to convince me that I *really* wasn't up to McGavin anymore. I talked to Melindez."

"Good, I'm glad you did. What'd he say?"

"Oh, at first—what I expected. He wanted me to stay teamed up with McGavin, said I was a good influence on the kid."

Joan chuckled knowingly. "He just knows no one else will have Danny. Good old wishy-washy Melindez."

"Jeez, you sound like you work down there."

"I *do.*"

Hodges laughed and patted the swell of her hip beneath the sheet. "Point taken."

"So what's the captain going to do?"

"Well, eventually he caved in—especially when I said I'd even take a transfer to Communications if need be."

She paused. "Is that such a bad idea until you can file your papers?"

"What?"

"Communications?"

"Oh, shit, honey, I'd be bored to death on one of those consoles. That was just something to jack up Melindez."

She decided to say nothing more about it. "Well, good, then, you're getting a new partner."

"Yeah, but . . ." His voice trailed off into a remorseful silence.

"You're not having second thoughts, are you? That's all I've heard these past weeks—how Danny McGavin is killing you."

Hodges exhaled. "You know, I had it set in my mind that he was such a baby *reptile*. But this afternoon, when I told him we were kaput, well . . . it hurt him . . . I think it hurt him real bad."

"Bob, you can't be father to the world."

"I know, I know."

"And if he wants to win the war all by himself—let him. The battles are tough enough. And you owe it to me and the kids to get through them. Especially these last few. All right?"

First thing after unlocking the front door, Danny didn't have to race around his apartment picking up underwear and tossing Budweiser empties in the plastic can under the kitchen sink. The place was always neat; he liked it that way.

"Nice," she said, looking a little surprised. Then a question burst out of her mouth: "Were you ever married, Danny?"

He laughed. "You've got to be kidding."

She frowned at the way he said this, but then he kissed the sad expression off her lips. "I mean, Louisa, nobody even came close to qualifying . . . until now."

That melted her a little, and her arms snaked around his neck. "Oh, Danny . . ." She had a stark way of looking at him that made him feel desired without her seeming aggressive in the least. "You can be so nice when you want."

Gently, he broke off the embrace to dim the floor lamp. And when that wasn't enough, he found a votive candle in a kitchen drawer and set it to flickering in a saucer on the breakfast counter. The wash of golden light made her lithe shadow tremble against the wall.

He came back to her, kissed her neck, her shoulders, even ran his lips over the small butterfly.

"Danny, I want us to be good together . . . to be happy."

"We will be, I promise."

He led her into his bedroom, undressed her at the foot of his bed. And when her beauty was fully revealed to his sight, he smiled. "My *God* . . . Louisa."

She looked happy when he said this, his voice slightly raspy with desire.

Somehow the tension between them had broken, and Hodges found himself even enjoying their late morning cruise through the streets of Newton Division in the crinkled yellow Pontiac.

"You hear from Louisa yet?" he asked while munching on a fiery burrito.

McGavin was doing a decent job of driving with one hand and feeding a hard-shell chicken taco into his mouth with the other. "Nah, she's still up north."

"Joan sure liked her."

McGavin nodded, a hint of appreciation in the gesture.

"How you gonna see her when we start working nights here?"

"We'll work it out." McGavin licked the reddish grease off his fingertips. "How about the D.A.?"

"What?"

"The D.A. You hear any word?" McGavin eyed a Hispanic youth in a passing car, and Hodges read his thoughts. He tossed the burrito down into the wax paper in his lap and unhooked the microphone off the dash.

"Control, One CRASH Thirty-two."

"CRASH Thirty-two, go ahead."

"Requesting wants, warrants, DMV on California plate: One Nora Frank Union Three Zero Nine . . . Buick Skylark."

"One Nora Frank Union Three Zero Nine—stand by."

"The district attorney, man," McGavin said somewhat impatiently. "What'd he have to say on our case?"

"Yeah, yeah. The deputy D.A.—forget the jerk's name right now—said Oso's testimony won't mean shit in court. And it seems good old Hightop's got himself a lawyer he can't afford."

"But someone else can."

"So what's new? That's fucking life."

For once, McGavin didn't argue.

The radio speaker squawked to life: "Unit requesting California plate: One Nora Frank Union Three Zero Nine—no wants, no warrants. Ortiz, Hidalgo, 2411 San Rafael Street, this city."

"One CRASH Thirty-two, roger." Hodges hung up the mike and reached for his burrito.

"Well," McGavin said, "at least we're costing the sons of bitches some time and money."

"That's the spirit. We do what we can . . . when we can . . . if we can." Hodges knew what McGavin was going to say next by the way his eyes turned reflective. He also clenched the wheel with both hands.

"You know that talk we had, Bob?"

"Right."

"I've been thinking. If I was you, I'd want a new partner, too. Might do us both some good in the nerves and bad-gut department."

Hodges would have offered his hand—except that McGavin was wolfing down his third chicken taco. "No hard feelings, then?"

"Nah, I deserve it."

"Hey, we finally agree." But over the next few minutes, when McGavin's mood swung suddenly toward glumness, Hodges added: "You know I do have the feeling—someday you're gonna be a good cop. If you live that long. And if they change all the rules."

McGavin smiled, then reached down to the floor mat for a large chocolate milk shake.

CHAPTER 13

"H EY, *TINTO* BOY . . ."

It began with a shove, a school-yard affront.

The gangly black youth who had been shoved didn't answer the challenge from the Chicano in kind. Instead, he flew back at him with a vicious side-kick, which splintered ribs and brought a howl from the injured gang-banger.

His cry of pain alerted his homies, who abandoned the weightlifting stations at which they'd been straining and closed in on the black youth. Iron-pumping street fighters one and all, they menaced the youth with martial arts stances.

"What this shit?" The sight of the esseys throwing up a ring of karate fists around the lone brother brought the black gang-bangers into the fray, which then began in earnest.

Yet, within a few seconds, the racial lines became confused. Some of the blacks, Crips by affiliation, suddenly realized that they were defending a known Blood—and wanted no part of that. They began fighting simply to withdraw, although two of them used the confusion to get a few licks in on the gangly Blood, who—in being pummeled from all sides—was hanging like Jesus off the ten-foot chain-link barrier that enclosed the jail's rooftop exercise area.

"Feel good, motherfucker?" one of the Crips snarled before backing out of the way—the deputies were wading into the edge of the melee swinging their riot clubs, which were a foot longer than a patrolman's baton.

Dazed, the black youth lost his grip on the fence and dropped to the decking.

A huge Hispanic with a Sur tattoo—advertising his kinship to the Mexican Mafia, which reigned in Sur, or southern California—seized the youth by the hair and twisted his head as far as it would go, grinding his face into the mesh. Then he let go—a deputy had momentarily paralyzed him with a baton blow to the backs of the knees.

Drunkenly, the black youth held up a palm to tell the same deputy that he was finished. He looked it: the diamond mesh of the chain-link fence had been imprinted as crosshatch abrasions on his face. "Help me up, man—please."

Within minutes, he was standing on his own strength, almost fully recovered.

He was tough. Tough as oak.

Detective Chuck Foster had been assigned to the Sheriff's Office anti-gang unit, Operation Safe Streets, long enough to know that only limited windows of opportunity existed for interrogating gang-bangers. These windows usually opened up after some spate of violence, when the bangers involved were slightly off-balance because of anger, physical injury, wounded pride, or a sense of betrayal.

Swiftly, a gang investigator had to make use of these episodes; if he delayed even a few hours, any pliant behavior on the part of the bangers set like concrete—and once again they became their usual sullen, pig-headed selves. Faces like stone walls, eyes like agates.

As was his habit, Foster spent a minute or two alone in the interrogation room, seemingly meditating but actually reminding himself that he wasn't here to prove anything, to make converts to reason, or to browbeat the object of his questions. He was here to get information.

Then he rose and cracked the door: "Bring in him please, Deputy."

The rawboned black youth strutted in, and the deputy removed the handcuffs.

"Hello, Hightop—long time no see," Foster said, his usual precise diction replaced by a careless street slur. "What happen your face? Somebody try to make you his punk? Some Crips try to corn-hole you up on that roof?"

Hightop flopped down into a chair. "I want a doctor."

"Why they do you, Hightop?"

"Shee-it, nobody do me, Foster."

"Those scratches say otherwise."

"Don't mean nothing."

"You sell bad shit out on the street?"

Hightop shook his head disdainfully, then pulled on his lower lip with his fingers as if to say that this kind of talk was beneath his dignity. "I wanna talk to my lawyer."

"Give it up!" Foster raised his voice for the first time. "That faggot can't bunk with you here, man!"

"My lawyer, homes!"

Foster flung open the door and shouted, "Deputy!"

And when the jailer appeared a moment later, the detective said to him, winking so that Hightop couldn't see: "Christ, even his homeboys can't deal with his shit. I got reason to believe his own Bloods are trying to do him in."

The deputy caught on right away. "That's what it looked like to us. A Blood done that to his face."

"Then it fits. I think Hightop here's a hook Blood. He hustling for Crips on the side—I'm sure of it. Maybe he'd be safer bunking with some Crips."

"I think that can be arranged, Detective."

"Do it."

"No!" As hoped, Hightop resisted being taken away, and the deputy had to throw a twist-lock on his arm to get him back into the chair. Still Hightop went on shouting, his voice raw with panic: "Hold it! Hold it, man! Foster jiving! Don't put me with no Crips! I'm telling you, man—I get jammed if you put me with Crips!"

Foster waved for the deputy to back off.

Hightop sat staring at him, his eyes large and quick in his face.

"Wanna get outta the gang module?"

Hightop harrumphed at the futility of the notion.

"Wanna get back in the general population?" Foster sat down across the table from him, never once letting go of Hightop's frightened gaze. "Tell me something I don't know."

"What? 'Bout this get-down on the roof?"

"Shit, homeboy, I don't care about that. That's intramural sport around this place."

"Then I don't know nothing."

"You may beat your rap, Hightop—but there's all kinds of justice in this world. And you're in our hood now."

"Don't I fucking know it?"

"I don't know what you know. You going to have to tell me, Hightop."

"Like what?" His voice cracked a little under the strain. A good sign.

Foster's eyes grew cold. "Gimme something tasty. Some of that nasty cheese you got."

Hightop steepled his thumbs together on the table, his expression doleful as he pitted his quivering thumbs against each other.

"Cold world, Blood," Foster went on. "No mercy. Ain't that what you write on walls?" He paused, if only to make Hightop glance up again. "Who got Robert Craig? Who put the gauge on him, man?"

The night was almost too cool for short sleeves, and Hodges had already mentioned twice that he looked forward to wearing ties and long sleeves. He said they made a cop look more professional.

Danny just kept driving; he didn't say a thing. He hated goddamn ties. But he liked being back on the neon-lit streets.

Somehow, night made it feel more like cop work, not like some gritty kind of social work. More often than not, the bad things happened under cover of night. And a good cop wanted to be where those heavy things went down, just as a career soldier secretly prayed for battles. Without these often violent challenges, cop work quickly turned tedious, an endless stream of public-service bullshit: see the lady—malicious mischief mailbox, a stolen bicycle report at . . . return to station, see watch commander for station tour, reference Boy Scouts . . . pure meaningless caca.

The night was sharp with a sense of expectation that even affected Uncle Bob, made him sit forward in the shotgun seat, his eyes darting from car to car and down the alleys, too.

Something good was buzzing in the underlit smog. At least, something a real cop would think good, Danny mused.

An on-the-ball sheriff's detective had turned Hightop. Danny had no idea how the dick had persuaded the savage gang-banger to drop the dime, but he wasn't about to look a gift horse in the mouth. At long last they could link a vehicle to the Robert Craig homicide.

And now all of Southeast, even the homicide dicks assigned to the division, were out looking for the van.

"Hold it," Hodges said tensely.

Danny hit the brakes.

"Back up to the alley again . . . yeah, okay, right here—stop." Hodges aimed a hand-held spotlight down the length of the dingy passageway. A dark-colored Ford van was parked at its far end, but it proved to be the delivery vehicle for the florist shop that fronted on the street. "Shit," Hodges said, sounding genuinely disappointed.

"You getting into this, Uncle Bob?"

"Shut the fuck up," he said good-naturedly, tucking the Ithaca back under the front seat after Danny had hotrodded up the alley to check out the van. "You hungry?"

"Fucking famished."

"Let's hit the Denny's up on—" A radio alert tone silenced him.

"Units in the area: Eighteen William Three reports the suspect One-eighty-seven van, dark green Ford, Three Adam Boy Robert Zero Nine Seven, northbound on Avalon at Seventy-ninth."

"Rocket's van," McGavin said incredulously, dropping the gears into low and pinning the gas pedal against the firewall. "That dickhead Rusty Baines stumbled onto Rocket's van."

"Here we go!" Hodges attached the magnetic emergency light to the Pontiac's roof, then grasped the shotgun that he'd just secured. He made sure the safety was on before jacking a round into the chamber. "You got your belt on?"

"Yeah, yeah, yeah."

"All units: William Three is now in pursuit, northbound on Avalon approaching Florence . . ."

Hodges let it go with a groan, but Danny railed: "Fucking goddamn detective! Can't get within ten miles of a fucking suspect without being made!"

"Yeah, but he kinda grows on you."

They both laughed.

"Shut up a minute . . . I think we're the only sled in position." Hodges keyed the mike: "One CRASH Thirty-two, we're southbound on Avalon from Vernon, responding to the One-eighty-seven van."

"Roger, CRASH Thirty-two." Then the Communications sergeant could be heard in the background, murmuring something urgent to the dispatcher. "All units: William Three has TC'ed on at Avalon and Gage. Non-injury . . . repeat: non-injury. CRASH Thirty-two continue to roll as primary. William Three reports suspect vehicle last seen still northbound on Avalon."

"Roger, Control," Hodges said.

"Christ!" Danny howled, trying to nurse even more speed out of the Pontiac's screaming engine. "Not only can't Baines tail a car without being made, he can't drive worth a fuck either!"

"Slow down!" Hodges's head was swiveling this way and that, his eyes feverish for a glimpse of the dark green Ford van before it was swallowed by the heavy traffic of the southside night. "This is it! This is the area. Slow down!"

All at once it seemed as if God had pointed a finger at the Pontiac. Both men cringed as white-hot light poured down on them, lighting up the street scene as if they were living through the first seconds of a nuclear blast.

Then they heard the rotors thumping against the thick air.

"Unit that I have my light on . . ." a radio voice said.

"CRASH Thirty-two, Air Support, go."

"Suspect van on top of rise—behind liquor store. Go past, turn right, up the ramp. You'll kiss their bumper."

"Roger, Air Support." Hodges tossed the mike on the dash, then thrust the Ithaca shotgun through his open side window. "Right, McGavin! Up there! Go past it! Yeah, *right!*"

"I *heard* him!" Danny snapped over the massed wail of sirens from black-and-whites that were also converging on the lot. He unholstered his revolver and tucked it under his thigh as the Pontiac bounced over the curb and rocked up a steep driveway. The ramp gave him the feeling of topping a roller coaster.

Hodges seized the P.A. mike, but then, on second thought, chucked it into Danny's lap. "You take 'em down, hotshot."

"You bet." As the Pontiac flew over the top of the ramp, Danny stomped on the brake pedal, and the car landed with a smoking shudder—blocking the van's only exit.

He clicked on the high beams: the Ford was parked with its boxlike rear end facing them, as the chopper pilot had said it would be.

Hodges bailed out and crouched behind his door, which he angled to deflect any bullets that might spiral his way.

Danny did the same with his door, then stared over his sights at the driver's side of the van. With his left hand, he held the mike to his mouth: "Police! Put your hands out! All hands outside!"

Three pairs of hands were soon dangling outside the van, one pair from each of the front side windows and one from the partly open cargo door.

Danny also kept checking the rear doors for the slightest movement, although the windows were tinted, almost opaque. He couldn't forget the Uzi he had so recently faced.

And he half expected a fragmentation grenade to roll out of the dark green van—a National Guard armory in Boyle Heights was missing a whole case of them. "Driver! Wiggle your fingers if you understand me!"

The fingers fluttered emphatically.

"Now with your right hand slowly reach inside the van and take the keys out of the ignition!"

He did so.

"Throw them away from the van—twenty feet!" Out on the edges of his field of vision, Danny could see Ithaca-toting patrolmen racing into position, taking cover behind a retaining wall and a dumpster. The chopper continued to hover overhead, casting the scene into ghostly light that was probably frightening of itself to the suspects. "Driver, you're doing good. Now open your door from the outside—and get outta the van. Keep your hands up. Let's go!"

Surprisingly, a clean-cut black kid wearing horn-rimmed glasses inched out of the van. His knees had gone to rubber on him. Not the typical gang-banger Danny had expected. But appearances had deceived before, and scared-looking kids had blown away cops. He didn't care for this. It all seemed too disarming. "I want you to walk very slowly to the back of the van."

The kid tottered as he walked to the rear doors—was he actually going to faint? Or was he going to pretend to faint while the rear doors yawned open and a fusillade of automatic rifle fire stitched Hodges and Danny with enough tumbling lead to kill fifty cops?

Danny kept his forefinger firmly inside the trigger guard: something was odd as hell about this, and he had no intention of winding up on the short end of it. "Keep your left hand in the air. I want you to open the back of the van."

Closely monitoring the progress of the take-down, the chopper pilot banked down to a position directly behind Danny's back; his dazzling spotlight flooded the van's carpeted cargo space as soon as the driver swung the doors open.

Inside, the two passengers froze, their pupils glittering red like animals' eyes.

"Driver," Danny went on, feeling no better about the possibility that something bad was going to happen any instant, "move to your left now. Keep your hands up and don't move unless I say. Front passenger, nod if you understand me."

The youth dipped his head as if each of the police weapons aimed at him was tapping against his chest.

"Okay, front passenger, get out of the driver's seat with your hands up."

He emerged in a timid crouch.

"Don't hunker over like that!"

He braced like a West Point plebe.

"Good . . . Walk backwards to the rear of the van. You and the driver, get on your knees . . . hands up . . . that's it. Down on your bellies now. Move it!"

They prostrated themselves on the concrete.

"Keep your hands in front of you. Bury your heads in the ground and don't look this way." Finally,

Danny directed his attention on the kid in the cargo space, a pudge who just didn't fit the gang-banger profile. Like the other two, he looked like he was suffering from tremulous bowels. "You in the van—come out the back doors, slowly. Hands up!" This was a slight departure from S.O.P.: usually it was best to have all the suspects come out the same door. But Danny was afraid that, in passing between the high-backed bucket seats, the last kid might go for a weapon. "On your knees between your friends!"

He was crying. The fat kid was crying as he genuflected in the blaze created by the Pontiac's high beams and the helicopter's spotlight. This was no gang-banger. He looked like a rib shack gourmand.

"Lay down!" For a disconcerting split second, Danny wondered if, in the confusion of Baines's collision, the chopper had gotten onto the wrong vehicle. Half of the southside population moved in dark-colored vans. But, no—Three Adam Boy Robert Zero Nine Seven; the plate was righteous . . . unless Hightop had been stroking the sheriff's detective. "All three of you, now—spread your legs. Now, arms to your sides, palms up. Doing fine. Next, put your right hand in the small of your back. Your *right* hand, you stupid motherfucker!" Danny barked at the fat kid. "Now, same thing with the other hand."

At that point, six patrolmen trotted forward from the retaining wall, two on each suspect—one to cuff and one to leer down the length of an Ithaca at him.

"Shit." Rising, Danny knuckled a kink out of the small of his back. "These guys looks pretty scary to me."

Hodge shrugged that he didn't understand either. "I'd still bet this was the chariot old Rocket was driving when he lit up Robert Craig."

"Let's hope. . . . I don't like to choreograph this crap for nothing." Danny aimed his flashlight skyward and clicked it on and off four times—code four.

The unearthly light faded, and the chopper wheeled into the night.

CHAPTER 14

"H OW LONG YOU KNOWN ROCKET?" DANNY ASKED Willie Wright, the fat kid.

"I dunno."

"One year? Ten?"

"A year, I guess."

"Where's his lady live?"

"I dunno."

Danny shot up from the interrogation room table and loomed over Wright. "Hey, don't pull my fucking dick!"

"I don't know where she live!" Wright's eyes were moist, and a dew of sweat clung to his forehead. Every few minutes, his features would screw up into a sob, but somehow he was able to keep the sound from breaking out of his mouth. "I just dunno, man."

"What if you had to find him?"

"I don't need to find Rocket, never."

"Listen, dammit!"

Wright dropped his eyes—and then again the strange, silent sob.

"What if somebody wanted to kill him, Willie? And you had to let him know. Where would you find him?"

"I dunno."

"Hey, we can do this all night." Danny snubbed out a half-smoked Marlboro. "What's Rocket's girl-friend's name?"

"Her name?"

"You're not talking to some fool, man!"

Wright flinched.

"You think you're talking to a fool?"

"No . . . no, man."

"We are talking about your freedom! And you don't know her name? Okay, what's her girlfriend's name?"

Wright blinked in confusion. "What girlfriend?"

"Any one! Name one!"

"Name *who*, man?"

Danny chuckled, warmly almost. "Don't tell me you don't know the little ladies' names . . . a big strong player like you. What's the name of some of Rocket's girlfriends' friends?"

Wright mumbled something under his breath.

"What?"

"Annie," he croaked, a single decibel louder.

"Annie what?"

"I dunno."

"Jesus Christ!" Danny batted the ashtray off the table.

Wright began rubbing his eyes, his elbows turned in toward his chest like a boxer on the ropes. "I just know the lady as Annie."

"Who else? And don't be pulling my dick, now." Danny seized Wright's hands and pulled them away from his wet eyes. "I'll front you off right before all your friends. I'll hand you a fifty-dollar bill and say, 'Thanks for the information, Willie.'"

Wright glared at him in fear and disbelief.

"I'll do it, Willie. I've done it before."

"Man—"

"I've *enjoyed* doing it before." Danny grinned.

Wright heaved a sigh that left his shoulders sagging. "Cheryl . . . Cheryl Williams."

Despite his obvious fear, Lewis Clark, the driver of the dark green Ford van, kept some of his dignity. He peered at Hodges through his horn-rims, realizing that he was cornered but not quite ready to roll over yet.

"How did he get ahold of your van?" Hodges asked, patiently allowing a pause in which Clark might answer. "Please, Lewis, we know that he used your van. Now, if you don't want to get into trouble, just tell me how Rocket got it."

"I lent it to my brother."

"And . . . ?"

"Rocket took it from him at a party."

"He just took the van?"

"My brother was afraid."

"More afraid of Rocket than of you?"

Lewis didn't answer.

"Just so we understand each other—I don't want you. I want Rocket. But he and his cuzzes used your van in a drive-by. So I can book you, too, unless you want to help me—"

Then McGavin burst into the interrogation room, laughing.

Hodges frowned, wondering what was going on, ready to ask McGavin why he wasn't still with the fat kid in his own interrogation cubicle.

Clark didn't know what to make of the intrusion,

although he appeared to be taking McGavin's laughter personally.

"Relax," McGavin told him, "I'm not busting a gut at you." He turned to Hodges: "You know what fat Willie just told me?" He laughed again. "You know that foxy chick hangs out with Cheryl Williams and Annie?"

"I don't think so," Hodges said cautiously.

"Sure . . . you know who I mean. This is wild, man—sexy little thing, you know? Shit. Lewis, what the fuck is the name of that girl?"

"Sharon?"

"Right. Uh, Sharon . . ." McGavin began snapping his fingers. "Sharon . . ."

"Robbins?"

"Robbins!"

Slowly, Hodges came to his feet, then, still expressionless, tilted his head toward the door for McGavin to follow.

Outside in the corridor, he whispered, "Fucking inspired, McGavin!"

"Then I'm not a total screw-up?"

Hodges smiled. "Maybe not a total."

McGavin, Hodges, and Bill Young made a pact to say nothing to Rusty Baines about his having wrecked his car in pursuit of three scared kids whose only link to Robert Craig's homicide had been Rocket's power to intimidate everyone who lived on his turf. In saying nothing to the Homicide detective about his faux pas, the three CRASH cops figured they would get on his nerves more effectively than if they were to trade insults with him. The overgrown redhead thrived on insults the way a maggot prospered on garbage.

Baines would ramrod the raid on Sharon Robbins's house because it was Homicide's case. And so he assembled the detail of CRASH cops and Southeast patrolmen a few blocks from the target.

Still not sure what to make of the trio's polite silence, he stood alone at the open trunk of a borrowed unmarked car, snicking rounds into the magazine tube of his shotgun.

Despite his exhaustion, Hodges chuckled to himself. "Love it."

"Yeah," Young said, hushed. "This little TC may be enough to make that motherfucker humble for months."

"I doubt it." McGavin was strapping on a military-style flak jacket when Young shook his head.

"Don't wear it, baby."

"Why not?"

"I mean it's up to you, man. I know the department hands those things out and all. But we ain't going up against mortar and rocket shrapnel—I fucking *hope*. I learned about them green bastards in 'Nam. All one of them does is flatten out a bullet. It turns a ninemillimeter round you might survive into something as wide as a cannonball you *won't* survive."

McGavin shed the jacket. For once, he looked grateful. "Thanks, Bill . . . I didn't know that."

Hodges nodded. Maybe McGavin *was* coming around. He thought he might reconsider what he had told Captain Melindez. Joan would give him the devil for backpedaling, but it wouldn't be the first time.

The sun wasn't so much rising as appearing to bulge up through the leaden marine layer of clouds. It'd be a crappy morning to die, he thought, giving himself a chill. He came close to asking McGavin for a smoke before he calmed down again.

God, I'm sick to death of these things. To McGavin it's great fun . . . as it probably was to me once. But Bill Young and I have been far too lucky on far too

*many of these gigs not to know that one day a man's
luck runs out . . . and he leaves the scene in the coroner's white station wagon. And a year later not ten guys
in his unit can recall his name. . . .*

"All right," Baines said, "huddle up here and let's
get going." He tried to ignore the smiles the trio gave
him. "We are hitting a single-family dwelling, cinder-
block construction, red in color."

"I don't recall it right off," one of the Southeast
guys asked. "This a rock house?"

"Maybe."

"Meaning what, Baines?"

"Meaning it's got steel front doors, probably bought
surplus from Fort Knox."

"What about bars on the windows?"

"Negative. And that's why I say maybe on it being a
rock house. We'll sure as hell be the first to find out."

"What about letting Metro have this one?" someone asked uncertainly.

"No time. We got information Rocket is inside with
this Robbins broad. This morning. Now."

"How we gonna get through those doors, Baines?"

The detective turned and smugly pointed down the
street at a city tow truck waiting in the gray dawn
twilight. "Winch the motherfucker off. Any other
questions, you little whiny-ass sissies?"

Danny had worked a summer on a wrecker as a kid,
so he volunteered to attach the end of the cable to the
doors. And Bill Young offered to accompany him up
onto the sagging wooden porch.

In the last minutes before they kicked off, with the
freeway traffic whispering in the distance like a cold
wind, Young asked the tow-truck driver for a crowbar.
"This is how I put myself through fucking school," he
explained to Danny as he slipped it into his empty
baton ring.

Danny laughed softly.

"You think I'm kidding?"

Then they both crawled up onto the back of the truck.

Young rubbed a shiver off the backs of his bare arms. "My imagination or is it chilly out here?"

"No, it's cold . . . it's always cold under these low clouds." Danny was watching a corner of the red house, the only part of the structure he could glimpse from here. Down the block, Hodges, who'd already set up on the place with a gauge, hand-signaled that the patrolmen were in position along the sides and around the back.

The tow rig started inching forward noiselessly but for the faint rumble of the idle. The driver had been replaced by one of the Southeast blue-suitters, who had an Ithaca cradled across his arms as he steered.

Hodges, having taken cover behind the engine block of a fenderless Valiant, kept his focus on the windows of the red house across the street.

He motioned with a flick of his fingers for the truck to keep coming; there was no sign of movement within.

Young twisted around and tapped softly on the cab with the butt of his handgun, signaling for the patrolman to halt.

He and Danny bounded off the truck. McGavin trotted to the front and knelt before the winch.

Young squatted beside him, his revolver trained on the front doors while Danny grasped the steel hook in his hands and began playing out the cable, duckwalking while Young continued to provide security for him.

He felt good about Young. It wasn't just that Bill had his head on straight: there was something in Young's manner this morning that told Danny he was getting a second chance. He honestly didn't want to blow it.

They made it to the porch with nothing happening other than a dog barking a few streets over.

Danny was preparing to loop the cable around the door handles when Young whispered, "Hang on a sec. Think I can get this with old Jim Crow here. Less noise that way."

Danny nodded—it'd be sweet to get the absolute drop on the bastards inside. That way, nothing would make it to the toilet bowl. Not an ounce.

Young was busy prying when he suddenly froze. Then, squinting in confusion, he pressed his ear against the clammy steel of one of the doors.

Then Danny could hear the sound, too. The urgency in it make him drop the cable and unholster his sidearm.

"Jesus," he said, hushed, "is somebody getting *killed* in there?"

Young snorted, controlled himself, then laughed helplessly again.

"What?" Danny asked.

Young leaned close to his ear: "Who you been fucking? Helen Keller?"

Danny stared at him a moment. "You mean that's fucking?"

"I mean that's *fucking*, homes." Then Young compressed his lips and gently tapped the point of the crowbar under the lock plate.

Danny glanced back. Hodges was hunching his shoulders as if to ask what Young and he were hearing. McGavin formed a circle with two fingers and ran the middle finger of his other hand through it several times.

Hodges nodded appreciatively.

Danny kept watch on the front windows, the doors, even listening for movement under the porch.

A grinning Bill Young then gave the high-sign—he'd cracked the door.

Hodges and Baines came trotting flat-footed across the street, the detective whispering into his radio handset. This would send two patrolmen crawling through the bathroom window, whose glass they would ream out at any instant with their batons.

Danny stood up, ready to barrel through the door. This would be a no-knock warrant, his favorite kind. He shifted his Smith and Wesson to his left hand for a moment, wiped his sweaty right palm on his trousers before closing it around the grips once again.

He could sense Hodges behind him, but didn't look back. His entire being was transfixed on the steel doors.

Then, smoothly, Young slid one door open, and Danny charged through, keeping low as he wheeled his revolver at eye level completely across the small living room.

"Police!" he bellowed. "Nobody moves!"

Empty. He saw right away that the room was empty.

He finished the sweep by covering the hallway while Hodges, Young, and Baines thundered in, guns held at the ready.

"This one's clear," Danny told them.

From the bathroom down the hallway came the sounds of shattering glass and then another cry of "Police!" from the Southeast patrolmen making the second entry.

Unbelievably, through all of this racket, the moaning and wails of ecstasy went on, rising to even more fervent crescendos. Unless the young woman was being subjected to water torture, Young was right: this was indeed fucking. World-class, Olympic-caliber fucking.

Then Danny quit making jokes inside his head. His mouth was too parched for him to feel like laughing.

On Hodges's terse nod, Danny advanced to the first door along the corridor—the one from which issued the amorous screaming.

Sliding his forefinger off the trigger for a jarring instant, he kicked the door in.

"Freeze!" This time he had two people in his sights.

The young man, whose naked back was presented to Danny's muzzle, went motionless, as did the young woman peeking huge-eyed around his shoulder—except for the hysterical batting of her lashes at the blue suit looming over the foot of her bed.

"Shit," Hodges said behind Danny, "that's not Rocket . . . we don't have Rocket!"

"What?" Baines could be heard lumbering around in the hallway. "Don't fucking tell me! I did everything but blow the judge for this warrant!"

What happened next was over and done forever in a split second.

Less than a split second.

A microsecond.

And only later, in boozy retrospection, was Danny able to shave that microsecond into individual slices of time, each a still frame capturing an action that in reality had come and gone before the more judicious side of his brain could apprehend what had happened.

The black youth sprawling atop Sharon Robbins was not the sullen Rocket.

He was the more affable Killer Bee, who turned his head, looking sheepish. And, in his defense, there was a feeling in the dim bedroom that the confrontation was over.

While the wrinkle lines were crinkling the back of Killer Bee's neck as he twisted around to have a look, Danny could hear shoes crunching across broken glass on the bathroom floor.

And it seemed that while all this was still happening, unfolding like a horror movie in slow motion,

Danny started to scream for Killer Bee not to budge, but before the words could get out of his mouth the youth was hopping up off the mattress and reaching for something under the bed.

Danny began to squeeze back his trigger.

He visualized a gun. He fully expected Killer Bee to come up with a roscoe blazing.

Later, it seemed to him that he saw the white muzzle flash but didn't hear the explosive report. And then, puzzlingly, he realized that the flash had come out of the bathroom door, which was now bouncing off the bedroom wall, having been thrown open by one of the Southeast cops who'd just crawled through the window.

Killer Bee was bent over, a misty spout of blood coming out his back and spraying the wall behind him.

"Hold it!" Hodges shouted somewhere in the swirling midst of all this. "Stop! *Fuck!*"

He fell on his knees beside the bed and tried to help Killer Bee stem the bleeding, which was the most shocking red Danny had ever seen.

But it was no good.

Killer Bee knew he was dead, and his face got small and pinched and scared like a hurt kid's. Danny knew right then that this was the face Bee's mother would see whenever she closed her eyes from now on.

"Homes, homes . . ." Hodges sounded like he was crying, although his eyes were dry and hard. "Why'd you move? Why!"

Killer Bee's face was no longer a rich brown. It was the color of peanut shells. And it looked more amazed than anything else. "I was putting my fucking pants on, Hodges."

Then he died.

Hodges groaned and backed away. "Shit!"

Still bewildered by what had happened, not trusting

his own eyes, Danny broke open his cylinder as quickly as his trembling hands would allow.

Six undented primers—he hadn't fired.

He'd thought so, but now he was positive. . . . It had all happened so fucking *fast.*

Yet, oddly enough, Sharon was glaring at him and not at the stunned-looking patrolman standing on the shards of glass in the bathroom. She glared at Danny McGavin as she shook Killer Bee by the slack shoulders as if trying to awaken him. "No! No!" But at last she accepted, and her eyes turned icy. "You motherfucker! *Pac-Man!* I kill you, Pac-Man!"

As if drifting out of a trance, Danny realized that he was still aiming his revolver at her.

Mechanically, he returned it to his holster and snapped the safety strap over the hammer.

He tried to think of something to say. But nothing came to mind.

Then he stepped past Baines in the doorway and went out for some air.

A fucking microsecond.

CHAPTER 15

THEY RECLINED IN A CLUTCH OF OLD CAR SEATS AT THE dead end of an alley, the homies from Crip de Ville and Sharon Robbins.

She had a rock pipe between her pouty lips, and T-Bone held the match for her. Smiling, she clamped her hand around his wrist to keep the flame steady as she inhaled. "Thanks, Bone."

He smiled back at her—but it was a hook smile without much feeling in it.

Rocket was leaning against a brick wall close by, on the edge of the gig, looking down, because his main man, his ace cool—Killer Bee—was dead. But maybe he looked that way, too, because Killer Bee had been porking his lady when the cops lit up his ass.

Now Sharon was giving T-Bone warm, slanty looks, and T-Bone didn't really like it all that much, because he knew something she didn't: Rocket was packing today. That lump under his colors was a four-five, Mr. Colt. And when Rocket jammed somebody, that body could wind up dead, fast.

"Shit," Sharon whispered, suddenly looking straight up at the little bit of blue sky that showed—maybe like there were ghosts in that wispy blue or something. Her eyes got all wet around the lids, and she sniffled loud enough to make Rocket glance over her way. "Poor old Bee . . ." She wiped her nose on her jacket sleeve. "He didn't have no roscoe. He didn't have shit. Old Bee just kicking back . . ." She was looking at her red-painted nails when she said this last thing, and Rocket turned away, disgusted.

"Motherfucker," somebody said low, meaning The Man, the one who'd blown away Killer Bee.

"Lately that fucker bump titties with everybody. . . . He gone . . . he gone now."

"I hear he jacking up the esseys, too."

"Jacking the whole fucking town . . . all the hoods, man."

"He gone."

"That righteous." Rocket spoke for the first time in a long while. His eyes were all shiny, and his lips curled like he had a bad taste inside his mouth. "Cops . . . like cockroaches . . . can't never kill them all. Ain't possible . . ." Without warning, he grinned, a terrible grin that reminded T-Bone of all the things he'd seen Rocket do: the hits and the other things he called *discipline*. "But you can kill the biggest roach . . . that you can do, my cuzzes."

"He gone . . . he gone . . ."

The trouble with night watch was that it made for empty, restless afternoons.

Danny awoke around eleven with painfully bright sunlight streaming in through his bedroom window.

He fried two eggs, smothered them with salsa, and downed the steaming mess with a cold beer.

After cleaning up, he realized that he had nothing else to do until work tonight.

Once again, breaking a resolution not to do so, he picked up the phone and dialed Louisa's house. And again, no answer.

She should have returned from Sacramento two days before.

Maybe she was really enjoying her sister's company, Danny told himself, although this rationalization was beginning to wear thin.

Or maybe something was wrong with her phone.

No way would he drop by her house again. He'd already put her in danger by that first confrontation with the White Fence homeboys. And maybe that explained her continued absence: she was scared to come home and wanted to let the hood cool down a bit.

He wished like hell that he'd asked her for her sister's number. He didn't even know the woman's married name.

"Christ . . ." Danny drifted around his apartment, hands stuffed in his pockets, a Marlboro dangling from the corner of his mouth.

Strange—but after watching Killer Bee die, he'd really needed to hold Louisa in his arms. It was still bothering him: the picture of blood spouting out of the Bee's bare back. And he somehow believed that the image wouldn't leave him alone until he could erase it with Louisa's tender presence.

Then an idea hit him. He grabbed his leather jacket and hurried down to the carport. He fired up his Mustang and sped toward the freeway.

Twenty minutes later he was pulling up in front of the chicken shack.

He was glad to see that Louisa wasn't working. He

wouldn't know what to do or say if he found out that she'd returned and not told him.

Smiling through the order window at the Chicana waitress, he said, "I'm Danny."

Her eyes revealed nothing.

"When's Louisa coming back to work? You heard?" She shrugged noncommittally.

"See, I'm dating her . . . going with her, I guess. Is she back from her sister's yet?"

Finally, the waitress said something, but her voice was low, seething almost.

"What?" Danny leaned closer.

She repeated what she'd said.

After a moment in which he just stood there, his face expressionless, he wheeled angrily and rushed back to his car. "Thanks, sis!"

It'd been a long time since he'd gotten the *no habla* business from anybody in this barrio.

"Porter, my man," T-Bone said to the black patrolman who'd just blocked the Crip's path by parking his LAPD hoopty where an alley crossed the sidewalk. He jutted his chin at the Hispanic cop who was getting out of the cruiser, having radioed in the F.I. "They still got you teamed with the essey?"

"Hey, he's my main man, Bone."

T-Bone figured that this was a field interrogation. Just a few minutes of jiving with The Man; then he could be on his way.

But suddenly, smoothly, Porter whipped out his cuffs. Before T-Bone could mutter "shit," his hands were manacled behind him.

A few yards away a peewee sat at one of the picnic tables in front of a Burger King. T-Bone red-eyed him to make sure he would listen up and report this back to Rocket, without fail.

"Shee-it, Porter, what you on me for, man?"

"I'm not, Bone. I *got* to take you in."

"Jesus, man, I took care all them warrants. You know that. Cost me seven hundred dollar."

"Different kind of hold." Porter began guiding T-Bone toward the caged backseat of the black-and-white. "Something else entirely, homes."

"Say what?"

"Hold come down from your P.O."

"Who?"

"Remember that dude you're supposed to check in with every now and again?"

"I seen that mother just last week."

"Oh, well, in that case . . ." Porter opened the back door and cushioned the top of T-Bone's head as he ordered him to get in.

"This chickenshit, man."

"P.O. thinks so, too. Says you promised him you'd find a different class of friends."

"Shit, what's a brother to do down here? You gonna invite me for dinner next Sunday, Porter? Where you live, man? Out San Fernando Valley? Should I bring my own lady, or you got a daughter you fix me up with?"

The patrolman just laughed.

"This hook bullshit—I know it," T-Bone went on, catching the peewee's eye one last time. "Something else going on, Porter. Maybe you hear some hoo-rah about a war coming and now you taking everybody down . . . *fuck!*"

Rocket sat atop a packing crate, caressing the Uzi submachine gun with an oily piece of felt.

Moonlight streamed down through the high windows of the abandoned warehouse, fell in pale squares across the dirty cement floor, and caught his Crips sleeping on mattresses set down in rows.

Crip de Ville had taken to the mattresses.

Rocket had gotten the idea from *The Godfather,* his favorite movie, which he'd seen more times than he could count. His real name was Michael, too, and like Michael Corleone he probably spent too much time brooding. But he had his people to watch over, and these sleeping forms were his people, his soldiers.

Each had his weapon laid out beside him within reach: revolvers and pistols and gauges and rifles and a few full autos, like the Uzi he was clutching.

In the corner were canned goods and other foodstuffs—enough to last a week, if need be. And the water still ran in the rest room taps.

Crip de Ville had enemies on all sides, and Rocket wasn't sure which of them would attack first. But he and his cuzzes were ready.

He heard a car coming and went quietly to the window to look down on the alley around whose far end headlamps came glancing.

A yellow Pontiac crept into view.

He cracked the window and tracked the battered vehicle over the sights of the Uzi.

But he didn't open fire, and the Pontiac finally made a left turn onto the street south of the warehouse.

Rocket lowered the Uzi and sneered.

In lordly silence, Leo Lopez was playing hearts with three other *veteranos* in the dayroom area of the jail dormitory—and half-listening to two *tintos* shooting the shit with each other, one on a top bunk, one on a lower.

"I heard that, T-Bone," the one on the lower bunk said. "I sure did."

"Shit," the other drawled. "I got cool with these niggers, you know? So I take up they enemies, right? I represent the set. Wherever I go, I *am* the set. . . ."

The *veterano* sitting across from Leo must have

been eavesdropping, too, for he suddenly shook his head and said quietly, "Fucking *tinto.*"

Leo cut him short with a glare: he wanted to hear this. A stupid traffic warrant following a stupid ticket he couldn't afford to pay had landed him in these blue denim "counties" and *puto* slip-on *carcos*—with no *zacate,* Corona, or pussy for another four days. As long as he was stuck here, he wanted to learn something, something to trade later, maybe.

"Okay with me, Frog," the *veterano* said, his eyes drifting back to his cards.

". . . Kicking back with the homeboys," the one called T-Bone went on, chuckling at his cool self, "pulling that crazy shit."

"Right on, my man."

"I like that crazy shit, you know. Go bust, you know. Catch somebody—stick 'em, bust 'em, stabbing—"

"Mobbing the houses, beating fools down, blasting my enemies. Yeah!"

The two *tintos* slapped hands.

"Go partying, you know," T-Bone said. "Go this freak house over here, cuz. You know, leave cuz over here . . . go over this freak house, cuz over there. Cuz sleeping on the floor."

"Say what?"

"Yeah, Rocket hiding out. Po-lice got Killer Bee . . . shit." Then T-Bone giggled. "Caught cuz putting his fuel in Rocket's lady, right? Fuck—shot that nigger full of lead man. Motherfucker is a pencil man. Police come in . . . say *shit*—he hands up, bare-ass naked . . . and blew him away!"

"That's cold, man."

"Fuck, right on. That's Pac-Man, though," T-Bone lowered his voice, but Leo Lopez still heard him say: "We gonna be biting on his ass . . . soon."

* * *

Loud knocking startled Danny out of a fitful nap.

His hand fumbled under the sofa for his revolver as he rolled off the cushions onto the carpet.

The television was murmuring on low volume, not the game show host who'd made Danny drowsy, but Malloy and Reed being their squeaky-clean professional selves in another rerun of *Adam 12*. He switched off the set and padded quietly to his front door, stood to one side.

"Who's there?" he demanded.

"Put the fucking gun down and open the door!" came Hodges's impatient voice.

Danny glanced at his revolver, smiled, then sprang the dead bolt.

Hodges strolled in, eyeing the wheelgun. "Good guess, huh?"

"Just lucky."

"You always sleep in your clothes?"

"I faded, man."

"Me, too . . . years ago," Hodges confessed, sinking into the armchair with a sigh, closing his swollen eyelids. "Sweet Jesus."

"You look like shit."

"Feel like shit." He opened his eyes when he sniffed the smoke from the Marlboro Danny had just lit. "Gimme one of those motherfuckers."

Danny's eyes widened a little. "You sure?"

"Yeah, yeah . . . come on." He ran the cigarette under his nose before lighting up. "Just don't ever tell Joan. She'll hire two hitmen outta that quit-everything-you-love-to-do treatment center to tear out my lungs. Cost a small fortune to get me off these the first time." He took two puffs, then grimaced and crushed it in the ashtray. "What the crap do I mean first time? Son of a bitch."

"You doing okay, Bob?"

He smiled, but it was a sick and tired smile. "Just ducky. How about yourself?"

Danny met Hodges's gaze for a moment, then rose and got them each a beer from the refrigerator. "I don't know how I'm doing."

The sarcasm left Hodges's voice. "How's that?"

Danny gave him a lopsided grin. "You know, I thought I'd be tickled shitless to see that asshole laying dead there in his own blood. . . ." He took a long swallow instead of going on.

"And how *do* you feel?" Hodges asked after a moment.

"I wish Louisa was here."

"She's not back yet?"

Danny shook his head.

"Still up north?"

"I guess."

"She'll be back soon."

"Sure." Then Danny brightened. "Hey, do you like to play pool?"

"Love it—but not today. Don't you answer your phone?"

"What do you mean?"

"Lieutenant's been trying to call you all morning."

"I was out . . . driving."

"Well, we got a Use of Force Review hearing at one—in case you forgot."

Danny slapped his forehead. "Shit!"

"Once again I save your worthless career for you . . . snatch you out of the pink jaws of termination."

"Christ, I don't know how it could have slipped my mind."

"I do," Hodges said, his voice soft and grim. Then he looked as if he wanted to bring up something else, but quickly changed his mind.

* * *

"Louisa?" her mother's Spanish came through the door. "Are you in there? Are you well?"

She lifted her face off the moist pillowcase. "I'm fine. Go away."

"Do you know why the telephone has been unplugged? Louisa, do you hear me?"

She buried her face in the pillow again, stopped her ears with her fingertips.

"*Hija,* we are not going to have *this* again now, are we? Not after two years now, are we? Louisa?"

After a while, her mother went away from the door.

As Danny joined the other officers on the bench in the corridor outside the hearing room at Parker Center, the cop on the end cracked the swinging door a little so they could all listen. The witnesses were being excluded from the room so each man wouldn't have the opportunity to tailor his testimony to that given by his brother officers—and to whitewash the man who'd been compelled to use lethal force. Yet nobody on the bench objected when the guy at the end of the bench opened the door a bit.

It was all bullshit anyway. The commanding officer of Personnel and Training was intoning like he was conducting a high mass: "The use of a firearm is in all probability the most serious act in which a law-enforcement officer will engage. It has the most far-reaching consequences for all of the parties involved. A reverence for the value of human life shall guide officers in considering the use of deadly force. . . ."

Rusty Baines, his wide buttocks occupying enough space for two cops, cupped his hand above his lap and began stroking.

"Don't be shitting us, Rusty," Bill Young said. "Get that hand closer in where it belongs."

"Fuck you, Young."

"With that itty bitty thing? Be a waste of my time, baby."

Danny reached inside the blue blazer he wore for court, but then realized that this corridor had recently been designated a no-smoking area. Ninety-eight percent of California was now a no-smoking area. Put the no-smoking activists in charge of arms control and there'd be no nukes in five years, tops.

". . . As long as members of the public," the echoing voice went on, "are victims of violent crimes and officers in the performance of their duties are confronted with deadly force, it will remain necessary for police officers to be properly armed for the protection of society and themselves. . . ."

Danny yawned. Day sleep was never as good as night sleep.

". . . An officer is equipped with a firearm to protect himself or others against the immediate threat of death or serious bodily injury or to apprehend a fleeing felon who has committed a violent crime and whose escape presents a substantial risk of death or . . ."

Danny leaned forward to glance down the glimmering waxed corridor: as soon as they'd arrived, Hodges had pulled Captain Melindez and Lieutenant Reed aside for a whispering gig that was still in progress. Chalking it up to paranoia, Danny sensed that they were talking about him.

". . . Justification for the use of deadly force must be limited to what reasonably appears to be the facts known or perceived by an officer at the time he decides to shoot. . . ."

"Aye, there's the rub," Bill Young whispered under his breath.

Baines sneered. "I didn't know you people were into Shakespeare."

"Shit, baby, what you think Othello was? Shanty fucking Irish like you?"

Baines was thinking up a retort when the door suddenly whooshed shut on the sound of approaching footfalls, then opened again a few seconds later.

"Reginald Baines," an impeccable lieutenant from the Office of Operations summoned.

"Present, sir."

"Present, sir," one of the guys mimicked, but in a voice two octaves higher than Baines's voice.

"Hold it down out here," the lieutenant warned.

Everyone's face went to granite until he and Baines were gone inside.

"Oh shit oh dear," Young mumbled.

The door was cracked opened once again, and Baines's bullshit wafted out into the corridor: "Yes, sir, that is correct. We knocked. We identified ourselves as Los Angeles police officers . . ."

Young tossed his eyes. "That was a *no-knock* warrant. That stupid fuck lies even when he don't have to!"

Feeling increasingly antsy, Danny got up and strolled down the corridor to the swinging door that gave access to that half of the hearing room. He gazed through the small, chicken wire–laced window at the poor bastard who'd done the capping and caused all this inconvenience.

He looked like the loneliest man in the world. Either that or he was suffering from the intestinal flu—he had about that much color left in his face.

There but for two more pounds of pressure on the trigger go I.

On the drive over, Hodges had confessed that in his third year, while with Seventy-seventh Street Patrol, he'd broken up an armed robbery and wasted the perp. Blown his head clean off his shoulders with a gauge. "And from that moment on, for months afterward, McGavin, it was like my whole life was a sack of garbage . . . like somebody had turned it upside down and dumped it on the fucking floor for dogs to root in."

Danny turned as somebody came up behind him—Captain Melindez, looking severe as hell as he said, "A word, McGavin."

"How many syllables and how many guesses I got, sir?"

Melindez red-eyed him for a few seconds until he seemed to realize that it was a pathetic stab at a joke—Danny was more nervous than he'd thought; still, the captain didn't smile. "Let's go."

Hodges looked so hangdog and Lieutenant Reed so apologetic that Danny immediately figured he'd been bumped as Uncle Bob's partner sooner than he'd planned. And, as if he were reading Danny's thoughts, Hodges planted a firm hand on his shoulder. "Listen, McGavin—"

"Yeah?" Danny interrupted, not meaning to. His heart was racing.

"I'm gonna tell you something now. Some bad news I got this morning."

Danny felt the blood drop out of his face: something else, something far worse, had occurred to him.

Louisa was dead. He was sure of it.

And suddenly everything fit: no word from her over these past days; for the first time ever, Hodges had dropped by his apartment this morning; and Bob had seemed on the verge of broaching something he'd then tabled. Fucking White Fence had snuffed her for taking The Man as her lover—and poor Hodges had wanted moral support from the captain and the lieutenant before breaking it to Danny.

"Is it . . . is Louisa okay?"

Hodges looked confused for a moment. "Sure, I suppose. Have you heard anything?"

"No, it's just that—"

"Shit." Hodges said, realizing what Danny was thinking. "No, man . . . this has nothing to do with her. Jesus, sorry I gave that impression."

Danny nodded. "All right then, what gives?"

Hodges glanced at both Melindez and Reed before coming back to Danny. "It's out on the street that you shot Killer Bee."

Danny gave a bewildered chuckle. "What?"

"McGavin," Reed said, "it wasn't you, now, was it?"

"Me? Hell no, I even cleared my weapon with the Shooting Investigation Team."

"Did he?" the captain asked Hodges.

"Absolutely. Killer Bee suffered only one thoracic bullet wound—and died of it. S.I.T. came up with only one spent casing. It was still in the Southeast patrolman's cylinder."

"Wait a minute," Danny said. "Shouldn't this discussion be going on *inside* the hearing room? At least in there I can have an attorney beside me."

Melindez spun on him, but kept his voice to a whisper: "We're trying to help you, man! Maybe even trying to save your fucking life—you understand?"

"No, sir, I honestly don't."

"I'll try to explain, Captain," Hodges said. "Look McGavin, my informant overheard a conversation he wasn't supposed to. They've marked you. They're going to ride on you."

"Wait, wait . . ." Danny ran his fingers through his hair. "Obviously I am missing something here. I did not shoot Killer Bee. Now, granted, things were pretty fucking confused in that bedroom. But I did *not* do it."

"Doesn't matter." Hodges's tone of voice was so matter-of-fact that Danny felt a flash of anger.

"Who says?"

"Bob's got a point," Reed said, looking more worried than Danny could recall. "Truth is just the consensus out on them streets. You shot the Bee because every swinging dick out there *thinks* you dropped the hammer. That's just the way it is, McGavin."

"They are not gonna shoot a cop!"

The three older men simply stared at him for a moment. Then Melindez said to Hodges: "What about working the obvious angle on this?"

"Have my informant testify?"

The captain nodded. "Why not? Who told you this?"

"Rather not say."

"Then have it your way. We won't ask him to snizzle on his buddies."

"His cellmates—he's up at County right now on a traffic warrant. He's probably still banging from time to time, so he'll never testify. It's just that he owed me this one. And if we burn him, nobody in this unit will get shit for a long time to come."

"I hear you," Reed said.

"Well, that leaves me one option." Sighing, Melindez leveled his eyes at Danny's.

"You gonna have me ride a desk for a while, sir?"

"I can't afford another desk jockey—already have three men on light duty as is. No, we've got to transfer you, preferably someplace quiet with a minimal amount of gang-banging going on—West Valley, the airport substation, someplace."

"Look, Captain, why let them scare me off the street? Why let them think they've won? Why give them the satisfaction? Besides, I don't want somebody else taking my bullet—if it comes to that. How would you feel living with that, sir?"

For the first time, Melindez nodded as if he understood. Reed even grinned at him.

"Look, sir, I'm okay."

Melindez looked to Hodges and asked the big question with a slight shrug.

Hodges didn't say a word for what seemed forever, then said like he meant it: "He's okay."

Melindez and Reed were on their way to afternoon coffee when the captain asked, "Shit, Wally, did I just do the right thing by those two?"

"Motherfucker!" Reed shouted out the window and leaned on the horn as a silver Mercedes cut him off. "Your ass be grass if I was back in Traffic." Then, instantly, he relaxed again. "I think so, Cap. Bob Hodges knows what he's doing."

"But what do you think of this McGavin kid?"

"Don't know. He's still in that formative stage. Can go either way—best man in the unit or fucking hoodlum in blue. Always that way with the thoroughbreds. And he's got spunk. See him stand up to us? If a man's scared of us potbellied old poops, what those gang-bangers going to do to him?" He smiled slyly. "Hodges was that way. That's why they're not getting along worth a shit. Too much alike, deep down. 'Nobody but me's taking my bullet'—that's vintage Hodges. Not many folks remember way back then, but Bobby Hodges was nine parts piss to one part perfume, until something good clicked inside. Until the *man* came alive. He won't deny it neither."

"You know what I just did in there, don't you, Wally?"

"What's that?"

"By letting McGavin go back out, I just forced us to batten down the hatches. I threw down the gauntlet."

Reed considered this for a moment, then asked, "Georgia Street, then?"

"Yeah . . . Christ."

Reed turned back for Central Police Facility on Georgia Street in the heart of skid row. This windowless monolith housed Metro division. "Shake, rattle, and roll," he voiced Metro's unofficial motto.

CHAPTER 16

THE SPECIAL OPERATION BEGAN AS A FLURRY OF TELE-
phone calls coming into Central Police Facility on the
evening before.

The background noise was the homey sound of a
television or the clinking of bar glasses or the hollow
knocking of bowling pins or a church organ or traffic
whooshing past a booth. But all the callers asked the
same thing: "Mode of dress and detail?"

And to each the young woman on Georgia Street
said: "Uniform and CRASH, South Bureau."

Some exclaimed, "All right!"

Others were less enthusiastic: "Shit, can't they keep
their own nest clean?"

Nevertheless, by 2300 hours that evening, the men
of Platoons B and C—the department's crime sup-
pression field units—had a rough idea what the next

day had in store for them and went off to their rest, or lack of it. Metropolitan division had an inordinate number of divorced men in its ranks; but some considered alimony and child support an acceptable price to pay to belong to the most elite division in L.A.P.D., arguably the best division of its kind in the entire U.S. law-enforcement community.

At 0700 hours the next morning, two police buses sallied forth from Central Police Facility, trailed by a navy blue delivery van containing enough shotguns, M16 rifles, ammunition, and non-lethal chemical agents to occupy Luxembourg or Monaco or even Belize indefinitely.

Inside each bus were fifty cops in blues. Some were dozing, trying to catch up on some of the sleep they'd done without the night before. Others were wolfing down doughnuts or Twinkies in the name of breakfast, although none was fat. One was attempting to entertain his hung-over buddy with armpit farts—and not succeeding: "Knock that shit off, Hutch."

But as the convoy pulled into the parking lot of Southeast station, a transformation came over them. The interiors of the buses went quiet as the platoons surveyed the black-and-whites and paddy wagons that had been assembled here for their use. Then, calmly, the men began reaching for their personal gear.

Metro was ready to shake, rattle, and roll.

And by 0900 hours that same morning, the southside gangs were feeling much like Luxembourg or Monaco or Belize would if suddenly invaded.

Spooky sprinted down the alley, hoping that he'd shaken off the two cops who'd ordered him to halt and then given chase when he refused. But he wasn't ready to stop yet, even though his lungs were burning and a metallic taste was coating the inside of his mouth.

Never before had he seen The Man in such numbers

—and not just the Southeast pigs, but unfamiliar ones who took no shit off anybody and could run damn near as fast as a fifteen-year-old cuz.

Spooky knew where he was headed, but also realized that he couldn't go there directly, especially with two cops hot on his ass.

Checking out the street from the building corner at the end of the alley, he could see a cruiser several blocks distant, its lights blinking red and blue. But those cops were busy shaking down some cuzzes next to the school yard, so he darted across the asphalt and scaled a six-foot chain-link fence, dropped into a small field of dry weeds, which rustled against his jeans as he trotted through them. On the far side he ran up a wooden fence, which was tottering and ready to fall, and followed the alley beyond into a row of houses that had been condemned for a new freeway—except that the freeway dudes then ran out of money, so these places had been vacant a long time now. Rocket said that they'd always be empty, that there'd be less and less money and more and more vacant houses, and that a cuz had to stick to his set, his brothers, because things were getting worse all the time and the set was all a cuz really had in this cold, fucking world.

Spooky glanced over his shoulder: for once, no cops in sight.

However, he purposely jogged beyond the house with faded blue stucco and dirt-clod pocks all over its walls before doubling back at the next corner and coming down the frontage, finally stopping past the shattered windows on the side of the blue house. "It's me . . . it's Spooky, man," he whispered.

Last night about ten, when they were all holed up in the old warehouse off Central Avenue, Rocket had said that he'd had a vision, and that it was no good to

stay inside that place on account of too many brothers
—and not all of them Crips—being on to the place.
So two of the cuzzes went out and hot-wired a Buick
Electra, all gleaming and pretty, sitting in a church
parking lot, and Rocket ordered everything moved in
shifts to this new place.

The Electra was now hidden in the garage on the
alley behind the house. Checking the alley first,
Spooky knocked five times on the back door. He
could hear the two-by-four wedged against the door
being taken down.

Rocket himself opened up, ready to pop caps with
his Uzi. "Get your ass in here quick." He pulled
Spooky inside by the sleeve of his T-shirt, and two
cuzzes propped the two-by-four back in place.

Spooky took a lot of fast breaths so he could talk.

"What you running for like that?" Rocket asked, his
eyes mean and narrow.

"The Man everywhere, like four to a hoopty, and
these black-and-whites is all over the place."

Rocket digested this, frowning.

"And new cops . . . these new cops I never seen."

"Metro, then. They jamming us with Metro. What
else?"

Spooky didn't want to say what had to be said next,
but knew that Rocket would beat him if he found out
about it from somebody else. "They asking about the
hit on Pac-Man."

Rocket's eyes caught fire—it made Spooky glance
down at the dirty linoleum.

"What?"

"The Man *knows.*"

"You tell him?"

"No! No, Rocket! No fucking way I drop the dime!"

Rocket stared at Spooky a chilling moment longer,
then seized him by the back of his hair and dragged

him into the living room and started kicking the bare feet of the cuzzes who were still sleeping on the mattresses there.

"Spooky say they on to the hit!" he raged.

The cuzzes inched back against the walls like worms in their sleeping bags.

"Who been talking?"

Everybody clammed up, and the only way Rocket got somebody to speak was to cuff him hard across the face with the back of his hand.

"Rocket, my man," Shooter said, wiping the blood away from the corner of his mouth, "we all been here with you . . . just you all the time."

This made Rocket think for a few seconds. "Yeah . . . yeah . . ."

He backed away from Shooter, who looked relieved that Rocket was finished pugging. "Then who ain't here? That's the fucking question."

"T-Bone, he be up at County," another cuz quickly volunteered.

"Yeah . . ." Rocket said, like he was on to something now. "That's righteous." His eyes fixed on Spooky's. "You got no tattoos yet, do you?"

"Not yet."

"Good, you going out again."

Spooky wanted to groan, but knew better.

"Take off that black T-shirt, get one what's white from somebody. Leave your rag here. And no colors no how."

"Where I go, Rocket?"

"Find one of T-Bone's ladies. Whoever you find, she gonna visit the Bone up at County today."

Frog ambled down the steps in front of the county jail, Looney Tunes and Ron Delauney flanking him. "This is a matter of fucking honor—that traffic cop was full of shit. I told everybody I don't pay."

"You didn't pay," Delauney said.

Frog halted and opened his palms to the heavens. "Then what am I doing out here, *vatos?*"

"Your brother paid."

"Felipe paid?"

"I got him a job for after school."

"Doing what?"

"Bagging groceries. And he told me he didn't want his big brother having no birthday inside the old *condado.*"

"That little *lambion . . .*" Frog called him a kiss-ass, but then his eyes softened. "He said that?"

"Yeah," Delauney chuckled.

"'Froggie went a-courting,'" Looney Tunes began singing, "'and he did ride, uh-huh . . .'" He was acting so goofy, so unlike his usual cool self, that Frog suspected he was slightly shermed. "'Went up to Miss Mousie's door, uh-huh . . .'"

Frog spun on him. "Will you shut the fuck up?"

Looney Tunes just laughed and went on singing.

"Check it out, Leo," Delauney said, lowering his voice. "The shit's heating up. Southside, mostly. But it's spreading north. Keep your people cool."

"Always, man."

They exchanged a barrio handshake.

Then Delauney said, "You'll have to get your own job now, huh? Pay your kid brother back?"

"We'll see what happens."

Looney Tunes threw his arm around Frog's shoulders and quit singing long enough to whisper: "You into Miss Mousie now? Gonna have to find you some pussy? Too much time in the slammer?"

"You calling me a *puto?*" Frog threw a roundhouse at him, but Looney Tunes easily danced out of the way.

Delauney parted company with them at the sidewalk. "All right, I'll leave you jokers to your own bullshit."

"Hey, thanks, Ron . . . no shit."

"Anytime, Frog. And, Larry, keep up the voice lessons . . . you're a fucking credit to your race."

Looney Tunes had a cold sixer waiting in his car. He and Frog clicked their bottles together: *"Por vida!"* And within seconds of firing up the engine, Tunes had the stereo maxed out. Frog dangled his hand out the window and drummed the beat against the outside of the Impala's door, which was mottled by a patch of body work still in progress two years after the collision.

"Oh, Tunes . . . man . . . Tunes," Frog said dreamily, closing his eyes against the flat rays of the late afternoon sun, "just cruise. . . . This is too fucking beautiful to end."

He turned down the speakers. "No can do."

"Why?"

"You'll see." And then after twenty minutes or so, Tunes said, "You know, man, I been thinking . . ."

"Oh, shit."

"You know, you esseys the most athletic folks in the whole fucking world," Tunes said, unmindful of his own barrio accent.

"Say *what?*"

"I mean it, man."

"Okay," Frog said for the sake of argument, "what about you *tintos,* man? Your Jesse Owens. Jackie Robinson. Shit, most basketball teams—take away you fucking *tintos* and you got the coach and the water boy left."

"Fine . . . I show you what I mean. I show you how you esseys rather train than any fucking thing else in the world."

"Oh, man . . . where you get this shit on the *raza?*"

Tunes slowed for a cluster of illegals waiting at a bus stop, a few of the men in sombrerolike hats and the women in shawls. *"Trucha!"* Tunes cried to them. *"La Migra!"*

They scattered at a dead run, even the oldest of their number sprinting.

"Shit," Frog said in disgust as Tunes laughed hysterically, "why you telling those poor *chuntaros* Immigration's on the way?"

"Sorry, man—I started early."

"Started what?"

"This!" Tunes whipped around the corner and sped down into the hollow.

From here Frog could see the clot of cars parked around his house on Twenty-first Street. Even the front lawn was jammed with vehicles. "All right, *primo!*"

"Your party been going since ten this morning!"

"Without me?"

"What can I say, *ese?*" Tunes parked four houses down the street; it was useless to try to get any closer.

The music coming from Frog's house became louder and louder and finally deafening as they hurried up the sidewalk. The air had turned pungent with the smell of *grifa.* "All right!"

Bird was squatting on the curb in the cool twilight, stoned out of his head. "I don't feel so good, Frog . . . but like happy birthday, man."

"Thanks." Grabbing a beer from one of his nephews posted at the driveway gate, Frog rushed up the front steps and through the door into the noisy, packed living room. "I hope this ain't supposed to be no fucking surprise party—because I could hear it going up at County!"

He was greeted by a cheer. The *vatos* clapped his back, and the *cholas* kissed him again and again, their perfume smelling like good times on the way, good times hanging in the air. "Hey, Chata, I be back for more of that later!" he told the warmest of them all.

Then he spied Felipe drinking in the corner and waved his brother over.

"Yeah?" Felipe asked, maybe not knowing what to expect—Frog's expression was stern.

"You piss me off."

"Y'que?"

Frog hoisted an eyebrow. "I tell you what I'm going to do about it . . ." Then he hugged his brother fiercely, his eyes squeezed tightly shut until he let Felipe go.

Another cheer followed.

Then, because it seemed right, Frog motioned for somebody to boost the volume, and he and Felipe began a crazy time-step, an elaborate *cholo* dance that went on at a dizzying pace until they both stumbled out of it in near exhaustion.

Frog was panting for breath when his bedroom door glided open and his second cousin stepped out into the living room and looked around, his handsome face calm and dignified.

Frog didn't treat his cousin with familiarity: more at issue than any blood tie was the fact that his *primo* was an important *veterano* of the White Fence gang, a visiting dignitary from an allied *clika*, the most elder *clika*, who deserved to be shown every respect and courtesy.

"Johnny."

"Frog."

They shook solemnly, and one of the peewees brought them each a fresh beer.

Johnny smiled thinly. "I'm celebrating two things this evening."

"How's that?"

"First, my cousin's birthday." He lifted his beer. *"Por vida!"* His toast was echoed around the room. "And then something else . . . me and my lady"—again, the thin smile—"after two years' misunderstanding, are back as one."

"I am happy for you both, Johnny," Frog said, turning to make sure that everyone from Two-One toasted the reunion.

Johnny acknowledged this with a nod, then said, "So you will excuse me now . . . There's much time to make up."

Smiling at the laughter, he turned and went back into the bedroom.

Rocket rode in the passenger bucket seat of the Buick Electra, his Uzi and three spare magazines on the floor mat between his sneakers, within a shove of his heels of being concealed under the front seat. Directly behind him sat Shooter, a Remington shotgun shoved down behind him into the backseat crack. A third passenger would have been superfluous: only two weapons could be safely fired out one side of the car.

Spooky was driving. "You want me start that way, Rocket?"

"Not yet—ain't dark enough."

The Uzi would do a good job of spraying the house, keeping any return fire to a minimum. But the five pumpkin balls—one-ounce lead slugs—loaded in the gauge would provide penetration into the house. A pumpkin ball could completely stitch a wooden structure, like the one they were riding on this evening.

Rocket could only be relatively sure that they were hitting the right people. As ordered, one of T-Bone's ladies had gone to see him up at County, and the Bone had confessed that he'd been jiving with a friendly

Crip and maybe he'd said something about the hit on Pac-Man . . . or maybe he hadn't—he couldn't rightly recall, the hook-ass nigger. Rocket would discipline him over that later. But if the Bone said anything like this, his lady had been told to ask if anybody else had been close by. T-Bone mentioned some esseys playing cards at a table in the dayroom, but said that they hadn't been listening. Rocket doubted that. Next, the Bone's lady asked him if, right after he spilled this shit about the Pac-Man hit, anybody asked to see the jail watch commander or got alone with one of the deputies or anything. No, but T-Bone said that one of the esseys who'd been playing cards—some homeboy called Frog—asked to see the jail nurse, even though a little while later he came back looking fine. Hearing that, Rocket had known as well as he could ever know that he had his snitch.

"Cop back there, man," Spooky said tensely.

"No sweat," Rocket said. "Keep your speed up and don't hit no brakes—or I kick your ass. Nobody look back, neither."

After a minute or two, a sheriff's patrol car drove past them at sixty in the freeway lane to the left of them.

"See, what I tell you?" Rocket chuckled contemptuously.

They had switched plates with another Electra in a University of Southern California parking lot that afternoon.

"What happen he did stop us?" Shooter asked.

"We do him, man. . . . They getting ready to do us, ain't they? The Pac-Man would do you, wouldn't he? Just like he done Killer Bee?" Rocket checked the fading sky, then glanced at the dash clock. "Okay, Spooky, head that way. We *ride*. Keep driving as we go by . . . don't stop for nothing. And, Shooter, don't be fucking with no cars. Go for esseys you can see or lit windows."

"Done, cuz."

"Better be."

Frog was buried deep in the overstuffed chair with Chata nestled in his lap. "God," he murmured in her ear, "you don't know how I missed you, baby."

"You weren't in there *that* long."

"Hey, when you're long the way I'm long, baby, it's always too long. Know what I mean?"

She just giggled.

He slid his hands around her breasts.

Everyone had had enough *grifa* to want to *listen* to the music, some smooth love music now, so it was turned much lower in the living room, although some peewee outside had some loud rock going on an auto stereo. "Shit," Frog grumbled, "pretty soon that asshole be laying Freddy Fender on me."

A few of the *vatos* took time out from making it with their girls to laugh.

Frog was raising his beer can to Chata's lips when his hand froze.

Another *veterano* lifted his head from the sofa.

A car approached in rapid acceleration, then suddenly decelerated. And in this hood that meant only one thing.

"Down!" Frog cried, spilling Chata onto the floor as he bolted up and lunged for the door frame, flipping off the light switch with one hand and pulling a *chola* out of the opening with his other. "Everybody down!" Only then did he flop on the carpet himself.

He could tell by the echoing of the first reports that the house next door was taking the rounds—a mistake because those people were straight, not bangers. The shooters then must have realized their error, because their car continued to roll down the street, and bullets began thudding against the front of Frog's house. Some even sounded like they were striking the interior wall behind him.

Then the front windows exploded, and Frog buried his face in his arms.

CHAPTER 17

I UNDERSTAND," DANNY SAID, FALLING IN BEHIND A LOW rider on Twenty-first Street, looking for a broken taillamp or any other pretext to stop the Chevy. He didn't find any. Maybe he was just too tired to tangle with the barrio tonight. His time on the hot seat before the Use of Force Review Board had exhausted him more than he'd imagined—it might be days before he felt like himself again. The nastiest questioning, the kind that could torpedo the career of the poor bastard from Southeast, had focused on Danny: from his vantage point, had he also believed that Killer Bee was going for a weapon? Danny's final answer—and the coy, brass-ridden sons of bitches had couched this same question in a dozen different ways—was that he had begun to squeeze back on his trigger when he saw the Southeast patrolman's bullet blow out the Bee's backside. So hell, yes, as far as he was concerned, the Bee had been going for broke. The patrolman had looked like he could have kissed Danny, and McGavin vowed to buy him a beer or baby-sit with his kids for him while he and his wife went out on the town when this manure-storm blew over.

"You understand what?" Hodges asked out of the depths of his own thoughts half a minute after Danny had spoken.

"Why you didn't want to burn Frog."

"I trusted you would." Still, Hodges sounded a little relieved. "If Leo hadn't dropped the dime . . . well, we'd still be in the dark. And Metro wouldn't be out trying to head this mess off. That's why I want to thank him tonight, if we can do it on the sly." He yawned, then stretched as much as the confines of the Pontiac would allow. "After that, coffee. . . . My body no longer adjusts to shift changes."

Then both men braced for the broadcast following an alert tone: "All units in the area: Shots fired at a dwelling, Two-one-one-four Twenty-first. Any unit in position?"

"One CRASH Thirty-two, Control . . . about one minute away." Hodges hung up the mike. "Shit."

"Any unit in position to assist CRASH Thirty-two?"

"Well," Hodges said, "looks like somebody thanked Leo before we got to."

Danny accelerated around the low rider. "That his address?"

"Yeah."

"Jesus."

Danny parked across the mouth of the driveway, preventing any of the dozen cars on the front lawn from leaving. Women were screaming; *cholos* were rushing down the narrow spaces between the tightly packed Chevrolets, trying to throw together some kind of response to the attack. A few were clutching handguns as Danny drove up, but these quickly vanished.

"Control, CRASH Thirty-two is there," Hodges said into the mike. "E.T.A. on a back?"

"Rolling from the station—about five. Advise on any injuries."

"Roger."

Danny said nothing as he waited for Hodges to decide if they would get out of the Pontiac without an assisting unit arriving within the minute.

"Christ," Hodges finally said, giving the squelch on his radio handset a quick test. "I know most of these assholes—let's do it."

Locking his door, Danny shouted to some homeboys lounging against the porch pillars like nothing had happened: "Anybody hit?"

They remained silent.

"Wait a sec," Hodges said, running his flashlight beam over the numbers on the mailbox. "I remembered wrong. Frog's place here is Two-one-one-*two.*"

"Reporting party next door?"

"Must be. Let's check there first."

"You go ahead," Danny said. "I'll see what's up with Frog."

Hodges hesitated for a moment, obviously reluctant to split up, even briefly.

"Go on . . . go ahead," Danny said over his shoulder, starting up Frog's driveway. "I haven't spray-painted any of these homies . . . *yet.*"

Hodges took off at a trot for the neighbors' place.

Clasping his baton where the rubber grommet was seated in his belt ring, Danny sidled through the *cholos* on the porch, ignoring how they red-eyed him.

The silence greeting him in the living room told

him that dope and weapons were close at hand. Otherwise, some of the homeboys would already be bad-mouthing him.

"Where's Frog?" he asked, keeping his voice calm and civil.

After a moment, somebody mumbled, "I dunno."

"Anybody hurt?"

"I dunno."

"Anybody see who did it? Anything on the car?"

"We was all in here, man."

"Yeah, right." Danny let it all slide. Tonight these were the victims; tomorrow night, when the hood's karma had tilted once again, they would be the suspects—welcome to the dark side of the barrio. But, shit, there was a dark side to Bel Air, too, probably darker—at least these *cholos* didn't pretend to be model citizens.

He whipped a small spiral notebook out of his shirt pocket. "All right, nobody moves until I get all your names—"

He stopped because the bedroom door had eased open.

At first he thought that his exhaustion was playing tricks on his mind, that he was finished for a while—it happened to everybody sooner or later. It was that disconcerting to glance up from his notebook and *believe* that Louisa was standing in the door frame looking like a pill-head whore with multicolored raccoon eyes, her cheeks roughened with red splotches scratched by a man's one-day growth of beard.

His grin was stunned—stupid-looking, almost—and his voice hesitant: "Louisa?"

For an instant he was relieved by the way the young woman sneered. He'd never seen Louisa do that. But then she spoke, and it was undeniably Louisa Gomez's voice. "What's the matter, Pac-Man?"

"Louisa?"

"What?"

Then, emerging from the darkened room, a *veterano* stepped up to her back. Danny recalled him from a field interrogation on the Fourth Street bridge, so he was White Fence. And now, with a serene smile, the *veterano* draped his arm around Louisa's shoulders possessively.

A few of the *cholos* must have known about Danny and Louisa, because they suddenly laughed.

Danny wheeled and pushed his way back out onto the porch.

He felt as if he'd been suffocating in that crowded room, and now he felt close to puking.

A cold-looking moon had risen over the rim of the hollow, and his moist eyes fixed on it as he drew in a couple of deep breaths.

Then somebody brushed rudely against his back, and he clamped his elbow down over his revolver to keep it from being ripped out of his holster. This was no time to be confused: one of these *cholos* could stick a shank in him before he knew what had happened.

But it was Louisa who had brushed against him. She shoved him again, several *cholas* giggling and offering her moral support from the background. "What's the matter with you, man? What's the matter, Pac-Man? Huh?"

She was weeping, but that didn't stop her from pummeling him with her small fists.

He caught her hands in midflight and held them down. After a few seconds, she stopped struggling against his grip.

Her shoulders were trembling, and her face was a miserable mess; but her lovely eyes were the same as always, and they tore through him to his yearning.

There was no anger left in him. His voice was a soft croak: "How's your sister?"

"What are you looking at?"

"I . . . nothing."

"You think you know who I am? All you see is what you want, man. You only want things one way. You don't like me this way? Huh? Well, this is *me*. This is the me you didn't want to see, Pac-Man!"

"I just . . ." He had to glance away. "What are you doing here?"

"Me? I *live* here." She sneered like a typical *chola* again.

"No, you don't live here. You live in White Fence."

"I go where I *want*. We got no fight with Two-One. Johnny and me are visiting his cousin."

"Who's Johnny?"

"My man," she said proudly, defiantly, although he had stopped trying to hold her hands—they remained cupped in his palms on her account, not his.

It was all so fucking confusing. What did she want him to do? Square off with her *veterano*?

Johnny, meanwhile, had followed her out as far as the open door. He slouched against it. He wore a sniggering expression Danny felt too sickened to want to slap off his face.

He could hear the patrol backups coming fast, one already a short distance up the street and a second barreling down into the hollow. Something in him wished that they might never arrive, that he would vanish forever in this angry vortex of *cholos* and *cholas*.

Then it hit him: he had to check on Hodges.

He had Hodges left.

At last Danny pushed away her hands. "I got to go."

"I was wrong about you, Danny. . . ."

He started walking backwards, the crowd following him, beginning to menace him with taunts and fighting stances.

"You don't just have a mean heart . . . you're a *murderer!*" Then, at last, she sobbed.

It was too much to explain . . . what had happened to Killer Bee. Perhaps it could never be explained to those who hadn't been there.

"No, Louisa." He wanted to touch her face, but by now other *cholas* were getting in the way, snarling at him like wildcats. "I'm probably everything *but* that. I'm an honest-to-god son of a bitch. But I'm not a murderer."

A screech of brakes told him that the first black-and-white had arrived.

Then inexplicably, even to himself, Danny flashed four fingers back at the cruiser.

But the Latino patrolman wisely ran up anyway, muttering, "Like hell you're code four, *'mano.'*" He drew his baton. "All right—everybody back!" And to make sure that no one gave him the *no habla* routine, he repeated the command in barrio Spanish.

Louisa was only partially visible in a huddle of *cholas* who were jostling her back toward the house. For some reason, she appeared to be resisting them.

"Danny!" she suddenly cried in a way that gave him chills, and her hand shot out of the midst of the young women, her fingers beseeching him.

"Good-bye, Louisa," he whispered. "I didn't mean to do this to you. . . . I'm sorry I'm so fucked up that *this* looked good to you."

Then the patrolman asked, "Where's your partner?"

"Next door, I think."

"You mean you split up . . . in *this* hood?"

"Yeah," Danny said, "it won't ever happen again." He started striding for the house next door.

"Better hurry, man. He radioed in for an ambulance and told dispatch to put County General on STAT!"

Surgical Team and Technicians.

Danny started running.

Hodges was gazing down into his bloody hands as if they were close friends who'd failed him.

The woman had been hit in the upper chest with something bigger than 9mm parabellum, the round fired by a Mini-Uzi submachine gun—now confirmed as the preferred automatic weapon of southside Crips. The entry wound was too large for even .45 caliber. Some monstrous projectile had devastated her flesh, which was now translucent, like petroleum jelly.

Hodges was in bad shape, and Danny was afraid that he was completely out of it. He peered into his partner's face.

Hodges stirred a little. "She was alive . . . breathing. I was keeping her alive . . . and then . . ." His eyes got glassy and he stared at his hands.

It was then that Danny realized a tiny girl was screaming her lungs out. Her father was clutching her, and both were jammed up against the blood-splattered refrigerator by the weight of their horror.

Hodges didn't budge when Danny pried the handset out of the leather holder on his Sam Browne. "Control, One CRASH Thirty-two," he said, hushed.

"Unit calling Control?"

"CRASH Thirty-two. Cancel the ambulance . . . roll coroner."

"Roger, CRASH Thirty-two."

Mention of the coroner started the man whimpering, his pale lips tight across his teeth as if he were afraid to cry in front of the two cops.

Without a thought, Danny crawled across the gore-strewn floor to him, slowly reached out, and held the man in his arms, the child nested in the shadow between their bodies. "I know, brother . . . I fucking know . . . let it out . . ."

A wail—a cry of utter inconsolable pain broke from the man, and Danny had to close his eyes against the sound.

Later, when he looked back to see if Hodges was doing any better, his partner looked as if he'd just glimpsed something unearthly, something mystical here in the carnage of a barrio kitchen.

It took a moment for Danny McGavin to realize that he was the reason for that strange look on Hodges's face.

"I don't know, man," Frog said. "I just don't know." He shifted uneasily in the rusted lawn chair, the nylon groaning as he moved. "I got scarce so Hodges wouldn't lay no *be fucking cool* shit on me. I never was no *juda*, so this oath shit with the law never like rested easy on me, you know. . . ." He accepted a *yesca* cigarette from Bird and tried to mellow out on a long hit. But it was no good. He was still wound tight, hungry for a release he knew was still hours away. The full moon was halfway to its zenith, shining harshly, like a motorcycle headlamp set on high beam.

"A crazy life," said one of the homies in the moon-bright backyard.

"A good life," another intoned, "if you don't fucking weaken . . ."

"Jesus next door—how's he doing?" Frog asked.

"He's staying with family over in Montebello," Looney Tunes said low, his *tinto* skin making him nothing more than a shadow against the faint purple sky. "I told him we'd watch his place."

"Good . . . we gotta do *everything* for him now. And then someday he'll be a big help to us. . . . You wait and see." Frog swirled the beer in his bottle thoughtfully before drinking. "Well, Bird, I've given you some time, like I said. You still sure it was this Shooter *vato* in the backseat?"

"Dead sure, Frog. Him and me was together at C.Y.A.—I'd know him anywheres."

"What he'd draw Youth Authority for?"

"Offing some dude. He's fucking crazy, man. And his pres is even crazier. Some dude called Rocket."

"I know him," Looney Tunes said.

"And the other thing you swore, Bird—you still swear by it?"

"It's righteous, Frog. We was working chopping weeds up in the mountains and Shooter was bragging on me about all the hideouts the Crip have here and there and everywheres."

"And you remember them?"

"I swear, man—as good as he told me."

Frog was silent for a moment. *"Wacha*—here's what you do, Bird. Take your mama's Toyota—"

"Okay, okay."

"Settle fucking down, now, and find out where this Rocket's holed up."

Bird had already come to his feet. "Right."

"But one thing—I want you back before noon or I kick your ass."

"Then that's it?" Tunes asked, meaning the decision to ride on these Crips.

"Ya stuvo," Frog said—it's over with, that's it.

"How does White Fence fit in this?" a soft-spoken *vato* asked from the back porch.

Frog sighed. "They been more than generous. Johnny offered us some manpower, but I said no."

"Why?" Bird asked. "They're *loco,* man."

"Because it's time we stand on our own. It's time we took our place among the hoods, man. If I'd said yes, next thing you know White Fence's using us like fucking *braceros* or something. Understand?"

Their silence spoke for them.

"But one of Johnny's *vatos* is dropping by a little

present for us—some fucking frags. Grenades for our Crip amigos, man."

"They die," Whitey said matter-of-factly.

Felipe had stepped in front of Frog's chair and was standing as straight as he could. "I want in."

"We don't need no peewees," Tunes said.

"I want in, fucker!"

Tunes howled in mock disbelief.

But Bird tried to touch Felipe's arm. "Hey, man, we gonna do some shit what—"

"You shut up, *puto!* I won't take this no more! *Es mi barrio!* I want in!"

Frog stared at his little brother as if seeing him for the first time.

Felipe met his gaze squarely.

"You know what you're asking?"

"Yeah, Frog."

"No turning back, man."

"I know."

"Yeah, but *I* don't know. . . ." Frog planted his chin on his fist and thought awhile. Then he exhaled and said, "Only one way to settle this: get your ass out on the lawn."

Felipe strutted out into the middle of the dead grass. He looked small in the moonlight, but with a flick of his hand Frog motioned for three of the younger homies to advance on his brother.

Clearly, Felipe knew what was coming, but showed no fear as the trio encircled him. He calmly waited for one of them to hurl the first punch—which came an instant later to his throat.

Felipe made a gagging noise, which turned into a growl. He punched back furiously, driving two of the homeboys before him with gut blows. But the third *vato* used this drive to deliver a kick to Felipe's kidneys.

He collapsed to his knees, but then came right back up and ignored two painful blows to the face, which drew the first blood of the fight ritual.

Looney tunes tapped Frog's shoulder and whispered: "Enough, maybe?"

Frog raised his voice so all could hear: "Anybody else wanna jump this little *puto?* I don't think he's tough enough. I don't think he has the heart."

These words turned Felipe into an animal. He clawed at their eyes, tried to bite any hands that came close to his mouth. His punches were so furious he eventually spun himself against the ground—and was kicked nearly senseless this time.

But again he dragged himself to his feet and began fending off two more attackers, fresh from the sidelines.

His face was blotted over with blood, which flowed black instead of red in the moonlight.

At last, Frog said, "All right."

There were tears in his eyes, but he quickly wiped them away.

Hodges knew damned well that this last cup of coffee with Wally Reed would ruin what little sleep he might have had without it.

But he felt too tired at the moment to leave Reed's office and drive home. "Jesus . . . Jesus . . . Jesus."

"Yeah, baby." And Reed looked as if he was in the same state. He stifled a yawn that threatened to lift off the top half of his head. "Shit, mama."

So at least there was a bit of camaraderie to be drawn from this four-thirty-in-the-morning exhaustion.

"Metro's being pulled off starting tomorrow."

Hodges was too tired to hide his irritation. "You think we have this thing sewn up?"

"Nowhere close. But B Platoon drew VIP protection for the Vice President at the airport and then the Bonaventure Hotel. And D Platoon'll be tied up trying to keep some Armenians from blowing away another Turkish consul—that's hush-hush, of fucking course."

"Of fucking course."

"So C Platoon's being held in reserve for a *real* emergency, unlike *our* chickenshit itty gig." Reed began riffling through the heap of papers on his desk, then smiled as he apparently found what he'd been hunting for. "Thought this might please you, Bobby."

It was the teletype from downtown mandating long sleeves and ties for all uniformed officers. Autumn had finally come to southern California. The teletype was almost as good as the smell of burning leaves in the air.

"About time."

Reed chuckled. "You know, it's optional the rest of the year, too, if that's what you like to wear instead of fucking beachcomber sleeves."

"I know."

"Then why don't you go ahead and be different, man?"

Hodges peered through the venetian blinds at the city lights. "Because the only thing that keeps the bastards from overrunning us is the illusion that if you kill a cop, another one *exactly* like him is waiting to take his place. And if they can't single us out, it stays impersonal for them—one fucking asshole against the entire system."

Reed laughed softly as he tried to sneak a nitro pill down with a swig of coffee. "What we gonna do without you, Bobby? You leave and the heart and soul will drop out of this fucking nuthouse."

"I doubt it. Enough for one watch, Wally." Groaning, Hodges hauled himself to his feet, but then hesitated at the door. "Do me a personal favor?"

"Name it."

"Square it with the captain—and put the kibosh on that request for a new partner."

"You sure?"

"After tonight, yeah. He'll pan out okay."

"Well, good," Reed said, grinning. "I'm glad. I really am."

"Oh, another thing—don't tell McGavin. I'm having him over on days off for a couple beers. I'd like to tell him then . . . I mean, ask him if it's okay with him."

"You got it, baby."

"*Ciao.*"

Reed leaned forward. "Say *what?*"

Hodges smiled in confusion. "I don't—"

"Neither of us has said that in damn near twenty years. Don't you remember?"

"No."

"That Italian kid in our academy class, killed in the line a year later in Newton?"

"Oh, yeah."

"He had us all saying that *ciao* shit to one another . . . the whole class doing it."

"Yeah, I guess he did. . . ." Then Hodges ambled down the corridor, his expression distracted.

CHAPTER 18

FELIPE'S FACE HURT. BUT IT HURT IN A GOOD WAY, because the aches reminded him of the thing he'd gone through last night, the thing that had changed him forever.

Yesterday he had been a boy, a peewee. Today he was a man.

A few minutes before noon, Bird had come back from the southside. Right away, Frog took him inside the house, and they talked with nobody to listen. When they came out again, Frog told everybody to work faster on account of the hit was now on for sure. The *clika* would ride on the Crips who'd lit up the hood last night and killed the woman next door.

Some of the peewees started shouting, *"Two-one, Rifa!"* but Felipe decided to stay cool like the older *vatos,* who shrugged and went on with getting ready for the ride.

"Felipe, come here," Frog said with a new tone of respect. Then Frog sent him down to the beer bar on the corner to look inside the trash bin for all the bottle caps he could find, the ones with cork or foamy stuff on the inside.

On the walk back home, he saw a black-and-white parked up on the lip of the heights, the *marrano* keeping an eye on the hollow through binoculars. As soon as he got back, he told Frog about this, but his brother said he already knew—and would do something about it later. "First things first," he said.

He took a power drill and carefully made a hole in the middle of each bottle cap. When he had a pile of them, he began sliding them down a metal tube. "Sssh!" he said, putting a finger across his lips.

Felipe hadn't said shit and told Frog so.

"I know, man." He laughed, his eyes warm but a little sad too. "I mean, this is a fucking silencer. See?" Then he showed Felipe how it screwed onto the barrel of a .22 rifle he'd sawed off earlier in the day.

And then Chata drove up the driveway and parked in the backyard so the *marrano* couldn't spot her car from the heights.

Her Impala had hook fur on the dash and a small chrome steering wheel, but otherwise it didn't look much like a low rider, which Frog had said was what he wanted today. While he was inside the house making the call for Angie to bring over her car, too, Chata came up to Felipe and looked at him like she never had before. Her cheeks were split by a big smile and she didn't say shit as she looked him over. He'd always liked her cheeks, but had been afraid to tell her this. Chata, whose name meant "puffy cheeks," was one of Frog's best *rukas,* so Felipe had always kept quiet about his dreams to lie with her someday. When he thought about lying with somebody, it was always Chata inside his head.

But now she suddenly kissed him on the mouth, her tongue flitting twice between his teeth.

Then, laughing softly, she broke away when he came back for more, the hunger tightening his belly.

She hurried toward the house, and Felipe watched the sway of her hips until she shut the door behind her.

Then Angie showed up with her straight-looking Chevy and it pulled alongside Chata's Ipala. She didn't kiss Felipe like Chata had done, but she gave him a long, tender hug for no longer being a peewee, squashing her big breasts against him—and that was just as good.

All through the afternoon, which got breezy later on, the *vatos* worked on the cars, using torches that hissed loudly to cut holes in the floor, which were then covered by the mats. These, Looney Tunes explained, would let the *vatos* ditch their weapons if The Man tried to stop them after the hit on the Crips.

Felipe stood by and handed tools to the homies who'd worked in body shops or garages. Maybe someday he would like to work in a body shop. He wasn't sure, but maybe.

After this, Bird showed him how to load and work a .45 pistol. Then Felipe dry-clicked the pistol on the old barrel cactus in the corner of the yard which he pretended was a stubby little Crip coming at him.

Around four, Frog came out of the house and said it was time.

Before this, he had said no *pisto* today and that he'd get *awetado* as hell and kick ass if anybody got fucked up. But now he brought out a pipe filled with *concentrada,* which he said would mellow out everybody some. "I want everybody to be relaxed . . . to go at this *smooth.*"

Felipe took plenty of deep hits, but they didn't do much for him.

Still, he looked around and saw for the first time that the smog was off the hollow and it looked pretty. So pretty he wondered if he'd ever see it again. He didn't feel scared, but wondered a little if he was ever coming back. That was all. He really didn't think that was the same as being afraid.

Frog said it was time to mount up.

Four *vatos* got in each car. Frog motioned for Felipe to join Looney Tunes, Bird, Frog, and himself in the Impala. Even before Chata fired up the engine, Frog told the guys to lie down, which made it cramped in the backseat. But Felipe was silent even when Bird let one right in his face and giggled for having done it.

No weapons could be seen; Tunes had hidden them in places even a smart *marrano* probably wouldn't look.

The car started rolling forward. Felipe felt a thrill on the back of his neck.

"You want me to go the other way?" Chata asked, chewing gum fast—Felipe could hear her jaws clicking.

"No, go right past The Man," Frog said, his voice muffled because he was doubled over, too. "If we go out the back side, he'll radio for another fucking car to check us out." After a moment in which the only sound was the rumbling of the Impala's exhaust, Frog asked Chata, "Angie hanging back some like I told the bitch?"

"Yeah."

"Good . . . good. And use your goddamn signals, Chata. This is no time for a fucking traffic stop."

"I will, goddammit." She sounded a little pissed, but then forgot about it because Felipe could tell by the way she had slowed down a couple miles per hour that they were nearing the black-and-white parked on the heights.

He shut his eyes. He started praying that nothing would go wrong with this, his first ride.

Then Chata let out a long breath. "Okay . . . we're okay."

"What about Angie?" Frog asked.

"She's through, too . . . We're all okay."

"Orale!" Bird yowled.

But Frog told him to shut up, that it was no time to start celebrating. "And stay down, you stupid *tontos!"*

Everybody settled in for the ride to the southside, which Felipe knew would take a long time, because Chata was driving like she was in driver's education or something.

He could look out Tunes's window and see silver jets drop down past the sun on their way into the airport. It would be almost dark when they arrived in Crip turf. Frog had planned it this way so the hit could be made in the last light of day and their escape under the cover of first darkness.

Frog had thought of everything.

Felipe saw that Tunes had his eyes on him. "What, man?"

"With that four-five you packing in a couple minutes . . ."

"Yeah?"

"Don't be ripping through all your rounds at once."

"But don't be stingy with them neither," Frog said from the front. "This hit'll be over and done in two minutes . . . one hundred and twenty secs. I'm running the clock on this gig, so you all cut when I say. Understand?"

Bird and Felipe muttered yes.

Looney Tunes just yawned.

"Central Avenue," Chata said, braking for a light.

"Okay," Frog said. "Angie still behind us?"

"Yeah." Chata spit her gum out the window, then accelerated again. "On my ass."

"Horale," Frog said—all right—his voice higher suddenly. "Streets look clear of The Man?"

"Nothing parked along here, baby."

"Do it, Larry."

Looney Tunes tore off the door panel on his side and started passing out arms: the silenced and sawed-off .22 to Frog, who jacked a cartridge into the chamber right away; two grenades and a .357 magnum revolver to Bird, who clicked the frags together like pool balls; the .45 pistol to Felipe; and a broke-down gauge for himself, which he put together double fast.

Frog sneaked a look over the dash. "Here's good."

Chata braked.

Felipe felt his heart pounding like it had forgotten how to beat, but told himself it was *nada*—just the *concentrada* he'd smoked before setting out.

"Let's go."

Felipe bailed out and stayed close to Tunes, like he'd been told. It was almost night and the breeze was chilly.

He begged Jesus that he wouldn't start shivering—or that if he did, the others wouldn't notice.

They were at the entrance to an alley behind some houses. The houses looked empty, like from a war or something.

Frog waited for the *vatos* from Angie's car to catch up with them, then—without saying shit—led the way up the alley. They had not gone far when Frog motioned for everybody to stop and stay where they were while he crept forward, walking on the toes of his Adidas.

Felipe suddenly remembered that he'd forgotten to

jack a round into the .45's chamber, but was afraid now to make any noise.

Frog slowed down along the back of a blue stucco garage, then wheeled around the corner. He fired twice.

Felipe saw no flashes, but heard a *pffft-pffft* sound, a little more than he'd expected from the silencer.

Waving the *vatos* to come forward again, Frog kept his eyes on the blue house.

Felipe used the soft tramping of shoes to cover the clacking he had to make to charge his pistol.

Rounding the corner, he saw a Crip sitting on a plastic milk crate, his trunk all cocked over to the side against the garage wall. He was bleeding from the chest and his forehead. His eyes were wide open and sparkly in his *tinto* face—it was getting dark fast.

But then, like the other *vatos*, Felipe ignored the dead Crip.

Frog tapped Bird on the shoulder to go, and the *loco vato* ran hunched over down the side of the house, which had no lights showing through the cracks in the boards nailed over the windows. Tunes had his gauge trained on these windows, so Felipe did the same. But he had to lower the handgun after a few seconds because his hands were shaking so bad.

This shamed him, and he hoped that things would start soon so he could prove himself . . . before he lost his courage.

Bird dropped a frag through a slit in the boards over the living-room window and then, running back toward the alley, tossed another grenade through the kitchen window.

From where he waited, Felipe watched Bird, expecting the Crips to blow him away at any instant.

After what seemed too long a time, Bird came jogging back to the garage like the Crips and their guns didn't mean shit to him, although his breath misted out of him fast and loud.

"They're in there," he said as the first explosion rocked the silent, vacant hood.

Holding the pistol between his knees, Felipe covered his ears with his palms. He saw Frog tap the light button on his wristwatch in the same instant the second blast came. This one, from the kitchen, flashed an orange pall over the backyard, catching the faces of the homeboys. Loose boards off the window tumbled across the dark sky and clattered into the alley.

Looney Tunes fired first.

The *vatos* started spreading out, shooting from the hip as they scattered for cover.

It came to Felipe that his brother's watch was ticking and these were the few seconds in which he must prove himself for all time. If he fucked up, he would be a *puto* until Jesus came back. He must do very well or die in this backyard. One or the other.

Squirming forward on his belly, drawing closer to the house than anyone else, he began squeezing his trigger. He was only shooting at a rear window until he realized with a shock that real live Crips were stumbling out the back door, their guns winking back at him through the darkness.

Something had gone wrong: it was darker than it was supposed to be during the hit. He could barely make them out against the night.

"Calmate, culo!" a voice inside him cried—*calm down, asshole.*

He picked out a silhouette and aimed with care.
Blam!

The silhouette disappeared.

But where?

Yet, after a moment, Felipe could see this Crip sprawled on the lawn, pumping his legs like a guy with the wind knocked out of him in a football game.

Another *tinto* jumped out of the smoky kitchen window, but he was spun around in midair—maybe by one of Tunes's big shotgun bullets—and landed on his head.

He didn't move again.

The Crips who'd run outside began to inch back inside.

Felipe smiled to himself. Two-one was winning. The hit would be a good thing, after all.

Then, through all the boom-booming, the unmanly screams of pain, he thought he could hear sirens.

Quickly now he looked for somebody else to kill.

Behind him Frog cried, "Split, Two-one!"

But at that instant a Crip bolted out the back door of the house, spraying the yard with something like a little machine gun. A burb gun, maybe. Felipe could hear bullets thud into the dry ground around him, but he took a deep breath and eased back his trigger—nothing happened!

The slide was all the way back.

This, Bird told him, meant that his magazine was empty.

The Crip kept rushing forward, even though somebody yelled at him from the house: "Get back here, Rocket!"

And then Frog shouted, "Felipe! Felipe!"

Felipe froze, although he could see from the corner of his eye that the homeboys were splitting—all but one were leaving him behind—he didn't know what to do. He was sure he was going to die, but told himself to be brave. To die brave like the homeboys on the murals over in White Fence.

Looney Tunes was striding forward like he didn't give a shit for anything, his gauge belching a white flash each time he let go at the Crip armed with the burb gun.

"Felipe, run!" Frog kept hollering. "Get out of there, you stupid fuck!"

Tunes dropped to one knee, and Felipe could tell by the way his head bobbed on his neck that he'd been hit.

But Tunes came right back up and blasted the Crip, whose machine gun flew out of his hands like it'd been yanked by an invisible wire or something.

The *tinto* landed on his ass, clutching his throat and making gurgling sounds that made Felipe feel sick.

Larry pumped the arm on his gauge and shot him again.

And then the Crip flopped over like he had no bones inside his body.

Rising, Felipe thought about making sure he was dead, but then thought instead about Tunes, who was hunkered over his knees like he was in church or something. One side of his face was flattened against the dry grass.

"Larry?" Felipe touched Tunes on the back, shook him a few times before finally giving up. His hand came away bloody.

All at once, there was more shooting after a spell of quiet, but it was only Frog capping blindly at the house to cover his own rush up to Felipe.

"Larry ain't doing so good, Frog."

"Larry's dead, man," he said, his voice kind of whispery and gentle. "And we got to go—*now.*"

Then he seized Felipe by the Pendleton and dragged him to his feet.

They started running for the cars; the girls were already gunning the engines.

The sirens sounded very close now.

After nightfall, the breeze began whirling moisture in off the ocean. And by midnight, that part of Aztlan—the occupied territories of Mexico—known as Sur lay under a dank cover of low clouds. Down in a ravine, in the depths of a hollow known only by the thoroughfare that ran through it—Twenty-first Street —a fire was burning in a rusted fifty-gallon drum. The wood being consumed was orange. It was well seasoned, the last vestige of a huge citrus grove that had once cloaked the hollow in waxy green, that had once been tended by their great-grandfathers fresh from Texas or Sonora. Now and again, the embers shot up big sprays of sparks, which startled the *cholos* and *cholas* gathered around the drum.

Frog gazed skyward: there was only a fuzzy white place in the clouds where the moon was supposed to be. A ghetto blaster was sending the raspy echos of a saxophone up the ravine.

"Hey, you know," Angie said, "that's life. That's the way it is, homes. You know? That's just life . . ." One of the *vatos* kissed her neck, and she reached back to caress his hair with her fingers without seeing who it was.

Bird was staring into the flames. He was shermed bad, and Frog was thinking about taking the sawed-off .22 away from him. Good for only a couple shots, the homemade silencer had been tossed on the way home from the hit, but as far as Frog knew, the rifle was still loaded.

"That fucking Looney Tunes, eh?" Bird said. "Fucking Rambo, man."

"Rambo don't ever die."

"You know what I mean, Frog . . . come on, man. *I* am fucking Rambo! If I go, I go like Larry—fucking *vato* cyclone *loco!*" He howled like a mad dog, then took another hit off the PCP joint before collapsing against a fallen eucalyptus log, laughing to himself.

Chata retrieved the sherm from the dust, then passed it along before it burned out.

"Yeah, sure . . . fucking whatever, Bird." Frog

glanced down at his brother, who was squatting in the dirt beside him, sucking on the collar of his Pendleton. Felipe still looked scared, but he had done well, amazingly well for such a small fuck. Frog just wished he felt better about it. Still, he ripped off his brother's *moco* rag and tousled his dried sweat-stiff hair. "Relax, man, you did great. You got great big balls, little brother."

Felipe smiled bleakly. Then somebody handed him the sherm and he tried to look tough smoking it.

Frog looked into the fire and then through it, beyond it, to he knew not what. "Shit, man . . . shit."

After a while, with the wriggly flames hypnotizing him, he saw himself like walking down a long desert road and he realized that he had somehow put the barrio behind him—but then he started fading like a spirit or a ghost going away from the world in a movie or something . . . and then he knew once again that he was nothing, nobody, *nada* outside this fucking hollow. Whatever came his way, he had to stay. Felipe, too, now. His brother had crossed the line and could never leave. Frog tried not to feel too bad about this. What choices had there been? Felipe a brain surgeon? A lawyer in a three-piecer? What hope was there, man? No, it was like written in a big book when you were born to the barrio, and you could never erase it. People born to Beverly Hills or Arcadia or San Marino could erase the past whenever they felt like it. But not somebody born to the barrio; if you left the hood, you yourself were erased.

Frog glanced up. Everybody around the fire had gone quiet.

Then he saw why: standing out where the orange flickers grew weak and trembly was Ron Delauney. His *tinto* face was glistening. He was sweating. In this chill he was sweating.

"I asked if I could talk to you first," he said, showing that he had no gun.

"Who'd you ask, man?" Frog said.

Delauney didn't answer. "I want you guys to stay cool, now. They got you. No way out of here . . . give it up, please. . . ."

And as if his words were not enough, a police chopper rose from behind the heights, its spot coming on and gushing whitely down on the scene.

They came down the ravine embankment in a rank, most of the patrolmen hefting shotguns. Behind them on the lip of the rise was a sniper team on loan from Metro, the triggerman equipped with night vision equipment.

Danny walked beside Hodges, who'd been grimly silent for hours now. McGavin decided it was time to stir his partner's lousy mood: "First night we get to wear long sleeves and ties—we got to thrash around in the brush."

"Yeah," Hodges said quietly. He was holding his revolver down against his leg.

"And this fucking Kevlar vest feels like a corset," Danny went on.

"Just might save your worthless life."

Danny could see Ron Delauney deep in the ravine, backlit by the homeboy's warming fire. He gave the high-sign for the cops to keep coming down the slope. The ex-gang-banger had more balls than Danny would have thought. And so far so good: the *cholos* weren't scattering and booking into the night.

Then Hodges said, "There's Frog. . . . He's got his brother with him."

"And the one called Bird," Danny whispered. "He's against that downed tree . . . looks whacked." He glanced aside at Hodges, whose face looked more angular than usual because of the firelight and the rotating spot from the chopper.

As planned, the rank of patrolmen halted about fifty feet above the Two-one *cholos,* and Danny and Hodges—as the CRASH men on duty in this division tonight—kept descending to join Delauney at the parley.

Danny hoped that the homies were out of grenades, even though the sniper would drop anybody who tossed so much as a cigarette butt and he himself was toting an Ithaca loaded with double-ought buck.

Frog was grinning as the two cops stepped out of the darkness. "Pac-Man, Hodges—we gonna have a little rapport here, huh?"

"I hope, Leo," Hodges said, still concealing his wheelgun behind his leg.

"How many of your blue *vatos* you got up there?"

"Enough not to make it a fair fight."

"Understood, man." Frog now sounded tired. "Understood."

Without being told, the *cholos* began kneeling, hoisting their hands.

"That's it, men," Delauney said. "That's the way to end this thing."

Frog spit into the fire. "Who'd you tell, Hodges?"

"No one."

"You're a fucking liar."

Hodges said nothing for moment. "I got a witness who puts your kid brother at the hit, Leo."

"Who, man?"

"Don't jack me off!" Hodges cried, then shook his head and lowered his voice again: "Christ, I wanted something better for Felipe." He stared at the peewee, who folded his hands between his knees and looked away. "I thought you did, too, Frog. But it looks like you don't give a shit if he winds up like Larry, who's cooling on a slab right now. I *cared,* Leo. But I guess that's always been my fucking mistake. . . ."

Frog's voice was now quivering with anger, perhaps with shame as well: "I try and do a favor for *your* lousy partner . . . and look what happens . . . look what happens to my hood." He laughed bitterly.

From the corner of his eye, Danny caught Hodges lifting his arm to signal a team of patrolmen to come the rest of the way down and begin taking the Twenty-first Street gang into custody—when in that split second movement near the fallen log made McGavin suddenly glance at Bird. The *cholo* had a sawed-off rifle and was swinging its muzzle around—toward Danny, toward the detested Pac-Man. Bringing up his gauge, Danny was a microsecond away from blowing a huge hole out Bird's back when Felipe darted up from the ground and batted the rifle aside.

A .22 round cracked.

Then from upslope two more cartridges sounded—much louder and from a rifle with a bigger bore.

The piddling .22 report had come from Bird's weapon, and the two thumpers had been issued by the sniper, killing Bird instantly, breaking his back and folding him over the log like a dishrag.

The *cholos* and their women started screaming that they were finished as a half-dozen patrolmen materialized out of the night and tapped the bases of their skulls with shotgun muzzles. Even though he was obviously dead, Bird was handcuffed and unceremoniously tossed on his slack face.

Danny turned to speak to Hodges, but didn't see him at first.

"Bob?"

"Yeah . . ." He was lying on the ground, propped up on an elbow, almost like a guy relaxing on a picnic blanket.

Then it came to Danny: Hodges had been hit. "Jesus!"

But Hodges held up a hand as if to indicate that he was all right.

The vest. Hodges had been saved by his Kevlar vest—and Danny felt relief wash over him.

Still, the man looked woozier than hell and would have pitched over on his chest had Danny not caught him. "You're okay, Bob—"

"Dan . . ."

"Don't try to shoot the shit . . . you've had the fucking wind knocked out, that's all."

Hodges's expression was agonized, as if he had to get something out or he'd explode. He growled as a patrolman ran his flashlight up and down the length of his body. Again, the intense expression: "Dan . . . *Danny* . . ."

"Knock it the fuck off, Hodges! What do I got to do to get you to shut up, huh?"

Then Danny noticed the frothy blood in the corners of his partner's lips. "Bob?"

Hodges nodded weakly. He was fading, and his eyelids kept trying to sag over his milky pupils.

Danny ripped open Hodges's long-sleeved shirt, still hoping to find a squashed pill of lead embedded in the first layer of bullet-resistant Kevlar.

The front of the vest was clean. "No! Where, Bob? Where, man!"

Hodges's eyes were now completely closed.

Danny slapped him hard, and he roused a little. "Stay with me, Bob, you hear? You're not checking out on me, motherfucker! You don't go anywheres without your partner! Remember?"

Danny grabbed the flashlight from the patrolman and widened the search on Hodges's torso for the entry wound.

At last he found it: under the arm—in the three-inch-wide Achilles' gap that ran down the wearer's side between the front and back panels of the vest. And there was no exit wound. No, that would have been too fucking clean—Danny screamed inside.

"He's gone," a patrol sergeant said simply.

Danny seized the dangling chin in his fingers and turned the already pallid face toward him. "Bob . . . brother . . . Bob . . . not like this . . . Uncle Bob . . ."

"He's gone, son . . . let him go . . ."

Danny pressed his cheek against Hodges's bald head. It was still warm. He knew this was crazy, but he would refuse to let go of Bob Hodges until his bald head grew cold. He would go that far down the way with his partner.

"Leave us the fuck alone," he warned the other cops, his eyes dry and fierce. "Leave us be."

EPILOGUE

Danny McGavin's new partner, a black four-year hotshot out of Wilshire Patrol, reached for the mike as he drove out of the Southeast station parking lot. Ordinarily, the man in the shotgun seat assumed the radio chores, but Lee took one look at McGavin and decided to handle this as well as the steering wheel: "Control, One CRASH Twenty-nine is in service, day watch."

"Roger, CRASH Twenty-nine."

Wordlessly, Danny watched the southside streets slip past.

Months had passed—but it still didn't seem as if Hodges was actually gone.

No . . . that night in the hollow, the slow torture of the shooting investigation, the funeral at which

Danny held both Joan and Linda Hodges's hands so tightly he feared breaking them—it was all part of some elaborate object lesson at whose conclusion Uncle Bob would pop up and say: "See, McGavin, *that* is what could happen if you really fucked up! Now, where you wanna eat? Vending machines okay?"

Danny chuckled to himself, sadly, reaching for a smoke—then realizing that he'd given them up. Forty-three days now.

Lee looked askance at him. "You want me to cruise these projects here or head more south?"

"Whatever."

"Yeah . . . right."

And in all these weeks Danny McGavin had never cried.

At the funeral, with the choppers streaming overhead and taps going and Hodges's sister trying to quiet down the baby and a lone piper playing "Amazing Grace" from afar, Wally Reed had cried like a kid. Even a barracuda like Captain Melindez had been silvery-eyed and runny-nosed and incapable of saying anything to Joan for fear of what might happen to his fucking macho image if he tried. Even Rusty Baines hadn't looked all that pleased with himself and had stumbled in the grass right after he laid his hand atop Tommy Hodges's head—maybe Uncle Bob had tripped the son of a bitch.

Danny chuckled again.

Everybody had showed what Hodges had meant to him—every swinging dick except Danny McGavin, who'd felt as empty as a dried gourd.

It was incredible, but from the moment they'd carried Hodges's body out of that stinking hollow, Danny could only recall the bad things. The mean-spirited words between them. The daily squabbles.

The slap in the booking tank. The outright battles. If only he'd never had a glimmer of what might have been between them, as friends, as brothers . . .

After the service, CRASH had gotten together for a couple beers, a wake of sorts, and Wally Reed had mumbled some jive about Hodges saying, the night before the end, that he had changed his mind about switching partners. Danny knew damned well that this was just Reed's big fucking heart talking; Hodges had never said a word about it in their final hours together before the shooting.

All at once, Lee was stomping on the brake pedal and Danny was holding himself off the dash with both arms. "Fuck! What the—"

"A deal going down!"

Danny could see a handful of gang-bangers scattering at least two blocks distant—an impossible distance for Lee and him to close—but the CRASH rookie was setting the parking brake and preparing to bail out and give chase.

"I'll sneak up this alley and how about you driving—"

"Hold up, guy."

"What?"

"Close your door and take it easy, for chrissake."

"I want those bangers!"

"I know, but let's go at it this way—"

"Hey, dude!" Lee cried, the cords standing out in his neck. "I grew up down here!"

"Right, Lee."

"So I don't need any lectures from some white cop . . . What you smiling for now?" Exasperated, Lee turned around and started the Pontiac's engine. "What's with fucking you, McGavin? You *all right?*"

"Couldn't be better." Danny faced forward. Without knowing why, he was fighting for breath. The back of his throat was raw, like he had a cold coming on. "Gonna tell you a little story."

"I don't need no fucking—"

"And you're gonna listen without interrupting, Lee. . . ." Danny paused for breath, surprised to realize that his eyes were beginning to smart, that they were burning to the point of brimming. "See, these two bulls are sitting on a hill . . . looking over these cows . . . and the young bull says, 'Hey, Pop, let's run down and fuck one of those cows . . .'" He couldn't go on for a few moments; his voice was no longer his own. He turned his face away from Lee. "But the old bull says, he says, 'No, son, let's *walk* down and fuck 'em all.'"

"What's that supposed to mean?"

The projects coasted past in a blur, but Danny suddenly laughed. "I gotta explain everything to you, man?" He could feel it: the emptiness was filling up with grief. A good grief too long deferred. He wiped his eyes on his long sleeve and asked, "You hungry, Lee?"